"A street poetess of pain and rage, Nancy A. Collins has cast an undeniable shadow across the tradition of dark and fantastic fiction."
—William P. Simmons, *Cemetery Dance*

"Sonja Blue is a punk vampire vigilante with a Clint Eastwood swagger who shows up the sensitive vampire antiheroes of most dark fantasy as refugees from a fern bar."
—*Publisher's Weekly*

"Nancy A. Collins turned the vampire genre upside down and inside out when she introduced her seductive and deadly female vampire character, Sonja Blue, in **Sunglasses After Dark** . Since then, there have been many Sonja clones, but Sonja still rules as the ultimate leather-clad, night-striding, predatory vamp-grrrl and vamp hunter."
—J.L. Comeau, *Creature Feature*

"[A] mix of gothic eroticism, the snappy dialogue of an old detective flick, and ass-kicking post-punk attitude. Sonja is sexy, smart, and not to be messed with."
—John C. Snider, *Sci-Fi Dimensions*

By the Same Author:
Sunglasses After Dark
Midnight Blue: The Sonja Blue Collection
A Dozen Black Roses
Darkest Heart
Angels on Fire

Nancy A. Collins
Dead Roses for a Blue Lady

A_SONJA_BLUE_COLLECTION

Two Wolf Press
A Division of White Wolf Publishing, Inc.
Atlanta, Georgia

Previous Editions:
Numbered Hardcover (Crossroads Press, 2002) ISBN 1-892300-07-9
Lettered Hardcover (Crossroads Press, 2002) ISBN 1-892300-08-7

ISBN: 1-56504-844-5
First Trade Edition: October 2003
Printed in Canada

White Wolf Publishing
1554 Litton Drive
Stone Mountain, GA 30083
www.white-wolf.com/fiction

knifepoint

Author's Note:

This story precedes the events chronicled in **Sunglasses After Dark** and does not, technically, feature Sonja Blue. However, it does involve Erich Ghilardi, the occult expert who would later go on to tutor Sonja in the fine art of vampire slaying. This is the story of how he acquired the silver knife that would one day become the switchblade she now carries.

The only thing the men had in common was the color of their skin. The older of the two was ginger-haired, with bristling facial ornamentation, and skin burned red as a beet from half a lifetime spent under the blazing tropical sun. He walked with a stoop, as if shouldering a great burden, and was dressed in a suit of rumpled seersucker.

The younger of the pair was tall and slender, dressed in primly starched bleached linens, his hair neatly oiled and parted down the middle of his skull as perfectly as if laid down with a ruler. A pencil-thin mustache graced his upper lip, which helped him appear slightly more than his one-and-twenty years.

The mismatched duo, the elder in the lead, made their way through the crowded bazaar, the younger of the two casting worried glances at the throng of native peasants who had gathered to buy and sell their wares.

The stoop-shouldered man led them down a winding side street, stopping before a house with a black lacquer door, above which hung a sign that read in Hindi, Sanskrit, English, and Chinese: *The Gate of Seven Dreams.*

The stooped man's companion roughly grabbed his arm, drawing him back from the threshold. When the young man spoke, it was with a Swiss accent. "Multoon! You did not tell me your contact was a fiend!"

The stoop-shouldered man in the seersucker suit turned and fixed the younger one with a bloodshot eye. "Fiend? I wudn't say that. But ole Naga *does* have a fondness for the poipe. But you needn't fear for yer reputation, young sorr. This here is a proper den, not like them *chandu-khanas*, where wogs and chinee are stacked like so much cordwood."

The black lacquer door opened onto a long corridor, and the younger man raised a perfumed handkerchief to his nose to mask the smell of unwashed human bodies, which rolled across the threshold. He hesitated for a moment, and then followed his companion inside The Gate of Seven Dreams.

The corridor turned, then turned again before opening onto a virtual labyrinth of small, dark, interconnected rooms, lit only by amber-glass lamps. The walls of the rooms were lined with multi-tiered wooden platforms resembling sleeping berths in a Pullman car, save that they lacked bedding of any kind. Each bunk was occupied by a man who lay as motionless as a stone, clutching an opium pipe, glazed eyes fixed on some unknowable point.

Multoon ignored the pipe-dreamers and motioned for his companion to follow him up a flight of stairs situated at the very back of the den. The upstairs of The Gate of Seven Dreams was reserved for wealthier patrons, as it was one big room, with mats spread about the floor for the comfort of the clientele, along with bolsters covered in cheap cloth for them to rest their heads. At the top of the stairs sat an old Chinese man behind a low table, upon which were a dozen or more opium pipes, all arranged in a large clay pot like dried flowers.

Although most of those sprawled about on the mats were of higher caste than those in the cramped bunks below stairs, there was little to tell one breed of smoker from the other. Both kinds lay on their sides, eyes lidded but not quite shut, as they chased the dragon whose smoke had enslaved them.

"We are lookin' for Naga," Multoon said to the pipe seller.

The old man pointed to the far corner of the room, where the shadows lay the heaviest, but said nothing.

The man Erich Ghilardi had traveled all the way from Bombay to see sat on his meager matt in the lotus position, dressed in what at first looked to be the robes of a Buddhist monk, save that they were black instead of saffron. The man Multoon called Naga was clean-shaven, with a hairless pate that shone like a peeled onion in the dim light of the Seven Dreams. The darkness of the monk's eyes and the tilt of his cheekbones suggested to Ghilardi one of the hill tribes of the lower Himalayas, yet there was something about his appearance that defied classification. Perhaps it was the vaguely greenish tint to his skin, although that could very well be explained by his taste for the smoke.

"Hello, Naga. 'Tis Multoon. You remember me, don't ye?"

Naga glanced up from his pipe and stared at the Irishman for a long moment, then nodded slightly.

"This here young gentleman is Mister Erich Ghilardi. Do you mind if we join ye?"

Naga motioned languidly with one hand for them to seat themselves on a nearby pallet, without removing the pipe from his lips.

"Bhoy!" Multoon called out to the old man behind the table. "Two poipes and a lay-out!"

The old man scurried forward, bringing with him a pair of pipes and then arranging a lay-out consisting of two yen hocks, a little glass lamp, a wet sponge in a china dish, a small tin dish, and a clamshell of black, tarry opium. Ghilardi grimaced in distaste as the items were placed before him.

"I don't... indulge."

"'Tis better to do as the Romans, as the saying is, young sorr," Multoon stage-whispered. "Now, if ye could be so kind as to settle with ole Hip Sung here..."

Ghilardi frowned but said nothing as he reached inside his wallet and handed the old man a five-pound note. Naga's glazed eyes suddenly glittered with interest at the sight of fresh opium. Multoon saw the change in the monk's demeanor and smiled.

"Consider this a gift—a sign of our friendship."

"White men bearing gifts have brought this land nothing but trouble," Naga said in surprisingly good English.

"And what is th' world outside to ye?" Multoon replied.

"It is less than a dream, little more than a shadow."

Ghilardi was unable to contain himself any longer. "It is true?" he blurted. "You know the location of the Black Shrine?"

Naga slowly turned his head in Ghilardi's direction. "I not only know of the Black Shrine's location, I have been there myself." Anticipating the young man's eagerness, the monk held up a languid hand. "First we smoke, then you may ask me questions."

Naga took up his own yen hock, which resembled a knitting needle flattened at one end that gradually receded to a point on the other, and grasped it between his thumb and the first two fingers of his right hand. He then dipped the point of the yen hock into the opium like a poet wetting his quill in an inkwell, removing a small bead of the black, tarry substance.

Naga held the drop of opium over the flame of the lamp until it swelled to the size of a chestnut. He carefully struck the opium against the globe of the lamp, causing a tiny burst of confined steam to escape, shriveling the ball like a raisin. After a minute or two of exposure to the lamp-flame, the opium's consistency became that of sealing wax.

Naga gripped his pipe in his left hand, warming its bowl over the lamp, and rolled the opium over the face of the bowl until it was shaped into a cone, its apex that of the yen hock's point. Once the cone was rendered soft, he pushed the yen hock into the small hole of the bowl, flattening the tip of the opium until it became a cylinder. He heated the bowl and pushed the needle into its hole, melting the opium. Naga then twisted the yen hock out of the bowl, leaving a small hole through the opium to the opening. He then leaned forward and held the bowl of the pipe over the lamp, so that the pill of opium was directly above the flame. The amount of time from the dipping of the yen hock to the taking of the opium smoke into his lungs was exactly a minute.

Naga held the heady smoke in his lungs for a long moment and then exhaled it from his nostrils. Ghilardi started at the sight of what appeared to be a second pair of nictitating eyelids slide across the monk's coal-black orbs. Ghilardi glanced at Multoon to see if his companion had noticed, but the Irishman was preoccupied with fixing his own pill of opium. When he looked back at Naga, the monk's eyes were once again normal. Ghilardi chalked up the slip in reality to the thick haze of opium smoke that filled the room.

"You say you have been to the Black Shrine," Ghilardi prompted.

Naga nodded his head as if it was about to roll off his shoulders. "I was born within its walls. For years it was the only world I knew. You see, I was not always as you see me now." He smiled at Ghilardi with the weary good humor of a man without hope. "Before the smoke claimed me, I was a high priest of the Order of the Holy Monster—the secret brotherhood that erected the Black Shrine and has served as its temple keepers and guardians since the Time of Pretending."

Ghilardi frowned. "Holy Monster? I thought the Black Shrine was dedicated to Kali the Destroyer."

Naga removed the pipe from his mouth long enough to spit in disgust. "The ignorant may call her Kali, but those versed in the history of the Real World know her as the Holy Monster. Some dare to call us heretics, but the truth is that all religions are but shadows cast upon the wall."

Ghilardi leaned forward, his eyes now gleaming as brightly as those of any opium addict. "Be that as it may, but what of the Demon Knife? Does it truly exist?"

Naga nodded sagely as he prepared another hit for his pipe. "The Demon Knife is very real, I assure you. But what is your interest in such things?"

"I am a collector of occult artifacts and other such arcane objets d'art," Ghilardi replied.

Naga lifted what would have been an eyebrow, had his forehead not been completely devoid of hair. "You mean you are a thief." Somehow the truth did not seem so offensive coming from the monk.

"But one prepared to pay a good price for good information."

"How good?"

"Enough to keep you wrapped in pipe dreams until your dying day."

Naga allowed himself a tiny smirk. "My people are very long-lived, Herr Ghilardi."

"And my people are the bankers of kings."

Naga regarded the neatly groomed European for a long moment, as if studying some aspect of his features invisible to the naked eye.

"The Black Shrine of the Holy Monster houses many sacred relics, things that date back beyond recorded history, to when some now vilified as demons or worshipped as gods bestrode the earth. The Demon Knife is one of these things.

"You see, long ago the forces of being and nothingness created servants to aid them in their battle for control of all things. Some of these servants were *devas*, others were *asuras*—what you Westerners call angels and demons. While the *devas* were of a uniform nature, the *asuras* came in a bewildering variety. Because these beings were born of Light and Darkness, they were collectively known as the Shadow Races, and they existed long before mankind learned to walk upright.

"It is uncertain which force was responsible for the creation of humans. The *asuras* believed mankind was created to serve as a source of food and amusement. The *devas*, however, saw humans as useful pets and protected them, more or less, much like shepherds tend their flocks.

"Then, for reasons known only to the universe, the forces withdrew from this mortal plane, leaving behind their living game pieces. Forgotten by their creators, the *devas* and *asuras* were thrown into chaos, uncertain as to what to do and what might befall them should they do it. The ensuing confusion lasted centuries, which meant little to the Shadow Races. However, the short-lived humans used the time to their advantage.

Once the *devas* and *asuras* finally resigned themselves to the fact that their makers were not coming back, humankind was well on its way to claiming its stewardship of Creation.

"Some of those amongst the Shadow Races recognized their opportunities as well, masking themselves as gods and goddesses in order to continue their ancient battles, forging alliances with tribal chieftains and shamans to utilize human armies to advance their agendas. In time, as human society became increasingly difficult to manipulate, the Shadow Races shrouded themselves in veils of superstition and folklore in order

asuras
dark

devas
light

to maintain their control. This gave them the illusion of disappearing, when in fact they never left. But I am getting ahead of myself...

"It was during those early days, known as the Time of Pretending, when the Shadow Races masqueraded as things they were not, that the Holy Monster was born. The *devas* and *asuras* always struggled against one another, but this time the *asuras* were led by a fierce warrior-prince known as Lord Raksa, who walked like a man but had the face and appetite of a beast. Raksa worked a spell that guaranteed him invulnerability in battle. If one drop of his demon blood struck the earth, he would be resurrected even stronger than before.

"The *devas* joined together to defeat Lord Raksa, raising an army of humans to follow them into battle, but the *asura* leader slew those who marched against him as if they were wheat before the sickle. The *devas* were equally unprepared for the savagery of their enemy, and many of their number were lost to Lord Raksa's sword.

"The surviving *devas* gathered following the rout of their army to decide what must be done. It was revealed to them by a captured *asura* foot soldier that the only way Lord Raksa's spell of invulnerability could be counteracted was if a female warrior of equal ferocity met him in battle. When the *devas* heard this, they became even more agitated, because *devas* are without true gender, being neither man nor woman. They knew that to send a human female against an *asura* would be worse than useless, for even if she succeeded in killing Raksa, his blood would still fall upon the ground and revive him.

"The more the *devas* reflected on their predicament, the angrier they became. Their wrath grew and grew, feeding on itself, until it leapt from their eyes and mouths like burning water. Out of the resulting pillar of flame stepped the figure of a woman, shaped in the manner of monsters, yet divine in nature. Her skin was black as the night, her eyes red as spilled blood. When she smiled, she showed teeth as sharp as knives and a tongue as long and pointed as a cat's. In one hand she carried a noose, in the other she bore a trident, the center trine of which was made of living fire.

"The *devas* looked upon the Holy Monster born of their righteous anger and were both elated and frightened by what they had wrought. They lost no time sending their newborn creation out onto the battlefield to face the enemy. The *asura* lord laughed when he saw the Holy Monster, for she was no bigger than a mortal woman, while he stood nearly twelve feet high. Lord Raksa was still laughing as he charged her, but his amusement ended as the Holy Monster plunged her trident into his heart and raised him above her head like a speared fish.

"As blood gushed from Lord Raksa's pierced heart, the Holy Monster opened wide her mouth and drank every drop. The *asura* army, seeing their leader drained like a wineskin, cast aside their weapons and fled in terror. However, the Holy Monster was now drunk on the blood of her enemy and not ready to stop at merely killing Lord Raksa. She pursued the fleeing demons and slew them all, from the grandest general to the lowliest cook.

"Once she was finished with the *asuras*, she turned her fearsome, demon-born bloodlust on the humans, adorning herself in the limbs and entrails of her victims. The Holy Monster drank streams of blood that became lakes that grew into rivers that expanded into oceans. And with every human she emptied, she left behind a trace of *asura*, so that they arose from the dead, changed from within. These creatures, born of the Holy Monster's bloodlust, were called *enkidu*—known to your race as vampires.

"Finally, the demon blood within the Holy Monster ran its course and her black skin split, like that of a snake, revealing golden light. Casting aside her monstrosity, she took her place amongst the *devas* who had made her. And like many before her, the Holy Monster was made a goddess in the eyes of humankind."

"And the Demon Knife? How does that fit into your story?"

"When the Holy Monster shed her skin, she cast aside her trident, the center trine of living flame having been transformed into a blade of purest silver as it was plunged into the icy heart of Lord Raksa. As time passed, the trident rotted away, leaving only the silver blade, which became known as the Demon Knife. The Black Shrine of the Holy Monster was built to house this and other precious relics, and there they have remained since the Ice Age, guarded by the descendants of those who once looked upon the Holy Monster in her terrible wrath and dedicated themselves to her worship."

"And you were once amongst their number?"

"I was their high priest," Naga replied simply, but not without a hint of pride in his voice. "If not for the pipe, I would still be with my brothers, offering bowls of blood and milk to She Who Strides Amongst the Dead. But I made the mistake of coming down to the city to trade for necessities and was introduced to the smoke of the dragon. Thus I became the debased creature you see before you—one willing to betray his heritage for *chandu* of the first chop."

"Not that we don't appreciate it, ole bhoy," Multoon chimed in.

Ghilardi studied the priest for a long moment. "How do I know you're telling me the truth?"

"Because I am damned, " Naga said, dipping his yen hock yet again into the black tar opium, "and the damned do not lie."

Ghilardi looked up from his work as Multoon entered the tent, bringing with him a gust of frigid Himalayan air. As usual, the ginger-haired Irishman seemed in a foul mood.

"Th' damned wogs are demandin' more money," Multoon spat. "Thim buggers won't go on if they don't get it."

Ghilardi sighed and massaged the bridge of his nose. "I thought you said Gupta could handle them."

"He can—under normal circumstances. But there's a point where even th' lash fails to motivate. They're afraid of evil spirits, sorr."

Ghilardi set aside the papers, a sour look on his face. Two weeks out of Simla, with an early winter on the way, and they had yet to locate the valley Naga had described. Ghilardi had far too much invested in the expedition to back out now, but he did not relish having to reach into his own pocket yet again. As it was, he had serious reservations about the character of Multoon, whom he suspected was lying to him about the bearers' demands for more money in order to gouge him even deeper. However, he needed Multoon as much as he needed the bearers, for the old soldier knew the language and the peoples of the Himalayas far better than he did.

"Very well," Ghilardi sighed, dropping his shoulders in resignation. "Tell Gupta his men will get their extra pay."

Multoon smiled, the gleam of greed in his eye confirming Ghilardi's suspicions. "Very good, sorr! I'll let thim know direct!"

Ghilardi drummed his fingers on the collapsible camp table, trying to figure a way out of the situation he had made for himself. While his inheritance was considerable, it was nowhere near large enough to finance a prolonged stay in India. There were matters concerning the family business he had been putting off for several months that could no longer be ignored, especially now that war had been declared between the Kaiser and the British king.

His father had always dismissed the occult as a fraud designed to separate the gullible from their money. Now that the mantle of family patriarch had been placed on his youthful shoulders, Ghilardi was beginning to wonder if the old man had not been right. Still, his father's passion for mountaineering, which had provided Ghilardi with his premature legacy, was proving useful to the expedition. No doubt Multoon had not expected his young business partner to be so at home in the higher altitudes.

Suddenly there was the sound of several highly agitated voices chattering away in Hindi outside his tent. Ghilardi groaned and rolled his eyes as he got to his feet to see what the devil was going on. He threw back the flap and saw Multoon standing in the middle of a swirling knot of bearers, most of whom looked like they were ready to bolt the camp. Multoon's man, Gupta, a hawk-faced Hindu with eyes as black and bitter as coffee and skin the color of milky tea, pushed his way through the mob, cursing the bearers while lashing out at them with a dog whip. Although surrounded by chaos, Multoon was beaming from ear to ear.

"Good lord, man!" Ghilardi shouted at Multoon above the din. "What is going on?"

"We done it!" Multoon bellowed in reply. "We done it! We found th' Black Shrine!"

The "we" was actually a bearer named Sarad who had set out in pursuit of a mule that had broken its tether. After an hour of searching, Sarad finally cornered the wayward pack animal in a box canyon. It wasn't until he had succeeded in harnessing the mule that Sarad noticed the huge edifice carved at the bottom of the canyon. Ghilardi could not fault the boy's perceptiveness, for he too had nearly overlooked it, even though he knew it was there.

The entrance was carved directly into the rock face but was so weathered by time as to appear natural at a distance. But upon closer look what at first appeared to be a collection of strangely grouped outcroppings proved themselves to the outline of a human head, the entrance to a cavern serving as its gaping maw, complete with a row of jagged stalagmites arranged like a row of pointed teeth.

"What do you think, Multoon?" Ghilardi asked, passing the binoculars to the Irishman.

"Looks peaceful enough," he replied, scanning the area with the slow, steady sweep of someone accustomed to reconnaissance. "No sign of ole Naga's bunk-mates, as far as I can see. But I can tell ye one thing, sorr, and that's thim black buggers back there won't come down into th' canyon, much less set foot inside that cave."

"I expected as much," Ghilardi said. "What of Gupta?"

"He sez he'll guard th' entrance, but he refuses to come inside."

"Then it's up to us to get in there, find the Demon Knife, and get out in one piece. Speaking of Naga's brothers, what do you think they would do to us if they caught us?"

"'Tis a heathen land," Multoon said with a dour frown, "and heathens ain't ones for blasphemin'."

The interior of the cave was unlike anything Ghilardi had ever seen. The first few yards or so were on level ground, then the floor of the cavern sloped steeply downward. But what made this cave remarkable were the stairs that led into the darkness below. The steps were wide as those of the British Museum in London, and made of huge, unbroken slabs of black marble, lit by a row of metal braziers that smelled of sandalwood. Ghilardi noticed the groove worn into the center of the steps by the passage of countless feet.

After several minutes of descent, they came to a wide underground pool as flat as glass, to the right of which, in a natural grotto, stood a statue of the dread goddess atop a dais fashioned of volcanic glass.

"Mein Gott," Ghilardi whispered under his breath.

"God has nothin' to do with this, me bhoy," Multoon rasped.

Unlike many of the idols Ghilardi had seen in his travels, the Black Shrine's Kali was of human scale, lacking the multiple arms and faces so common among the Vedic deities. However, despite its size, the idol of the Holy Monster was indeed marvelous to behold.

The figure was frozen in mid-dance, knee bent and foot raised, and although it was black as night, it seemed to shine in the flickering light from the huge braziers that flanked the dais, each big enough to hold a man. A garland of skulls fashioned from whole pieces of ivory hung about its neck, and about the waist was a skirt of hands made from milk-white jade. Otherwise, the Holy Monster was naked. Twin rubies twinkled in the eye sockets and a grotesquely long and pointed tongue, carved from a single piece of red jade, jutted from the mouth. In the left hand of the idol was a noose fashioned from the finest silk, and in the right was a dagger.

Ghilardi's heart leapt like a fish as he looked upon the fabled Demon Knife, forged from the fire of divine wrath and tempered in the blood of a demon king. In the flickering light from the braziers it shone like the morning star, bedazzling him with its serpentine shape and simple beauty. As he climbed the dais his ears were filled with a strange ringing, like the tolling of crystalline bells.

As Ghilardi stood face to face with the idol and stared directly into its ruby eyes, a queasy sensation of horror replaced the exhilaration in his heart, for he could plainly see that the idol of the Holy Monster was not carved from wood or stone, nor cast from metal, but was, instead, an astonishing example of taxidermy.

Swallowing the bitter ball of grease rising in his throat, Ghilardi turned his attention to wresting the Demon Knife from the effigy's hand. He fumbled with the rigid fingers for what felt like a small eternity before finally succeeding in breaking its grip.

Ghilardi turned his back to the idol and held his prize up to the light, where it shone and sparkled like ice. Despite being fashioned from silver, it weighed no more than an ordinary pocketknife and was perfectly balanced. The wavy blade, similar to that of a kris, was fitted to a hilt of finest ebony, and its dual edges gleamed like freshly whetted razorblades. Looking at its pristine glory, it was not hard to imagine such a weapon laying waste to legions of the damned. Indeed, the legends concerning the Demon Knife claimed that there was no devil that could not be killed with it—not even Evil Incarnate itself.

A raucous rattling sound, like that of a wooden chime, shook Ghilardi from his reverie. He turned and saw Multoon removing the garland of ivory skulls from the idol's neck and stuffing them into a canvas bag.

"What are you doing?" he yelped, his voice sounding young and foolish even in his own ears. "Put that back!"

Multoon paused in his looting long enough to favor his partner with a sneer. "What 'is it to thee, bhoy? Ye got yer loot, eh? Ye didn't think I spent all this time an' effort just t' steal a fancy pig-sticker, did ye? Besides, in for a penny, in for a pound, I allus say." Multoon removed the skirt of jade hands and then yanked free the red jade tongue that jutted from between the idol's lips.

Ghilardi's eyes widened in alarm when Multoon took out his pocketknife and locked its blade into the open position. He grabbed the older man's arm, staying his hand. "Are you mad!? This isn't just looting, it's desecration!"

Multoon shoved the younger man aside. "Mad? I'll tell ye what's mad!" he snarled. "It's skinnin' some poor dear, dyin' her blacker'n Queen's Victoria's mournin' dress, then stuffin' her like she was some bloody huntin' trophy!" He plunged the pocketknife into the idol's right socket, popping the ruby eyeball free in a spray of horsehair and packed sawdust.

"Good lord, man—don't you understand? What if the skin truly *is* that of Kali the Destroyer?"

"Yer daft! All that book learnin' has turned yer brains t'mush! Now let's clear off before Naga's bhoys learn we're here!"

Ghilardi pointed to the subterranean pool, the middle of which had begun to bubble like a pot on the boil. "Something tells me we're too late."

Their argument forgotten, the two men fled back up the steep black marble stairs toward the dim semicircle of light that was their only means of escape to the outside world. Ghilardi's heart was lodged just below his tonsils as they reached the entrance, and for once he was glad to see Gupta.

"Did ye place th' charges?" Multoon wheezed, his face so red it looked like he had painted it with tandoori paste.

"Yes, sahib," Gupta replied.

"Good man!" Multoon grinned.

"Charges? What charges?" Ghilardi asked, baffled by the exchange.

"I took th' liberty of plannin' against the likelihood of our bein' pursued," Multoon explained. "But this 'tisn't the place to stand an' talk about it."

The Irishman took off in a dead run in the direction of camp, Ghilardi at his heels. Seconds later there was a thunderous explosion. The entire canyon shuddered as if in the grips of an earthquake, knocking both men to the ground. When Ghilardi looked again in the direction of the entrance of the Black Shrine, all there was to see was a pile of rock. Gupta came trotting up, a demolitionist's detonation box tucked under one arm.

Ghilardi sat in the dirt and stared at where the Black Shrine had been. It was impossible to tell whether the blast had merely sealed the tunnel or demolished the entire cave. Not that it mattered. Something inside him shriveled and died as he realized he had played a major part in destroying all traces of the greatest archeological discovery since the unearthing of Tutankhamen's tomb.

All for the sake of a silver knife.

Upon returning to camp, Ghilardi was so depressed it was all he could do to wash the grime from his face. Multoon and Gupta, on the other hand, seemed in exceedingly high spirits. Ghilardi retired to his tent early, leaving the other two to regale the bearers with tales of their daring exploits in the search of treasure.

Too weary to write in his journal, Ghilardi placed the Demon Knife under his pillow and stretched out, fully clothed, on his camp cot. His mistrust of Multoon was now greater than ever, but he was simply too exhausted to sit up half the night waiting for the Irishman to drink himself into a stupor before going to bed.

Within moments of lying down, he fell into a deep sleep. His dreams were troubled, and he found himself back inside the Black Shrine, kneeling before the image of the Dark Mother. As he looked upon her, Ghilardi realized that she still wore her garland of skulls and skirt of hands, her eyes and tongue were still intact in her head, and the Demon Knife was once again in her hand.

Erich Ghilardi...

The voice that spoke in his ear was as clear and pure as the peal of a crystal bell, yet it filled him with a dread unlike any he had known before.

Behold the Mother of Vampires; She Who Cannot Be Turned Aside; She Who Is Terror; Queen of Night and Slayer of Demons. Behold her in her fierce glory and be afraid, and through your fear made brave.

As his dream-self stared up at the miraculously restored idol, the figure lowered its upraised foot and turned so that its ruby-red gaze was fixed directly on him. Ghilardi felt the dread in his heart blossom and become a terror as pure and primal as a mother's love. As the Holy Monster descended the dais and moved toward him, he saw that the skulls she wore about her neck were no longer made of ivory, but the bone of actual dead men, and that the severed hands fashioned of jade that encircled her waist had metamorphosed into the genuine articles as well. Even though he knew he was dreaming, Ghilardi closed his eyes and turned his head away

Look upon me, Erich Ghilardi, and fear me as you have feared no other thing. For only then can you open your third eye and look into the Real World without losing what you humans call sanity. Open yourself to the Real World, my son, for Kali-Yuga is upon us, and the avatar's arrival is at hand.

Although he knew what would greet his gaze would be horrible beyond all mortal ken, Ghilardi could not keep himself from opening his eyes. With the inevitability of nightmare, he turned his face to that of the Holy Monster. And screamed as hard as a woman giving birth.

Ghilardi awoke with a start so violent it was as if he had been jolted with electricity. After the horrid vividness of his nightmare, it was almost

a relief to find himself staring up the barrel of Gupta's pistol. Despite the gravity of his situation, he found himself wondering whether he had actually cried out in his sleep.

"Sorry to awaken you, sahib," Gupta said, his smile displaying no sign of regret. "But Sergeant Multoon says you are to die now."

"Sergeant Multoon...?"

As if summoned by incantation, the Irishman stepped out of the darkness, holding aloft a camp lantern like a perverse Diogenes. "*Master*-Sergeant, if ye please! Me an' Gupta go back to rigimint days. We was cashiered for attemptin' t'loot some rajah's summer palace. We been workin' together ever since. Ain't that right, Gupta?"

"Yes, Master-Sergeant."

"And now that we got what we come for, 'tis time to close shop. With th' haul from th' shrine we got enough to live like bloody princes for th' rest of our days. Gupta here already drugged th' men, so's we're saved the trouble of payin' 'em—or havin' 'em bear tales of what went on durin' th' expedition. If they ain't knackered already, they'll be so by sun-up. Then everything will be tidied up nice an' proper. Once yer took care of, of course. "

"Of course," Ghilardi said, echoing his assassin. He was astounded by how calm he felt. Although he realized his situation was indeed a dire one, no panic crowded his brain.

"Just so's ye know, sorr," Multoon said with a crooked grin. "There is no hard feelings on me part. 'Tis business only." He paused, a frown creasing his brow, and lifted the lantern higher. "Here now—what's that hissin' sound?"

Gupta's eyes bulged in their sockets like hard-boiled eggs and he abruptly screamed, jerking his pistol away from Ghilardi's head and firing at his own foot. Gupta fell to the floor of the tent, clutching his calf with both hands.

Ghilardi saw the unmistakable outline of a king cobra, its upper body raised to strike, limned against the canvas wall of the tent. Multoon must have seen it, too, for he cursed and whirled about, dropping the lantern as he emptied his gun at the creature that had appeared from nowhere. The cobra silhouette snapped forward like a whip. Multoon screamed even louder than Gupta and then dropped heavily to the ground, clutching his cheek, his florid face already grown black and swollen from the serpent's venomous bite.

Ghilardi remained on the camp cot, staring in confused horror as his would-be murderers died before his eyes. Still possessed of his eerie calm, he watched as the head of the cobra, its hood flared, rose above the foot of his cot. The deadly serpent swayed like a reed in a gentle breeze as it balanced itself on its tail, until it was easily six feet tall, fixing Ghilardi with unblinking eyes. The form of the cobra blurred and was replaced by the figure of a man. Ghilardi recognized the shaved head, black robes and shiny black eyes immediately.

"Naga? What are you doing here?"

"I may have fallen from grace, but even a depraved addict could not sell his god for the price of a year's supply of *chandu*. After you left with the map I drew for you, I could no longer find paradise in the smoke. My pipe dreams were replaced by nightmares. Where once there was peace, all that remained was torment. I cannot rest until I have paid for my transgressions—just as Multoon has paid for his."

"Naga—please—you must believe me, I had no idea what Multoon was up to."

"Indeed," Naga said, the greenish-gray scales covering his naked arms and upper torso glittering like armor. "*Your* motives, of course, were pure. All *you* were interested in was stealing a solitary item, not looting an entire temple and then wiping it off the face of the earth as if it was no more than an anthill. Tell me, thief, when you saw your good friend Multoon gouge the eyes from the Holy Monster, did you stay his hand, or did you merely stand and watch?"

The priest opened his mouth, revealing a pair of short, sharp fangs. Hissing like a fakir's basket, he lunged at the prone Ghilardi.

The silver blade of the Demon Knife flashed like a meteor in the dim light, slicing through the serpent-priest's neck. Ghilardi flinched in disgust as a gout of blood, far darker and nowhere near warm enough to be that of a human, splashed across his face.

As he staggered to his feet, the calm that had kept his mind clear and his hand steady receded at last. His heart felt like a captive bird battering itself against the bars of its cage. Ghilardi peeked out the hole Multoon's bullet had poked through the tent and saw shadowy figures dressed in robes similar to Naga's sliding in and out of the bearers' tents. Clearly the Black Shrine had another exit aside from the one Gupta had sealed. Naga's brothers were looking for something they had yet to find. Their agitated hissing was as loud as that of a steam engine sitting at the station.

Ghilardi tore open the back of the tent and fled headlong into the night, too frightened to think of anything but escape.

When Ghilardi awoke all he could see was white. After his eyes focused, he saw that he was staring at a whitewashed wall. He attempted to lift his head and look about, only to have a gentle, yet firm, hand place itself on his shoulder.

"Lie still, my son," said a man's voice. "You are safe here."

As Ghilardi relaxed and dropped back, he realized that the voice had spoken in German. *"Wo bin ich?"* he croaked.

"You are at the Lutheran Mission of the Lower Himalayas," replied his benefactor, a tall, raw-boned man with a salt-and-pepper beard and piercing blue eyes. "I am Brother Heinrich."

"How long have I been here?"

"You have been with us for over a week, my friend. One of the parishioners found you unconscious amongst the goats in his pasture and brought you to me."

"Did I—did I have anything on my person when I was found?"

Brother Heinrich lifted an eyebrow. "You mean the kris? It took three strong men to pry it from your hand. "

"Where is it?"

"There will be time enough for that, later, friend. First you must rest—"

"You don't understand!" Ghilardi said, his voice raised in agitation. "Where is it?"

The door to the sick room opened and a native hill-tribesman, a hand-carved cross dangling from a thong about his neck, stuck his head inside, a look of concern on his face.

"Brother? There is trouble?"

"No, Kakar, there is no trouble!" Brother Heinrich said reassuringly. "Could you be so kind as to bring me the kris our friend was carrying?"

Kakar disappeared from the doorway, only to return a couple of minutes later, carrying a small bundle wrapped in oilcloth. He glanced at the missionary before handing the package to Ghilardi. Brother Heinrich smiled and nodded, signaling to the hill-man that it was safe to do so. Ghilardi threw back the fold of oilcloth, sighing in relief at the sight of the silver blade.

"How is it you came to our valley, my friend?" Brother Heinrich. "Kakar and the others believed you set upon by bandits. Is that true?"

"Yes," Ghilardi said, sliding into the lie as easily as bathwater. "The party I was traveling with was attacked by thieves. They slaughtered them to a man—I was the only one who managed to escape."

"Kakar said there was blood upon the kris."

"Yes. I had to fight my way out." That, at least, was true.

"Most unfortunate, but praise be to Our Lord and Savior for delivering you from such evil! I have heard tell of the cutthroats and brigands that haunt the passes. You were indeed saved by the grace of God."

"And a sharp knife," Ghilardi said flatly.

He slept with the Demon Knife under his pillow that night and every night during his convalescence at the mission. When he finally boarded the ship that would take him from Bombay and back to the ordered world of bankers and clockmakers he had left behind, the silver blade was still close to his hand.

As the steamer left the harbor, Ghilardi stood at the railing and wondered if he could ever truly escape the nightmare. Something told him that no matter how hard, or long, or far he might try to run, in the end he would find it patiently awaiting his arrival.

cold turkey

Oh I'll be a good boy,
Please make me well,
I'll promise you anything,
Get me out of this hell.

—*Cold Turkey*, John Lennon

She had to give the dead boy credit. He had the trick of appearing human nailed down tight. He'd learned just what gestures and inflections to use in his conversations. His surface gloss and glitz weren't there merely to disguise basic shallowness, but an utter lack of humanity.

She'd seen enough of the kind of humans he imitated: pallid, self-important intellectuals who prided themselves on their sophistication and knowledge of "hip" art, sharpening their wit at the expense of others. Like the vampiric mimic in their midst, they produced nothing while draining the vitality from those around them. The only difference was that the vampire was more honest about it.

Sonja worked her way to the bar, careful to keep herself shielded from the dead boy's view, both physically and psychically. It wouldn't do for her quarry to catch scent of her just yet. She could hear the vampire's nasal intonations as it held forth on the demerits of various artists.

"Frankly, I consider his use of photomontage to be inexcusably *banal*. If I wanted to look at photographs, I'd go to Olan Mills!"

She wondered where the vampire had overheard—or stolen—that particular drollery. A dead boy of his wattage didn't come up with witty remarks spontaneously. When you have to spend conscious energy remembering to breathe and blink, there is no such thing as top-of-your-head snappy patter. It was all protective coloration, right down to the last double entendre and Monty Python impersonation.

It would be another decade or two before this vampire with the stainless steel ankh dangling from one earlobe and the crystal embedded in his left nostril, could divert his energies to something besides the full-time task of insuring his continuance. Not that the dead boy had much of a future in the predator business.

She waved down the bartender and ordered a beer. As she awaited its arrival, she caught a glimpse of herself in the mirror backing the bar. To the casual observer she looked to be no more than twenty-five. Tricked out in a battered leather jacket, with a stained Circle Jerks T-shirt, patched jeans, mirrored sunglasses, and dark hair twisted into a tortured cockatoo's crest, she looked like just another college-age gothic chick checking out the scene. No one would ever guess she was actually forty years old.

She sucked the cold suds down, participating in her own form of protective coloration. She could drink a case or three of the stuff with the only effect being she'd piss like a fire hose. Beer didn't do it for her anymore. Neither did hard liquor. Or cocaine. Or heroin. Or crack. She had tried them all, in dosages that would have put the entire US Olympic Team in the morgue, but no luck. There was only one drug that plunked her magic twanger. Only one thing that could get her off.

And that drug was blood.

Yeah, the dead boy was good enough he could have fooled another vampire. Could have. But didn't.

She eyed her prey. She doubted she'd have any trouble taking the sucker down. She rarely did, these days. Least not the lesser undead that lacked major psionic muscle. Sure, they had enough mesmeric ability to gull the humans in their vicinity, but little else. Compared to her own psychic abilities, the art-fag vampire was packing a peashooter. Still, it wasn't smart to get too cocky. Lord Morgan had dismissed her in just such a high-handed manner, and now he was missing half his face.

She shifted her vision from the human to the Pretender spectrum, studying the vampire's true appearance. She wondered if the black-garbed art aficionados clustered about their mandarin, their heads bobbing like puppets, would still consider his pronouncements worthy if they knew his skin was the color and texture of rotten sailcloth, or that his lips were black and shriveled, revealing oversized fangs set in a perpetual death's-head grimace. No doubt they'd drop their little plastic cups of cheap Chablis and back away in horror, their surface glaze of urbanite sophistication and studied ennui replaced by honest, old-fashioned monkey-brain terror.

Humans need masks in order to live their day-to-day lives, even among their own kind. Little do they know that their dependence on artifice and pretense provides the perfect hiding place for a raft of predators like the vampire pretending to be an art-fag. Predators like Sonja.

She tightened her grip on the switchblade in the pocket of her leather jacket.

"Uh, excuse me?"

She jerked around a little too fast, startling the young man at her elbow. She was so focused on her prey she had been unaware of his approaching her. Sloppy. Really sloppy.

"Yeah, what is it?"

The young man blinked, taken aback by the brusqueness of her tone. "I, uh, was wondering if I might, uh, buy you a drink?"

She automatically scanned him for signs of Pretender taint, but he came up clean. One hundred percent USDA Human. He was taller than her by a couple of inches, his blonde hair pulled into a ponytail. There were three rings in his right ear and one in his left nostril. Despite the metalwork festooning his nose, he was quite handsome.

Sonja found herself at a loss for words. She was not used to being approached by normals. She tended to generate a low-level psychic energy that most humans found unnerving, if not actively antagonistic. In layman's terms, she tended to either scare people away or piss them off.

"I— I—" She shot her prey a glance out of the corner of her eye. *Shit!* The bastard was starting to make his move, hustling one of the more entranced hangers-on toward the back door.

"I realize this is going to sound like a really dumb, cheap come-on," the young man with the nose ring said, giving her an embarrassed smile. "But I saw you from across the room—and I just had to meet you. Please let me buy you a drink."

"I, uh, I—"

The vampire had his prey almost out the door, smiling widely as he continued to discourse on modern art.

"There's something I have to take care of—I'll be right back! I promise! Don't go away!" she blurted, and dashed off in pursuit of her target for the night.

She scanned the parking lot, checking for signs of the vampire's passage. She prayed she wasn't too late. Once vamps isolated and seduced humans from the herd, they tended to move quickly. She knew that much from her own experience at the hands of Lord Morgan, the undead bastard responsible for her own transformation.

The vampire and his prey were sitting in the backseat of a silver BMW with heavily tinted windows. Their blurred silhouettes moved like shadows reflected in an aquarium. There was no time to waste. She'd have to risk being spotted.

The imitation art-fag looked genuinely surprised when her fist punched through the back window, sending tinted safety glass flying into the car. He hissed a challenge, exposing his fangs, as he whipped about to face her. His victim sat beside him, motionless as a mannequin, his eyes unfocused. The human's erect penis jutted from his open fly, vibrating like a tuning fork.

Sonja grabbed the vampire by the collar of his black silk shirt and pulled him, kicking and screaming, through the busted back windshield. The human didn't even blink.

"Let's get this over with, dead boy!" Sonja snapped as she hurled the snarling vampire onto the parking lot gravel. "I got a hot date waiting on me!"

The vampire launched himself at her, talons hooked and fangs extended. Sonja moved to meet the attack, flicking open her switchblade with a snap of her wrist. The silver blade sank into the vampire's exposed thorax, causing him to shriek in pain. The vampire collapsed around her fist like a punctured balloon, his body spasming as his system reacted to the silver's toxin.

Sonja knelt and swiftly removed the vampire's head from his shoulders. The body was already starting to putrefy by the time she located the BMW's keys. She unlocked the trunk and tossed the vampire's rapidly decomposing remains inside, making sure the keys were returned to his pants pocket.

She looked around, but there were no witnesses to be seen in the darkened lot. She moved around to the passenger side and opened the door, tugging the human out of the car.

He stood slumped against the rear bumper like a drunkard, his eyes swimming and his face slack. His penis dangled from his pants like a tattered party streamer. Sonja took his chin between her thumb and forefinger and turned his head so that his eyes met hers.

"This never happened. You do not remember leaving the bar with anyone. Is that clear?"

"N-nothing h-happened," he stammered.

"Now go back in the bar and have a good time. Oh, and put that thing away. You don't want to get busted for indecent exposure, do you?"

She was buzzing by the time she reentered the bar. She liked to think of it as her *après*-combat high. The adrenaline from the battle was still sluicing around inside her, juicing her perceptions and making her feel as if she was made of lightning and spun glass. It wasn't as intense as the boost she got from blood, but it was still good.

Someone jostled her, and Sonja looked down into the face of a drab, mousy woman, her face set into a scowl. She paused, studying the schizophrenia that radiated from the other woman like a martyr's halo. The scowling woman blushed, drew her shoulders in, ducked her chin, and hurried away as if she'd suddenly woken up and discovered herself sleepwalking in the nude. Sonja shrugged and continued scanning the bar for the young man who'd spoken to her earlier.

Give it up, he's forgotten you and found another bimbo for the evening.

Sonja fought to keep from cringing at the sound of the Other's voice inside her head. She had managed to go almost all night without having to endure its commentary.

She found him waiting for her at the bar. Sonja made a last minute spot-check for any blood or telltale ichor that might be clinging to her, then moved forward.

"You still interested in buying me that drink?"

The young man's smile was genuinely relieved. "You came back!"

"I said I'd be back, didn't I?"

"Yeah. You did." He smiled again and offered her his hand. "I guess I ought to introduce myself. I'm Judd."

Sonja took his hand and smiled without parting her lips. "Pleased to meet you, Judd. I'm Sonja."

"What the hell's going on here?"

Judd's smile faltered as his gaze fixed itself on something just over Sonja's right shoulder. She turned and found herself almost nose-to-nose with a young woman dressed in a skin-tight black sheath, fishnet stockings, and way too much make-up. The woman's psychosis covered her face like the caul on a newborn, with pulsing indentations marking her eyes, nose and mouth.

Judd closed his eyes and sighed. "Kitty, look, it's over! Get a life of your own and let go of mine, alright?"

"Oh, is *that* how you see it? Funny, I remember you saying something different! Like how you'd *always* love me! Guess I was stupid to believe that, huh?"

Kitty's rage turned the caul covering her face an interesting shade of magenta. The way it swirled and pulsed reminded Sonja of a lava lamp.

"You're not getting away *that* easy, asshole! And who's this slut?" Kitty slapped the flat of her hand against Sonja's leather-clad shoulder in an attempt to push her away from Judd.

Sonja grabbed Kitty's wrist, careful not to break it in front of Judd.

C'mon, snap the crazy bitch's arm off, purred the Other. *She deserves it!*

"Don't touch me," Sonja said in a clipped, cold voice.

Kitty tried to yank herself free of the other woman's grip. "I'll fucking touch you anytime I want! Just you stay away from my man, bitch! Now let me go!" She made to rake Sonja's face with her free hand, only to have that one grabbed as well, forcing her to look directly into her rival's face.

Kitty's features grew pale and she stopped struggling. Sonja knew the other woman was seeing her—*truly* seeing her—for what she was. Only three kinds of humans could perceive the Real World: psychics, poets and lunatics. And Kitty definitely qualified for the last category.

Sonja released the girl, but kept her gaze fixed on her. Kitty massaged her wrists, opened her mouth as if to say something, then turned and hurried away, nearly tripping over her high heels as she fled.

Judd looked uncomfortable. "I'm sorry you had to go through that. Kitty's a weird girl. We lived together for a few months over a year ago, but she was incredibly jealous. It got to the point where I couldn't take any more, so I moved out. She's been dogging my tracks ever since. She scared off the last two women I was interested in."

Sonja shrugged. "I don't scare easy."

He wasn't afraid of her. Nor did she detect the self-destructive tendencies that usually attracted human men to her kind. Judd was not a tranced moth drawn to her dark flame, nor was he a closet renfield in search of a master. He was simply a good-natured young man who found her physically attractive. The novelty of his normalcy intrigued her.

He bought her several drinks, all of which she downed without effect. But she *did* feel giddy, almost lightheaded, while in his company. To be mistaken for a human woman was actually quite flattering. Especially since she'd stop thinking of herself as human some time back.

They ended up dancing, adding their bodies to the surging crowd that filled the mosh pit. At one point, Sonja was amazed to find herself laughing, genuinely *laughing*, one arm wrapped about Judd's waist. And then Judd leaned in and kissed her.

She barely had time to retract her fangs before his tongue found hers. She slid her other arm around his waist and pulled him close, grinding herself against him. He responded eagerly, his erection rubbing against her hip like a friendly tomcat. And she found herself wondering how his blood would taste.

She pushed him away so hard he staggered backward, nearly falling on his ass. Sonja shook her head as if trying to dislodge something in her ear, a guttural moan rising from her chest.

"Sonja?" There was a confused, hurt look on his face.

She could *see* his blood beckoning her from just beneath the surface of his skin: the veins traced in blue, the arteries pulsing purple. She turned her back on him and ran from the bar, her head lowered. She shouldered her way through a knot of dancers, sending them flying like duckpins. Some of the bar's patrons hurled insults in her direction, a couple even spat at her, but she was deaf to their anger.

She put a couple of blocks between her and the bar before slumping into a darkened doorway, staring at her shaking hands as if they belonged to someone else.

"I liked him. I honestly *liked* him and I was going to... going to..."

Like. Hate. What's the difference? Blood is the life, wherever it comes from.

"Not like that. I never feed off anyone who doesn't deserve it. *Never.*"

Aren't we special?

"Shut up, bitch."

"Sonja?"

She had him pinned to the wall, one forearm clamped against his windpipe in a chokehold before she recognized his face. Judd clawed at her arm, his eyes bugging from their sockets.

"I'm... sorry..." he gasped out.

She let him go. "No, I'm the one who should be sorry. More than you realize."

Judd regarded her apprehensively as he massaged his throat, but there was still no fear in his eyes. "Look, I don't know what it is I said or did back there that put you off..."

"The problem isn't with you, Judd. Believe me." She turned and began walking away, but he hurried after her.

"I know an all-night coffeehouse near here. Maybe we could talk?"

"Judd, just leave me alone, okay? You'd be a lot better off if you just forgot you ever met me."

"How could I forget someone like you?"

"Easier than you realize."

He was keeping pace alongside her, desperately trying to make eye contact. "C'mon Sonja! Give it a chance! I—damn it, would you just take your shades off and *look* at me?"

Sonja stopped in midstep to face him, her expression unreadable behind her mirrored sunglasses. "That's the *last* thing you want me to do."

Judd sighed and fished a pen and piece of paper out of his pocket. "You're one weird chick, that's for sure! But I like you, don't ask me why." He scribbled something on the scrap of paper and shoved it into her hand. "Look, here's my phone number. Call me, okay?"

Sonja closed her fist around the paper. "Judd—"

He held his hands out, palms facing up. "No strings attached, I promise. Just call me."

Sonja was surprised to find herself smiling. "Okay. I'll call you. Now will you leave me alone?"

When Sonja revived the next evening, she found Judd's phone number tucked away in one of the pockets of her jacket. She sat cross-legged on the canvas futon that served as her bed and stared at it for a long time.

She'd been careful to make sure Judd hadn't followed her the night before. Her current nest was a drafty loft apartment in the attic of an old warehouse in the neighborhood just beyond the French Quarter. Save for her sleeping pallet, an antique cedar wardrobe, a Salvation Army-issue chair, a mini-fridge , a cordless telephone, and the scattered packing crates containing the esoteric curios she used as barter, the huge space was otherwise empty. Except for those occasions when the dead came to visit. Such as tonight.

At first she didn't recognize the ghost. He'd lost his sense of self in the years since his death, which blurred his spectral image somewhat. He swirled up through the floorboards like a gust of blue smoke, gradually taking shape before her eyes. It was only when the phantom produced a smoldering cigarette from his own ectoplasm that she recognized him for who he once had been.

"Hello, Chaz."

The ghost of her former renfield made a noise that sounded like a cat being drowned. The dead cannot speak clearly—even to Pretenders—except on three days of the year: Fat Tuesday, Halloween, and Candlemas. The ghost-light radiating from him was the only illumination in the room.

"Come to see how your murderer is getting on, I take it?"

Chaz made a sound like a church bell played at half speed.

grinding herself against him. He responded eagerly, his erection rubbing against her hip like a friendly tomcat. And she found herself wondering how his blood would taste.

She pushed him away so hard he staggered backward, nearly falling on his ass. Sonja shook her head as if trying to dislodge something in her ear, a guttural moan rising from her chest.

"Sonja?" There was a confused, hurt look on his face.

She could *see* his blood beckoning her from just beneath the surface of his skin: the veins traced in blue, the arteries pulsing purple. She turned her back on him and ran from the bar, her head lowered. She shouldered her way through a knot of dancers, sending them flying like duckpins. Some of the bar's patrons hurled insults in her direction, a couple even spat at her, but she was deaf to their anger.

She put a couple of blocks between her and the bar before slumping into a darkened doorway, staring at her shaking hands as if they belonged to someone else.

"I liked him. I honestly *liked* him and I was going to... going to..."

Like. Hate. What's the difference? Blood is the life, wherever it comes from.

"Not like that. I never feed off anyone who doesn't deserve it. *Never.*"

Aren't we special?

"Shut up, bitch."

"Sonja?"

She had him pinned to the wall, one forearm clamped against his windpipe in a chokehold before she recognized his face. Judd clawed at her arm, his eyes bugging from their sockets.

"I'm... sorry..." he gasped out.

She let him go. "No, I'm the one who should be sorry. More than you realize."

Judd regarded her apprehensively as he massaged his throat, but there was still no fear in his eyes. "Look, I don't know what it is I said or did back there that put you off..."

"The problem isn't with you, Judd. Believe me." She turned and began walking away, but he hurried after her.

"I know an all-night coffeehouse near here. Maybe we could talk?"

"Judd, just leave me alone, okay? You'd be a lot better off if you just forgot you ever met me."

"How could I forget someone like you?"

"Easier than you realize."

He was keeping pace alongside her, desperately trying to make eye contact. "C'mon Sonja! Give it a chance! I—damn it, would you just take your shades off and *look* at me?"

Sonja stopped in midstep to face him, her expression unreadable behind her mirrored sunglasses. "That's the *last* thing you want me to do."

Judd sighed and fished a pen and piece of paper out of his pocket. "You're one weird chick, that's for sure! But I like you, don't ask me why." He scribbled something on the scrap of paper and shoved it into her hand. "Look, here's my phone number. Call me, okay?"

Sonja closed her fist around the paper. "Judd—"

He held his hands out, palms facing up. "No strings attached, I promise. Just call me."

Sonja was surprised to find herself smiling. "Okay. I'll call you. Now will you leave me alone?"

When Sonja revived the next evening, she found Judd's phone number tucked away in one of the pockets of her jacket. She sat cross-legged on the canvas futon that served as her bed and stared at it for a long time.

She'd been careful to make sure Judd hadn't followed her the night before. Her current nest was a drafty loft apartment in the attic of an old warehouse in the neighborhood just beyond the French Quarter. Save for her sleeping pallet, an antique cedar wardrobe, a Salvation Army-issue chair, a mini-fridge , a cordless telephone, and the scattered packing crates containing the esoteric curios she used as barter, the huge space was otherwise empty. Except for those occasions when the dead came to visit. Such as tonight.

At first she didn't recognize the ghost. He'd lost his sense of self in the years since his death, which blurred his spectral image somewhat. He swirled up through the floorboards like a gust of blue smoke, gradually taking shape before her eyes. It was only when the phantom produced a smoldering cigarette from his own ectoplasm that she recognized him for who he once had been.

"Hello, Chaz."

The ghost of her former renfield made a noise that sounded like a cat being drowned. The dead cannot speak clearly—even to Pretenders—except on three days of the year: Fat Tuesday, Halloween, and Candlemas. The ghost-light radiating from him was the only illumination in the room.

"Come to see how your murderer is getting on, I take it?"

Chaz made a sound like a church bell played at half speed.

"Sorry, I don't have a Ouija board, or we could have a proper conversation. Is there a special occasion for tonight's haunting, or are things just boring over on your side?"

Chaz frowned and pointed at the scrap of paper Sonja held in her hand. "What? You don't want me to call this number?"

Chaz nodded his head, nearly sending it floating from his shoulders.

"You tried warning Palmer away from me last Mardi Gras. Didn't work, but I suppose you know that already. He's living in Central America right now. We're very happy."

The ghost's laughter sounded like fingers raking a chalkboard. Sonja grimaced. "Yeah, big laugh, dead head. And I'll tell you one thing, Chaz: Palmer's a damn sight better in bed than you ever were!"

Chaz made an obscene gesture that was rendered pointless since he no longer had a body from the waist down. Sonja laughed and clapped her hands, rocking back and forth on her haunches.

"I *knew* that'd burn your ass, dead or not! Now piss off! I've got better things to do than play charades with a ghostly hustler!"

Chaz yowled like a baby dropped in a vat of boiling oil and disappeared in a swirl of dust and ectoplasm, leaving Sonja alone with Judd's phone number still clenched in one fist.

Hell, she thought as she reached for the cordless phone beside the futon. *If Chaz doesn't want me to call the guy, then it must be the right thing to do....*

The place where they rendezvoused was a twenty-four hour establishment in the French Quarter that had once been a bank, then a show-bar, then a porno shop, before finally deciding on being a coffee house. Judd's hair was freshly washed and he smelled of aftershave, but those were the only concessions made to the mating ritual. He still wore his nose— and earrings, as well as a Bongwater T-shirt that had been laundered so often the silk-screened image was starting to flake off.

Judd poked at the iced coffee with a straw. "If I'm not getting too personal—what was last night all about?"

Sonja studied her hands as she spoke. "Look, Judd. There's a lot about me you don't know—and I'd like to keep it that way. If you insist on asking about my past, I'm afraid I'll have to leave. It's not that I don't like you—I do—but I'm a very private person. And it's for a good reason."

"Is there someone else?"

"Yes. Yes, there is."

"A husband?"

She had to think about that one for a few seconds before answering. "In some ways. But, no. I'm not married."

Judd nodded as if this explained something. It was obvious that some of what she said was bothering him, but he was trying to play it cool. Sonja wondered what it was like, living a life where the worst things you had to deal with were jealous lovers and hurt feelings. It seemed almost paradisiacal from where she stood.

After they finished their iced coffees, they hit the Quarter. It was after midnight, and the lower section of Decatur Street was starting to wake up. The streets outside the bars were decorated with clots of young people dressed in black leather, sequins and recycled Seventies rags. The scenesters milled about, flashing their tattoos and bumming cigarettes off one another, as they waited for something to happen.

Someone called Judd's name, and he swerved across the street toward a knot of youths lounging outside a dance bar called Crystal Blue Persuasion. Sonja hesitated before following him.

A young man dressed in a black duster, his shoulder-length hair braided into three pig tails and held in place by Tibetan mala beads carved into the shapes of skulls, moved forward to greet Judd.

Out of habit, Sonja scanned his face for Pretender taint, but it came up human. While the two spoke, she casually examined the rest of the group loitering outside the club. Human. Human. Human. Hu—

She froze.

The smell of *vargr* was strong, like the stink of a wet dog. It was radiating from a young man with a shaved forehead like that of an ancient samurai. The hair at the back of his head was extremely long and held in a loose ponytail, making him look like a punk mandarin. He wore a leather jacket whose sleeves might well have been chewed off at the shoulder, trailing streamers of mangled leather and lining like gristle. He had one arm draped around a little punkette, her face made deathly pale by face powder.

The *vargr* met Sonja's gaze and held it, grinning his contempt. Her hand closed instinctively around her switchblade.

"I'd like you to meet a friend of mine—"

Judd's hand was on her elbow, drawing her attention away from the teenage werewolf. Sonja struggled to conceal the disorientation from having her focus broken.

"Huh?"

"Sonja, I'd like you to meet Arlo, he's an old buddy of mine…"

Arlo frowned at Sonja as if she'd just emerged from under a rock, but offered his hand in deference to his friend. "Pleased to meet you," he mumbled.

"Yeah. Sure."

Sonja shot a sideways glance at the *vargr* twelve feet away. He was murmuring something into the punkette's ear. She giggled and nodded her head, and the two broke away from the rest of the group, sauntering down the street in the direction of the river. The *vargr* paused to give Sonja one last look over his shoulder, his grin too wide and his teeth too big, before disappearing into the shadows with his victim.

That's right. Pretend you didn't see it. Pretend you don't know what that grinning hellhound's going to do with that girl. You can't offend lover-boy here by running off to do hand-to-hand combat with a werewolf, can you?

"Shut the fuck up, damn you," she muttered under her breath.

"You say something, Sonja?"

"Just talking to myself."

After leaving Arlo and his friends, they headed farther down into the French Quarter.

As they passed one of the seedy bars that catered to the late-night hardcore alcoholic trade, someone's mind called out Sonja's name. A black man, his hair plaited into dreadlocks, stepped from the doorway of the Monastery. He wore a black turtleneck sweater and immaculate designer jeans, a gold peace sign the size of a hood ornament slung around his neck.

"Long time no see, Blue."

"Hello, Mal."

The demon Malfeis smiled, exposing teeth that belonged in the mouth of a shark. "No hard feelings, I hope? I didn't want to sell you out like that, girlchick, but I was under orders from Below Stairs."

"We'll talk about it later, Mal...."

The demon nodded in the direction of Judd. "Got yourself a new renfield, I see."

"Shut up!" Sonja hissed, her aura crackling about her head like an electric halo.

Mal lifted his hands, palms outward. "Whoa! Didn't mean to hit a sore spot there, girly-girl."

"Sonja? Is this guy bothering you?" Judd was hovering at her elbow. He gave Mal a suspicious glare, blind to the demon's true appearance.

"No. Everything's cool." Sonja turned her back on the grinning demon and tried to block the sound of his laughter echoing in her mind.

"Who was that guy?"

"Judd—"

"I know! I promised I wouldn't pry into your past."

Sonja shrugged. "Mal is a—business associate of mine. That's all you need to know about him, except, no matter what, *never* ask him a question. *Ever.*"

They walked on in silence for a few more minutes, and then Judd took her into his arms. His kiss was warm and probing and she felt herself begin to relax. Then he reached for her sunglasses.

She batted his hand away, fighting the urge to snarl. "Don't do that."

"I just want to see your eyes."

"*No.*" She pulled away from him, her body rigid as a board.

"I'm sorry—"

"I better leave. I had a nice time, Judd. I really did. But I have to go."

"You'll call me, won't you?"

"I'm afraid so."

Why don't you fuck him? He wants it bad. So do you. You can't hide that from me.

The Other's voice was a nettle wedged into the folds of her brain, impossible to dislodge or ignore. Sonja opened the mini-fridge and took out a bottle of whole blood, cracking its seal open like she would a beer.

Not that bottled crap again! I hate this shit! You might as well go back to drinking cats! Wouldn't you rather have something nice and fresh? Say a good B negative mugger or an O positive rapist? There's still plenty of time to go trawling before the sun comes up... or you could always pay a visit to lover-boy.

"Shut up! I've had a bellyful of you tonight already!"

My-my! Aren't we being a touchy one? Tell me, how long do you think you can keep up the pretense of being normal? You've almost forgotten what it's like to be human yourself. Why torture yourself by pretending you're something you're not simply to win the favor of a piece of beefsteak?

"He likes me, damn it. He actually likes *me*."

And what exactly are you?

"I'm not in the mood for your fuckin' mind games!"

Welcome to the fold, my dear. You're finally one of us. You're a Pretender.

Sonja shrieked and hurled the half-finished bottle of blood into the sink. She picked up the card table and smashed it to the floor, jumping up and down on the scattered pieces. It was a stupid, pointless gesture, but it made her feel better.

She kept calling him. She knew it was stupid, even dangerous, to socialize with humans, but she couldn't help herself. There was something about Judd that kept drawing her back, against her better judgment. The only other time she'd known such compulsion was when the thirst was on her. Was this love? Or was it simply another form of hunger?

Their relationship, while charged with an undercurrent of eroticism, was essentially sexless. She wanted him so badly she did not dare do more than kiss or hold hands. If she should lose control, there was no telling what might happen.

Judd, unlike Palmer, was not a sensitive. He was human, blind and dumb to the miracles and terrors of the Real World, just like poor, doomed Claude Hagerty had been. Rapid exposure to the universe in which she lived could do immense damage.

To his credit, Judd hadn't pressed the sex issue overmuch. He wasn't happy with the arrangement, but honored her request that they "take it slow."

This, however, did not sit well with the Other. It constantly taunted her, goading her with obscene fantasies and suggestions concerning Judd. Or, failing to elicit a response using those tactics, it would chastise her for being untrue to Palmer. Sonja tried to ignore its gibes as best she could, but she knew that something, sometime was bound to snap.

Kitty wiped at the tears oozing from the corner of her eye, smearing mascara over her cheek and the back of her hand. It made the words on the paper swim and crawl like insects, but she didn't care.

She loved Judd. She really, truly loved him. And maybe after she did what she had to do to save him, he'd finally believe her. He needed proof of her love. And what better proof than to rescue him from the clutches of a monster?

Dearest Judd,

I tried to warn you about That Woman But you are blind to what she Really Is. She is Evil Itself a demon sent from <u>Hell</u> to claim your Soul. I knew her for what she truly <u>was</u> the moment I first saw her and she knew I knew, too! Her hands and mouth drip blood. Her eyes burn with the fires of Hell. She is surrounded by a cloud of red energy. Red as blood. She means to drag you to Hell, Judd. But I won't let her. I love you too much to let that happen. I'll take care of this horrible monster don't you worry. I've been talking to God a lot lately, and He told me how to deal with demons like her. I Love you so very, very much. I want you to Love me too. I'm doing this all for you. Please Love Me.

Kitty

Judd woke up at two in the afternoon, as usual. He worked six-to-midnight four days out of the week and had long since shifted over to a nocturnal lifestyle. After he got off work he normally headed down to the Quarter to chill with his buddies or, more recently, hang with Sonja until four or five in the morning before heading home.

He yawned as he dumped a couple of heaping tablespoons of Guatemalan into the hopper of his Mr. Coffee.

Sonja. Now there was a weird chick. Weird, but not in a schizzy, death-obsessed art-school freshman way like Kitty. Her strangeness issued from something far deeper than bourgeois neurosis. Sonja was genuinely *out there*, wherever that might be. There was something about the way she moved, the way she handled herself, which suggested she was plugged into something Real. And as frustrating as her fits of mood might be, he could not bring himself to turn his back on her.

Still, it bothered him that none of his friends liked her—not even Arlo, who he'd known since high school. Some of them even seemed to be *scared* of her. Funny. How could anyone be *frightened* of Sonja? Sure, she could be intense… but scary?

As he shuffled in the direction of the bathroom, he noticed an envelope that had been shoved under his front door. He stooped to retrieve it, scowling at the all-too-familiar handwriting.

Kitty.

Probably another one of her damn fool love letters, alternately threatening him with castration and begging him to take her back. Lately she'd taken to leaving rambling, wigged-out messages on his answering machine, ranting about Sonja being some kind of hell-beast out to steal his soul. Crazy bitch. Sonja was crazy, too, but not in such a predictable, boring way.

Judd tossed the envelope, unopened, into the trashcan and staggered off to the bathroom to take a shower.

Sonja Blue greeted the night from atop the roof of the warehouse where she made her nest. She stretched her arms wide as if to embrace the rising moon, listening with half an ear to the baying of the hounds along the riverbanks. Some, she knew, were not dogs.

But the *vargr* was not her concern. She'd tangled with a few werewolves over the years, but she preferred hunting her own kind. She found it vastly more satisfying.

The warehouse's exterior fire escape was badly rusted and groaned noisily with the slightest movement. Sonja avoided it altogether. She crawled, headfirst, down the side of the building, moving like a lizard on a garden wall. Once she reached the bottom, she pat-checked her jacket pockets to make sure nothing had fallen out during her descent.

There was a hissing sound in her head, as if someone had abruptly pumped up the volume on a radio tuned to a dead channel. Something heavy caught her between the shoulder blades, lifting her off her feet and knocking her into a row of garbage cans.

She barely had time to roll out of the way before something big and silvery smashed down where her head had been a second before. She coughed and black blood flew from her lips; a rib had broken off and pierced one of her lungs.

Kitty stood over her, clutching a three-foot-long, solid silver crucifix like a baseball bat. While her madness gave her strength, it was still obvious the damn thing was *heavy*. Sonja wondered which church she'd stolen it from.

The dead channel crackling in Sonja's head grew louder. She recognized it as the sound of homicidal rage. Shrieking incoherently, Kitty swung at her rival a third time. While crosses and crucifixes had no effect on her—on any vampire, for that matter—if Kitty succeeded in landing a lucky blow and snapped her spine or cracked open her skull, she was dead no matter what.

Sonja rolled clear and got to her feet in one swift, fluid motion. Kitty swung at her again, but this time Sonja stepped inside her reach and grabbed the crucifix, wresting it from the other woman's hands.

Kitty staggered back, staring in disbelief as Sonja hefted the heavy silver cross. It was at least three inches thick, the beams as wide as a man's hand, and at its center hung a miniature Christ fashioned of gold and platinum. Kitty watched expectantly, waiting for Sonja's hand to burst into flames.

"What the hell did you think you were going to solve, clobbering me with this piece of junk?" Sonja snarled.

Kitty's eyes were huge, the pupils swimming in madness. "You can't have him! I won't let you take his soul!"

"Who said anything about me stealing—"

"Monster!" Kitty launched herself at Sonja, her fingers clawing at her face. "Monster!"

Sonja hit her with the crucifix.

Kitty dropped to the alley floor, the top of her skull resting on her left shoulder. The only thing still holding her head onto her body were the muscles of her neck.

Way to go, kiddo! You just killed lover-boy's bug-shit ex-girlfriend! You're batting a thousand!

"Shit."

She tossed the crucifix aside and squatted next to the body. No need to check for vital signs. The girl was d-e-a-d.

What to do? She couldn't toss the corpse in the dumpster. Someone was bound to find it, and once the body was identified New Orleans Homicide would take Judd in for questioning. Which meant they'd be looking for *her*, sooner or later. And she couldn't have that.

I've got an idea, crooned the Other. *Just let me handle it.*

Stealing the car was easy. It was a '76 Ford LTD with a muffler held in place with baling wire and a *Duke for Governor* sticker on the sagging rear bumper. Just the thing to unobtrusively dispose of a murder victim in the swamps surrounding New Orleans during the dead of night.

She took an exit off the Interstate heading east out of New Orleans, to where there was what was to have been yet another cookie-cutter housing development built on the very fringes of the marshlands of Lake Pontchartrain. The contractors got as far as pouring the concrete slab foundations before the oil slump hit. The condos were never built, but the access road from the Interstate still remained, although there was nothing at its end but an overgrown tangle of briars and vines that had become a breeding ground for snakes and alligators.

She drove the last mile without lights. Not that she needed them. She could see just fine in the dark. Having reached her destination, she cut the engine and rolled to a stop. Except for the chirring of crickets and the grunting of gators, everything was quiet.

Sonja climbed out of the car and opened the trunk with a length of bent coat hanger. She stood for a second, silently inventorying the collection of plastic trash bags. There were six, total: one for the head, one for the torso, and one apiece for each limb. She'd already burned Kitty's clothing in the warehouse's furnace and disposed of her jewelry and teeth by tossing them into the river.

She gathered up the bags and left the access road, heading in the direction of the swamp. She could hear things splashing in the water, some of them quite large.

She paused for a second on the bank of the marsh. Something nearby hissed at her, then slithered out of the way. She tossed the bag containing Kitty's head into the murky water.

"Come and get it 'fore I slop it to the hogs!" she called.

The assembled gators splashed and wrestled among themselves for the tender morsels like ducks fighting for scraps of stale bread.

Sonja was tired. Very tired. After this was over she still had to drive the stolen car to a suitably disreputable urban area and set it on fire. She looked down at her hands. They were streaked with blood. She absently licked them clean.

When she was finished, the Other looked through her eyes and smiled.

The Other wasn't tired. Not in the least.

It hadn't been a very good night, as far as Judd was concerned. He'd gotten chewed out concerning his attitude at work, Arlo and the others had treated him like he had a championship case of halitosis, and, to cap the evening, Sonja pulled a no-show. Time to pack it in. It was four o'clock when he got home. He was in such a piss-poor mood he didn't even bother to turn on the lights.

His answering machine, for once, didn't have one of Kitty's bizarro messages on it. Nothing from Sonja, either. He grunted as he removed his shirt. Was she mad at him? Had he said or done something the last time they were together that ticked her off?

It was hard to figure out her moods, since she refused to take off those damn mirrored sunglasses. Judd wondered how she could navigate in the dark so well while wearing those fuckers.

Something moved at the corner of his eye. It was the curtain covering the window that faced the alley. Funny, he didn't remember leaving that open...

Someone stepped out of the shadows, greeting him with a smile that displayed teeth that were too sharp. Judd felt his heart jerk into overdrive as the adrenaline surged into his system. Just as he was ready to yell for help, he recognized her.

"S-Sonja?"

"Did I scare you?" Her voice sounded like something out of *The Exorcist*. She sniffed the air and her smile grew even sharper. "Yes. Yes, I *did* scare you, didn't I?" She moved toward him, her hands making slow, hypnotic passes as she spoke. "I *love* the smell of fear in the morning."

"Sonja, what's wrong with your voice?"

"Wrong?" The Other chuckled as she unzipped her leather jacket. "I *always* sound like this!"

She was on him so fast he didn't even see her move, lifting him by his belt buckle and flinging him onto the bed so hard he bounced. She grabbed his jaw in one hand, angling it back so the jugular was exposed. Judd heard the click of a switchblade and felt a cold, sharp pressure against his throat.

"*Sonja—?*"

"Do not struggle. Do not cry out. Do as I command, and maybe I'll let you live. Maybe."

"What do you want?"

"Why, my dear, I just want to get to know you better." The Other removed the sunglasses protecting her eyes with her free hand. "And vice versa."

Judd had often wondered what Sonja's eyes looked like. Were they almond-shaped or round? Blue, brown, or green? He'd never once pictured them as blood red with pupils so hugely dilated they resembled shoe buttons.

The Other smirked, savoring the look of disgust on Judd's face. She pressed her lips against his, thrusting his teeth apart with her tongue, and penetrated his will with one quick shove of her mind.

Judd's limbs twitched convulsively then went still as she took control of his nervous system. The Other disengaged, physically, and stared down at him. He couldn't move, his body locked into partial paralysis. Satisfied her control was secure, she moved the switchblade from Judd's throat.

"I can see why she finds you attractive. You're a pretty thing... *very* pretty." The Other reached out and pinched one of his nipples. Judd didn't flinch. "But she's much too old-fashioned when it comes to sex, don't you agree? She's afraid to let herself go and walk on the wild side. She's so *repressed*."

The Other shrugged out of her leather jacket, allowing it to fall to the floor. "I will explain this to you once, and once only. I *own* you. If you do as I tell you, and you please me, then you shall be rewarded. Like *this*."

She reached into his cortex and tweaked its pleasure center. Judd shuddered as the wave of ecstasy swept over him, his hips involuntarily humping empty air.

"But if you fight me, or displease me in *any* way—then I will punish you. Like *so*."

Judd emitted a strangled cry as he was speared through the pain receptor in his brain. It felt as if the top of his skull had been removed and someone had dumped the contents of an ant farm on his exposed brain. His back arched until he thought his spine would snap. Then the pain stopped as if it'd never been there at all.

"Hold me."

Judd did as he was told, dragging himself upright and wrapping his arms around her waist. The Other knotted her fingers in his hair, pulling his head back so she could look into his eyes.

"Am I hurting you? Say yes."

"Yes."

"Good."

She smiled, exposing her fangs, and he realized that it was just beginning.

They fucked for three hours straight, the Other skillfully manipulating his pleasure centers so that he remained perpetually erect despite his physical exhaustion. She randomly induced orgasms, until they numbered in the dozens. After the seventh or eighth climax, he was shooting air. She seemed to enjoy his wails each time he spasmed.

As dawn began to make its way into the room, she severed her control of Judd's body. He fell away from her in midthrust, his eyes rolled back behind flickering lids. The Other dressed quickly, her attention fixed on the rising sun. Judd lay curled in fetal position among the soiled and tangled bedclothes, his naked body shuddering and jerking as his nervous system reasserted its control.

"Parting is such sweet sorrow," purred the Other, caressing his shivering flank. Judd gasped at her touch but did not pull away. "You pleased me. *This* time. So I will let you live. *This* time."

She lowered her head to his neck, brushing his jugular lightly with her lips. Judd squeezed his eyes shut in anticipation of the bite. But all she did was whisper: "Get used to it, lover-boy."

When he opened his eyes again, she was gone.

The Other took a great deal of pleasure in telling Sonja what it had done to Judd, making sure not to leave out a single, tasty detail as it reran that morning's exploits inside her skull.

Sonja's response to the news was to scream and run headfirst into the nearest wall, then to continue pounding her skull against the floorboards until her glasses shattered and blood streamed down her face and matted her hair. She succeeded in breaking her nose and shattering both cheekbones before collapsing.

"Girly-girl! Long time no see! What brings you into my little den of iniquity this time?"

The demon Malfeis sported the exterior of a flabby white male in late middle age, dressed in a loud plaid polyester leisure suit with white buck loafers. A collection of gold medallions dangled under his chins and he held a racing form in one hand.

Sonja slid into the booth opposite the demon. "I need magic, Mal."

"Don't we all? Say, what's that with the face? You can reconstruct better than that...."

She shrugged, one hand absently straying to her swollen left cheek. The bone squelched under her fingertips and slid slightly askew. Heavy-duty facial reconstruction required feeding in order for it to be done right, and she'd deliberately skipped her waking meal.

"You tangle with an ogre? One of those *vargr* punks?"

"Leave it be, Mal."

Malfeis shrugged. "Just trying to be friendly, that's all. Now, what kind of magic are you in the market for?"

"Binding and containment."

The demon grunted and fished out a pocket calculator, his exterior flickering for a moment to reveal a hulking creature that resembled an orangutan with a boar's snout. "What kind of demon are you looking to lock down?"

"I wish to have myself bound and contained."

Malfeis glanced up from the calculator, a sour look on his face. "Are you shitting me or what?"

"Name your price, damn you."

"Don't be redundant, girlchick."

Sonja sighed and hefted a knapsack onto the tabletop. "I brought some of my finest acquisitions. I've got hair shaved from Ted Bundy's head just before he was to go to the chair, dried blood scraped from the walls of the LaBianco home, a spent rifle casing from the grassy knoll, and a cedar cigar box with what's left of Rasputin's penis in it. Quality shit. I swear by its authenticity. And it's all yours, if you do this one thing for me."

Malfeis fidgeted, drumming his talons against the table. Such close proximity to so much human suffering and evil was bringing on a jones. "Okay, I'll do it. But I'm not going to take responsibility for anything that happens to you."

"Did I ask you to?"

"Are you *sure* about this, Sonja?"

"Your concern touches me, Mal. It really does."

The demon shook his head in disbelief. "You really mean to go through with this, don't you?"

"I've already said so, haven't I?"

"Sonja, you realize once you're in there, there's no way you'll be able to get out, unless someone on the outside breaks the seal."

"Maybe."

"There's no *maybe* to it!" he retorted.

"The spell you're using is for the binding and containment of vampire energies, right?"

"Of course. You're a vampire."

She shrugged. "Part of me is. And I'm not letting it out to hurt anyone ever again. I'm going to kill it or die trying."

"You're going to *starve* in there!"

"That's the whole point."

"Whatever you say, girly-girl."

Sonja hugged herself as she stared into the open doorway of the meat locker. It was cold and dark inside, just like the Other's heart. "Let's get this show on the road."

Malfeis nodded and produced a number of candles, bottles of oil, pieces of black chalk, and bags of white powder from the Gladstone bag he carried. Sonja swallowed and stepped inside the meat locker, drawing the heavy door closed behind her with a muffled thump.

Malfeis lit the candles and began to chant in a deep, sonorous voice, scrawling elaborate designs on the outer walls of the locker with the black chalk. As the chanting grew faster and more impassioned, he smeared oil on the hinges and handle of the door. There was an electric crackle and the door glowed with blue fire.

Malfeis' incantation lost all semblance of human speech as it reached its climax. He carefully poured a line of white powder across the threshold, made from equal parts salt, sand and the crushed bones of human babies. Then he stepped back to assess his handiwork.

To human eyes it looked like someone had scrawled graffiti all over the face of the stainless-steel locker, nothing more. But to Pretender eyes, eyes adjusted to the Real World, the door to the locker was barred by a tangle of darkly pulsing *vévé*, the semisentient protective symbols of the *voudou* powers. As long as the tableau remained undisturbed, the entity known as Sonja Blue would remain trapped within the chill darkness of the meat locker.

Malfeis replaced the tools of his trade in the Gladstone bag. He paused as he left the warehouse, glancing over his shoulder.

"Goodbye, girly-girl. It was nice knowing you."

"I'm looking for Mal."

The bartender looked up from his racing form and frowned at Judd. After taking in his unwashed hair and four days' growth of beard, he nodded in the direction of the back booth.

Judd had never been inside the Monastery before. It had a reputation as being one of the sleazier—and most uninviting—French Quarter dives, and he could see why. The booths lining the wall had once been church pews. Plaster saints in various stages of decay were scattered about on display. A Madonna with skin blackened and made leprous by age regarded him from above the bar with flat, faded blue eyes. She held in her arms an equally scabrous Baby Jesus, its uplifted chubby arms ending in misshapen stumps. Hardly a place to party down big-time.

Judd walked to the back of the bar and looked into the last booth. All he saw was a paunchy middle-aged man dressed in a bad suit smoking a cigar and reading a dog-eared porno novel.

"Excuse me...?"

The man in the bad suit looked up at him, arching a bushy, upswept eyebrow, but said nothing.

"Uh, excuse me—but I'm looking for Mal."

"You found him."

Judd blinked, confused. "No, I'm afraid there's been some kind of mistake. The guy I'm looking for is black, with dreadlocks..."

The man in the bad suit smiled. It was not a pleasant sight. "Sit down, kid. He'll be with you in just a moment."

Still uncertain of what he was getting himself into, Judd slid into the opposite pew.

The older man lowered his head, exposing an advanced case of male pattern baldness, and hunched his shoulders. His fingers and arms began vibrating, the skin growing darker as if his entire body had suddenly become bruised. There was a sound of dry grass rustling under a high wind and thick, black dreadlocks emerged from his scalp, whipping about like a nest of snakes. Judd was too shocked by the transformation to do anything but stare.

Mal lifted his head and grinned at Judd, tugging at the collar of his turtleneck. "Ah, yes. I remember you now. Sonja's renfield."

"My name's not Renfield."

Mal shrugged indifferently . "So, what brings you here, boychick?"

"I'm looking for Sonja. I can't find her."

"That's because she doesn't want to be found."

"But I *have* to find her! Before she does something stupid. Kills herself, maybe."

Mal regarded the young human, a slight smile on his face. "Tell me more."

"Something—happened between us. She feels responsible for hurting me. She sent me this letter a few days ago." Judd fished a much-folded envelope out of his back pocket and held it out to Mal. "Here, you read it."

The demon took the letter out of its envelope like a gourmet removing an escargot from its shell. He unfolded the paper, carefully noting the lack of signature and the smears of blood in the margins.

Judd,

I can never be forgiven for what was done to you, even though I was not the one who did those thing. Please believe that. It was her. She is the one that makes me kill and hurt people. She is the one who hurt you.

I promise I'll never let her hurt anyone, ever again. Especially you. I'm going to try something I should have done years ago, before she became so strong. So dangerous. So uncontrollable. She's sated right now. Asleep in my head. By the time she becomes aware of what I'm planning to do, it'll be too late. I'm going to kill her. I may very well end up killing myself in the bargain, but that's a chance I'm willing to take. I won't let her hurt anyone ever again, damn her. I love you, Judd. Please believe that. Don't try to find me. Escape while you can.

"She doesn't understand." Judd was close to tears as he spoke. "I *do* forgive her. I *love* her, damn it! I can't let her *die!*"

"You know what she is." It wasn't a question.

Judd nodded. "I know. And I don't *care.*"

"So why have you come to me?"

"You know where she is, don't you?"

Malfeis shifted in his seat, his eyes developing reptilian slits. "Are you asking me a question?"

Judd hesitated, recalling Sonja's warning that he should never, under any circumstance, ask Mal a question. "Uh, yeah."

Mal smiled, displaying shark's teeth. "Before I respond to any questions put to me, you must pay the price of the answer. Is that understood, boychick?"

Judd swallowed and nodded.

"Very well. Tell me your name. All of it."

"That's all you want?" Judd frowned, baffled. "My name is Michael Judd Rieser."

"To know a thing's name gives one power over that thing, my sweet. Didn't they teach you that in school? Come to think of it, I guess not."

"What about my question? Do you know where Sonja is?"

"Yes, I do." The demon scrawled an address on the back of the letter Judd had given him. "You'll find her here. She's inside the meat locker on the ground floor."

"Meat locker?"

"I wouldn't open it if I were you."

Judd snatched up the address and slid out of the pew. "But I'm *not* you!"

Malfeis watched Judd hurry out of the bar with an amused grin. "That's what *you* think, boychick." He leaned back and closed his eyes. When he reopened them, he was white with shoulder-length hair pulled in a ponytail, a ring in his nose, and a four days' growth of beard.

It was cold. So very, very cold.

Sonja sat huddled in the far corner of the meat locker, her knees drawn up to her chest. Her breath drifted from her mouth and nostrils in wispy flumes before condensing and turning to frost on her face.

How long? How many days had she been here? Three? Four? Twenty? A hundred? There was no way of telling. She no longer slept. The Other's incessant screams and curses made sure of that.

Let me out! Let me out of this hellhole! I've got to feed! I'm starving!

"Good."

You stupid cunt! If I starve to death, you go with me! I'm not a damned tapeworm!

"Couldn't prove it to me."

I'm getting out of here! I don't care what you say!

Sonja did not fight the Other as it asserted its ascendancy over her body. The Other forced her stiffened limbs to bend, levering her onto her feet. Her joints cracked like rotten timber as she moved. She staggered in the direction of the door. In her weakened condition she had difficulty seeing in the pitch black of the meat locker. She had abandoned the sunglasses days ago, but as her condition worsened, so did her night vision.

Her groping hands closed on the door's interior handle. There was a sharp crackle and a flash of blue light as she was thrown halfway across the locker. She screamed and writhed like a cat hit by a car, holding her blistered, smoking hands away from her body. This was the twentieth time she'd tried to open the door and several of her fingers were on the verge of gangrene.

"You're not going anywhere. Not now. Not *ever!*"

Fuck you! Fuck you! I'll get you for this, you human-loving cow!

"What? Are you going to *kill* me?"

Sonja crawled back to her place in the corner. The effort started her coughing again, bringing up black, clotted blood. She wiped at her mouth with the sleeve of her jacket, nearly dislocating her jaw in the process.

You're falling apart. You're too weak to regenerate properly....

"If you hadn't pounded your head against the fuckin' wall trying to get out in the first place—"

You're the one that got us locked up in here! Don't blame me!

"I *am* blaming you. But not for that."

It's that fucking stupid human again! You think you can punish me for that? I didn't do anything that you hadn't already fantasized about!

"You raped him, damn you! You could have killed him!"

I didn't, though. I could have. But I didn't.

"I *loved* him!" Sonja's voice cracked, became a sob.

You didn't love him. You loved being mistaken for human. That's what you're really mad at me about. You're upset that I ruined your little game of Let's Pretend!

"Shut up."

Make me.

Judd checked the street number of the warehouse against the address that Mal had given him. This was the place. It was one of the few remaining warehouses in the district that had not been turned into an overpriced yuppie ghetto. There was a small sign posted on the front door that read Indigo Imports, and a heavy chain and double padlock wrapped about the handle. A quick check of the ground floor confirmed that all the windows were secured with burglar bars. Still, there had to be some way of getting in and out.

He rounded the side of the building and spotted the loading dock. After a few minutes of determined tugging, he succeeded in wrenching the sliding metal door open wide enough for him to slide under. The inside of the warehouse was lit only by the midafternoon sunlight slanting through the barred windows. The place smelled of dust and rat piss.

The meat locker was on the ground floor, just where Mal said it would be. Its metal walls and door were covered in swirls of spray-painted graffiti. What looked like a huge line of cocaine marked the locker's threshold. Judd grabbed the door's handle and yanked it open. There was a faint crackling sound and a rush of cold, foul air. He squinted into the darkness, covering his nose and breathing through his mouth to mask the stench.

"Sonja?"

Something moved in the deepest shadows of the freezer.

"J-Judd? Is that you?"

"It's me, baby. I've come to get you out of here."

"Go away, Judd. You don't know what you're doing."

Judd stepped into the locker, his eyes finally adjusting to the gloom. He could see her now, crouching in the far corner with her knees drawn against her chest, her face turned to the wall.

"No, you're wrong, Sonja. I know exactly what I'm doing."

"I let her hurt you, Judd. I could have stopped her, but I didn't. I let her—let her—" Her voice trailed off as her shoulders began to shake. "Go away before I hurt you again."

Judd kneeled beside her. She smelled like a side of beef gone bad. Her hands were covered with blisters and oozing sores. Some of her fingers jutted at odd angles, as if they had been broken and not properly set. She pulled away at his touch, pressing herself against the wall as if she could somehow squeeze between the cracks.

"Don't look at me."

"Sonja, you don't understand. I *love* you. I know what you are, what you're capable of—and I love you anyway."

"Even if I hurt you?"

"*Especially* when you hurt me."

She turned her head in his direction. Her face looked like it had been smashed, then reassembled by a well-meaning but inept plastic surgeon with only a blurry photograph to go by. Her eyes glowed like those of an animal pinned in the headlights of an oncoming car.

"What?"

Judd leaned closer, his eyes reflecting a hunger she knew all too well. "At first I was scared. Then, after a while, I realized I wasn't frightened anymore. I was actually getting into it. It was like the barriers between pain and pleasure, animal and human, ecstasy and horror, had been removed! I've never known anything like it before! It was *incredible!* I love you, Sonja! *All* of you!"

She reached out and caressed his face with one of her charred hands. She had turned him into a renfield. In just a few hours the Other had transformed him into a junkie, and now she was his fix.

"I love you too, Judd. Kiss me."

She sat behind the wheel of the car for a long time, staring out into the dark on the other side of the windshield. Nothing had changed since the last time she'd been out here, disposing of Kitty.

She pressed her fingertips against her right cheek, and this time it held. Her fingers were healed and straight again as well. She readjusted her shades, opened the car door and slid out from behind the wheel of the Caddy she'd bought off the lot, cash in hand.

Judd was in the trunk, divvied up into six garbage bags, just like Kitty. At least it'd been fast. Her hunger was so intense she drained him dry within seconds. He hadn't tried to fight when she buried her fangs in his throat, even though she hadn't the strength to trance him. Maybe part of him knew she was doing him a favor.

She dragged the bags out of the trunk and headed in the direction of the alligator calls. She'd have to leave New Orleans, maybe for good this time. Kitty might not have been missed, but Judd was another story. Arlo was sure to mention his suspicions concerning his missing friend's weirdo new girlfriend to the authorities.

It was time to blow town and head for Merida. Time to go pay Palmer a visit and check on how he and the baby were making out.

Palmer.

Funny how she'd forgotten about him. Of all her human companions, he was the only one she'd come closest to truly loving. Before Judd, that is.

She hurled the sacks containing her lover's remains into the water and returned to the car. She tried not to hear the noise the gators made as they fought among themselves.

She climbed back into the car and slammed a cassette into the Caddy's tape deck. Lard's *The Last Temptation of Reid* thundered through the speakers, causing the steering wheel to vibrate under her hands. She wondered when the emptiness would go away, or at least be replaced by pain. Anything would be preferable to the nothing inside her.

I don't see why you had to go and kill him like that. We could have used a renfield. They do come in handy, now and then. Besides, he was kind of cute....

"Shut up and drive."

tender tigers

The Ogre does what ogres can,
Deeds quite impossible for Man,
But one prize is beyond his reach,
The ogre cannot master Speech:
About a subjugated plain
Among it's desperate and slain
The Ogre stalks with hands on hips,
While drivel gushes from his lips.

—The Ogre, W.H. Auden

You don't hear much about ogres nowadays. There are tons of books and movies and other media tie-ins about fairies and elves out there. That's because they're supposed to be cutesy-poo make-believe shit the size of your thumb. Like hell they are.

The same goes for the proliferation of vampires in pop culture, except they've been reinvented as the ultimate misunderstood bad boy. It's hard to believe that humans can take reanimated corpses who feed on the blood of the living and turn them into romantic icons, but there you go.

It doesn't work for ogres, though. They're too scary for the modern nursery, and they certainly don't cut it as sex symbols. Not unless your idea of a cozy evening is a cuddle on the couch with Leatherface.

In a world that can produce the likes of Jeffrey Dahmer, stories of cannibal monsters who look enough like humans that they can marry into normal families without anyone being the wiser cuts a little too close to the bone. So ogres have been downgraded from superstition to folklore, along with all the other long-legged beasties and things that used to go bump in the night. Which suits them just fine. It's much easier to go about your work when nobody believes you exist.

As Pretenders go, ogres are something of a poor cousin. They lack the vampires' mesmeric powers and the were-races' ability to shapeshift. They do not possess the *strega* and the *sidhe*'s inborn talent for sorcery. What they do have in their favor is being very, very strong, and in the females' case, being for the most part indistinguishable from humans. However, the males can only pass while they're young. Once they start developing bull-ogre attributes, there's no way they can be mistaken for "normal" in human society—at least not without considerable camouflage.

If the stories are true, the ogres once battled with and preyed upon the Neanderthals, over whom they had significant advantages in the survival-of-the-fittest department. They were kings of Shit Mountain back then.

Then the Cro-Mags made the scene. Although the Cro-Magnons were considerably smaller and physically weaker than the ogres, they had the nasty habit of using tools. Especially sharp ones that could be used from a distance. Things soon got out of hand, and the ogres' stock began its steady decline.

Still, with their immense strength, hardy physique and smallish brains, ogres have found a place for themselves in Pretender society, mostly by providing muscle to those who require it. They make loyal servants and tireless watchdogs. And, in their own way, they are dedicated parents. As commendable as that might sound, you have to bear in mind that ogres raise their young by stalking human families, hollowing them out, and living inside them. Not literally, mind you, but close enough.

I've had more than a few run-ins with ogres over the years, but mostly because they were in the service of a vampire noble, or doing scut work for human crime bosses or foreign military dictatorships. But every now and again I come across the odd free-range ogre....

It is not that unusual to see unsupervised youngsters going to and from the Laundromat with bundles of clothes. What caught my eye was how young this particular child was. She couldn't have been any older than seven. She was far too small to be manhandling a shopping cart full of clothes and laundry supplies so late at night. She could barely see over its top, and she pushed it with both hands.

While she doggedly maneuvered the overloaded cart up the street, I scanned a half block before and behind her, trying to spot any adult who might be accompanying her. There was no one to be found. This made my antennae go up. Unattended children are the favorite prey of virtually every breed of Pretender, not to mention your average human monsters. As a precaution, I opened my sight even farther, scanning the pedestrians and other passersby in the area. While there were plenty of seedy types loitering on the surrounding doorsteps, none of them were werewolves or vampires.

When the child rounded the corner and headed up a side street, I decided to follow her. I kept to the shadows, trailing a safe distance behind—

not so close that I would be noticed, but near enough to act should a smiling stranger emerge from a doorway or lean out of a passing car.

Suddenly, one of the wheels on the overloaded laundry cart gave way, jack-knifing its contents onto the pavement. The girl gave a horrified gasp and clapped her hands to her mouth. There was a look of fear on her face that was more in keeping with someone who had foreseen her imminent death than a child who had had a small accident. That's when I decided to surrender the shadows and step forward.

"Hey, kid, you need some help?"

She spun to face me, panic in her bright blue eyes. Then, upon seeing I was a stranger, the fear was replaced by relief.

"Fiona's gonna be mad," she said simply, and then stooped to gather up the clothes.

"Is that so?" I replied as I righted the cart. "Is Fiona your mom?"

"No," she said, with an emphatic shake of her head. "My mommy's dead."

"Then who is this Fiona then?" I asked, taking an armload of laundry, still warm from the dryer, and dropping it back into the cart.

"She's my daddy's wife."

I lifted an eyebrow and tried to smile as openly as I could without showing my teeth. "My name's Sonja. What's yours?"

"Tiffany."

"That's a pretty name."

Tiffany shrugged shoulders as fragile as those of a baby bird. "My daddy says I'm named after a lamp."

"They're very beautiful lamps."

A look of curiosity crossed her pale face, transforming her weary features into those of child again. "Really? Have you seen one?"

I found her interest contagious, and I couldn't keep myself from chuckling. "Not only have I seen one, I actually *own* one."

"Wow! Could I see it sometime?" Tiffany asked, her eyes sparkling like her namesake.

"Nothing's impossible."

"Tiffany!"

The voice was as shrill as a dentist's drill and just as pleasant to experience. I looked up to see a woman with a towering bouffant, heavy thighs and ample bosom, dressed in skin-tight zebra-print leggings and an appliquéd kitty-cat sweatshirt, rapidly bearing down on us. Tiffany's face drained of all color and animation, returning to its previous gray slackness.

"Fiona," she said dully, in way of explanation.

As Tiffany's stepmother drew closer, I caught a scent not unlike that of the lion house at the zoo. It was clear that my presence had not gone unnoticed as well. The ogress froze in her tracks, her piggish eyes narrowing at the sight of me. She tossed her head and made a snorting noise, like a wild boar that had caught wind of a mountain lion.

In such close quarters, it was easy for me to spot the flaws in the ogress' camouflage. Her fingernails were unnaturally long and curled inward, with elaborate tribal totems etched into them, and her hairdo served to hide her peaked skull. Her skin was coarsely grained, like the leather of a well-oiled catcher's mitt, and she gave off a raw, animal stink not unlike a big cat. Her teeth were small and sharp, and there were far too many of them, which accounted for her clipped manner of speaking.

"Tiffany," Fiona said, lowering her voice so it no longer sounded like a table saw cutting through sheet metal. "What's been keeping you, child?"

Tiffany glanced in my direction before answering. "The wheel on the cart came off again, and this lady was helping me fix it."

"I'll take over from here, if you don't mind," Fiona said brusquely. She took a step forward, extending her hand toward Tiffany. "Come along, dear. Your dinner's getting cold."

Tiffany frowned, clearly baffled by Fiona's behavior. The presence of strangers had probably never been enough to keep her stepmother's wrath at bay before. She looked at me again, her brow furrowed.

"No problem," I said, keeping my voice as even as I could. "I'll be more than happy to help push the cart the rest of the way."

Fiona's eyes clicked back and forth, trapped. She was unprepared to face a predator of my stature.

"Hey, Mama! S'up?"

The ogre who came to Fiona's side was young, probably no more than nine or ten years old, but he was already the size of a fifteen-year-old, with a jutting jaw, beetling brow, splayed nostrils and jagged teeth. His shoulders were wide and heavily muscled, sprouting long arms and oversized hands. His legs were bandy and his feet wide, although his build was hidden, for the most part, by ultra-baggy hip-hop pants and a matching shirt. A multi-colored knit stocking cap was pulled low over his thick brow. He was odd looking, but still capable of passing for human in public. Judging from the size of his feet and the width of his shoulders, he would be at least seven feet tall, possibly more, by the time he reached his full growth.

"No, Garth," Fiona said, patting her offspring's shoulder. "There's no trouble. *Now.*"

"Come along home, Tiffany, dear," Fiona said, displaying a fearsome set of sharklike teeth. "We mustn't keep your daddy waiting."

She knew I would not risk a public confrontation with two ogres. I had no choice but to relinquish my grip on the cart. There was nothing I could do but stand and watch as Fiona and her hulking son escorted Tiffany toward an apartment building on the corner. For appearance's sake, Fiona was actually pushing the heavily laden cart instead of Tiffany.

I knew the ogres would be watching me to see what I would do next, so I turned and headed back up the street without looking back. Once I rounded the corner, I broke into a run toward the street behind Tiffany's building. I entered the cramped lobby of the tenement that stood back to back with the apartment building the ogres had entered and pushed all the intercom buttons until I was rewarded with a buzz. I ignored the dingy elevator, taking the crooked stairs three at a time. I made the roof in less than ninety seconds.

A quick glance told me Tiffany's building had a courtyard that served as a holding bay for the tenants' garbage, which put at least thirty feet between her rooftop and the one I was on. I moved to the far end of the roof and made for the opposite ledge at a dead run. One moment I was bound by gravity, the next I was flying through the air, my nostrils filled with the pungent reek of rotting garbage rising from five stories down.

I hit the rooftop, rolling with the fall like a paratrooper, and came up on my feet. I quickly brushed myself off and trotted to the rear fire escape. I eased myself onto the metal stairs, careful to avoid the potted plants and hibachis illegally stowed on the landings by various tenants. I had learned a long time ago how not to be seen, but not being heard was another question. I had to be careful not to alert not only my prey, but their neighbors as well.

It didn't take me long to figure out which apartment was Tiffany's. The reek of cooped-up ogre radiating from their third-story window was strong enough to cut through the stench from the garbage below. Careful to remain in shadow, I peeked in through the window.

My first impression was that the room was full of jellyfish. Then I realized what I thought were tendrils drifting from the ceiling were actually scores of yellowed, insect-encrusted flypaper strips. The room looked to be the kitchen and living room, as well as the bathroom, judging from the tub located next to the decrepit stove.

Tiffany's father sat at the filthy Formica dinette table near the window. He was dressed in a dirty polo shirt and a pair of stained khaki pants. With his sallow complexion, bleary eyes and unshaven jaw, he looked like a junkie. He was strung out, all right. But not on smack or crack, or even that old standby, demon rum. No, the drug he was on was far more insidious than any that could be snorted, smoked, guzzled or run up.

As I peered in the window, the front door of the apartment opened and Fiona and Garth entered, followed by Tiffany, who was once again pushing the heavy cart. The moment the door closed behind them, Fiona's mouth pulled into a snarl that would have backed down a mandrill baboon.

"Stupid, horrid little bitch! How many times have I told you to *talk to no one*!"

She cuffed the girl's ear so hard Tiffany fell to the floor. The girl's father flinched as his daughter was struck, but did not open his mouth or try to stand up.

"Yeah," Garth said, grinning like a jack-o'-lantern, drool dripping from his lower lip. "You're stupid! Stupid! *Stupid!*"

Fiona whirled and slapped Garth in mid-taunt. The young ogre rubbed his jutting jaw, an uncomprehending look on his face.

"What'd I do, Ma?"

"You're no better than she is! You don't even realize how much danger we were in out there!"

Garth furrowed his brow and stuck his lower lip out. "I could have handled it...."

"She was *enkidu*, you witless fool! She would have torn you apart like fresh bread!"

Garth blinked a couple of times as he attempted to process the information he'd been given. He pulled the stocking hat off his head, revealing a bald, leathery pate stretched across a peaked skull.

"That was a *vampire?*" he said after a long pause.

Fiona did not bother to answer, but merely shook her head in disgust. Her gaze fell on Tiffany, who was still huddled on the floor, struggling to control her tears.

"Stop your whimpering, you little wretch! " She grabbed Tiffany's arm, roughly yanking the child onto her feet. "You still have chores to do before you're fed!"

"Let go! You're hurting me!" Tiffany cried as Fiona's birdlike talons bit into the flesh of her upper arm.

Tiffany's father's eyes flashed and his body jerked as if he'd been given a jolt of electricity. "Let her go, damn you!" he croaked.

Fiona let the child's arm drop and turned to face Tiffany's father. "My, my, *my*!" she sneered. "Looks like you need another fix, sweetie! I can't have you growing a backbone on me *now*, can I?"

Tiffany's father twitched and a look of anticipation mixed with sick fear crossed his wasted features. She was threatening him with what he both dreaded and lived for. He licked his lips with a dry tongue.

"Please," he whispered hoarsely. I couldn't tell if he was begging for mercy or pleading for more.

Fiona pulled her sweatshirt off, baring her upper torso. Her breasts were large and heavy, the nipples the size of a man's thumb and the areolas a bruised color.

Tiffany's father's twitch became a full-blown tremor, vibrating his chair like a tuning fork, as he stared at Fiona with lust and horror. Garth smirked as his mother removed her leggings. Tiffany lowered her head and hurried from the room, her cheeks burning bright red.

The ogress stood nude before her human husband, her taloned hands planted on her hips, legs splayed to better display her sex. Her lips pulled into a twisted smile as she studied her victim's face.

"Oh, yeah. You're jonesing bad, aren't you?"

She grabbed Tiffany's father by the throat, lifting him from his seat as if he weighed no more than his daughter. His eyes bugged slightly from the pressure on his carotid, and although his mouth worked like a goldfish's, he did not put up a struggle. Fiona tossed him onto the floor, where he laid on his back, the only signs of life the movement of his eyes and the erection tenting his pants.

The ogress straddled Tiffany's father, unzipped his fly and, after a few seconds of rummaging, freed his turgid penis. She laughed and glanced over at her son, who grinned and nodded his head, sharing an unspoken joke between them. Then, without further preliminaries, Fiona lowered herself onto Tiffany's father and began pumping her hips.

I was reminded more of a farmer milking a cow than of the sex act. This was something she had to do to keep control of her household situation, nothing more, nothing less. Tiffany's father's eyelids trembled like those of a junkie on the needle and his jaw dropped open.

The mucous membranes of an ogress's vagina are impregnated with chemicals that act like a cross between Spanish Fly, Viagra and crack, with a liberal dose of DMSO. The moment a human male sticks his dick in an ogress, he's in for the fuck of his life, no two ways about it.

Since the scattering of their tribes and the rise of the human empires, ogresses have managed to preserve the species by seeking out widowed or divorced human males and utilizing their desperation for sexual relations to gain control of them. The men they pick are usually passive types to begin with, and once the ogresses work their erotic arts, they are in complete and utter thrall. In time, the humans lose interest in bathing, eating, drinking... everything but the one thing they must have.

I grew bored watching the ogress rape her human and decided to see where Tiffany had gone. I eased myself over the fire escape railing and crawled headfirst around the corner, clinging to the brick face like a lizard on a garden wall.

I found Tiffany in a cramped bedroom, peering into a white crib with a picture of a yellow duck carrying a red umbrella emblazoned on the headboard. The floor of the room was littered with empty beer bottles and upended buckets of take-out barbecue ribs, the gnawed bones scattered about the floor like jackstraws. A plastic pail behind the door overflowed with dirty diapers.

"Look who's awake from his nap! Can you give Cissy a smile, Cully? That's a good boy!" Tiffany smiled down at the occupant and gave the Winnie-the-Pooh mobile hanging over the crib a spin. "What? You want me to play peekaboo?" She picked up a stained blanket draped over the foot of the crib and held it in front of her face. "Where's Cully? Where'd Cully go?" Whatever was in the crib gurgled in delight. "Peekaboo! There he is!" she said with mock surprise as she dropped the blanket away from her face. It was the first time I saw anything resembling a little girl shining in her eyes.

The bedroom door crashed open with such force it was knocked off its hinges. Fiona filled the threshold. She was still nude, her monstrosity exposed for all to see. Her toenails were long and curved, like the claws of an iguana, and her carefully maintained bouffant had unraveled, revealing her pointed skull. Still, as ogresses go, she was quite the looker.

"You know you're not supposed to play with the baby!" Fiona shrieked as she advanced on Tiffany. *"You're a bad girl!* You know what happens to *bad girls*, don't you?"

Tiffany mutely shook her head. She was too frightened to even cry.

"They get eaten up by monsters!" the ogress said, licking her lips with a pointed tongue.

As Fiona grabbed Tiffany's upper arm, the child finally found the breath to scream. It was a high, thin cry, like a kitten being tossed down a well. Fiona snarled and backhanded the girl, sending her flying across the room, where she dropped, unconscious, between the bed and the wall.

That was my cue.

I entered the apartment in a shower of glass. The ogress spun around, her lips drawn back in a jagged grimace.

"I told you to keep your distance, vampire! The morsel's mine!"

There was no point in trying to tell her I was not interested in Tiffany as food. She wouldn't believe me even if I tried. So I bared my fangs and growled deep in my chest. Before I could move on Fiona, I was slammed into the wall hard enough to shake the plaster loose.

"I've got her, Ma! I've got her!" Garth crowed.

Fiona's piggy eyes bulged. *"Garth! Get away from her!"*

"You should really listen to your mother," I said, then grabbed his head and jerked it in a direction it was not designed to go. There was a loud snapping sound, like a bundle of dry kindling being broken in half, and the young ogre fell to the floor.

I was lucky Garth was a preadolescent. Had he been a year or two older, there would have been no way I could have broken his neck so easily.

Fiona stared at the body of her son for a long moment, then looked directly into my face. Her lips pulled back even farther, exposing rows of needle-sharp teeth. She charged, her talons at the ready. She was fighting not only for her life, but the life of her remaining offspring.

The ogress' fingernails were hard as horn and sharp as knives, slicing through my leather jacket like it was tissue paper. I felt something warm and sticky spread across my belly, signaling the drawing of first blood. If I didn't want to find myself tripping over my own guts, I would do well to keep some distance between us.

I tried to reach into her mind, but Fiona had been around long enough to know what a psychic probe felt like. She furrowed her brow and snapped her teeth in rage, saliva flying from her lips. It would take too much time to wrest control of her motor center. Better to get this over with as quickly as possible, before the neighbors finally decided to call the cops.

I flexed my right arm, freeing the switchblade from its sheath inside the jacket's sleeve. It fell butt first into my cupped palm, and I ran my thumb across the dragon wrapped about the hardwood handle, pressing the ruby chip that served as its eye. I was rewarded by its silver blade springing forth, quick as a serpent's tongue. The ogresses' piggy little eyes narrowed in confusion as she spied the weapon. Vampires don't need to fill their hands in combat.

I feinted with the knife, making as if I were going to stab her in the belly. The ogress moved to block the blow, just as I knew she would. At the very last moment, I drove the blade into her left eye. Unfortunately, doing so put me within striking distance of her talons. I felt a sharp pain and then saw the end of my nose fly across the room in a spray of blood. Still, I did not dare let go of the switchblade as I twisted it in her eye socket.

The ogress shrieked like a wounded panther and pushed me away. She staggered drunkenly toward the crib, the switchblade still jutting from her eye, blood pouring from her nose and ears. Ogres are not allergic to silver like vampires and werewolves, but a knife in the brain is a bad thing, no matter what species you are.

Fiona's legs buckled on her third step. She grabbed the crib to keep from falling, smearing gore across the headboard. She gargled something in the language of her kind, doubtless a curse on my head, and collapsed, face first, onto the floor, the switchblade punching its way through the back of her skull like an ice pick going through a ripe cantaloupe.

I nudged her in the ribs with my boot, and then flipped her over in order to retrieve my blade, wiping it clean on my jacket sleeve. As I stood up, I touched the tip of my nose or, rather, where the tip of my nose *used* to be, and my fingers came away sticky with the thick, blackish-red ichor that passes for my blood. It would take a day's rest to reconstruct the damage, nothing more. I'd have to spend the rest of the night walking around looking like Michael Jackson, but that was far preferable to trying to get across town while holding my intestines in place with a borrowed dinner plate.

Now that Fiona and Garth were taken care of, the last thing on my "to do" list for the night was to dispose of the whelp. I leaned over the crib, knife at ready, but all I found was a tangle of bedclothes and a teddy bear with chewed-off ears.

"Don't hurt my brother."

Tiffany was standing in the farthest corner of the room, clutching a squirming bundle to her thin chest. I have to admit I was surprised the girl was still alive. Although there was a bruise spreading its dark bloom across her cheek, and her lower lip was swollen to twice its normal size, she seemed otherwise unharmed.

Realizing what I must look like, I tried my best to get the whelp away from her without frightening her. "Tiffany... honey. Give me the baby."

Tiffany tightened her grip and drew away, even though she knew she had no hope of escaping. "I won't let you hurt Cully."

"Tiffany... He's *not* your brother. Fiona tricked you father into thinking Cully was his so he would help feed and care for it. Once it got old enough to walk and talk, Fiona was going to *feed* you to it. It's an ogre... a *monster*... just like Fiona and Garth."

Tiffany shook her head, tears building in her eyes. "But he's just a *baby!* See—?" She flipped back the blanket, exposing the whelp's face.

To my surprise, it was actually cute, although in the same way baby rhinos and gorillas are cute. It looked human enough to fool the casual observer, although the width of its jaw and the shape of its skull and brow were somewhat odd. The fact it already had a full set of teeth was something of a giveaway, too.

"You love your Cissy, don't you, Cully?" Tiffany cooed. The whelp smiled broadly and reached out with a pudgy hand capped with tiny, pointed fingernails, and squeezed Tiffany's nose, giggling with babyish glee.

"See? He *loves* me!" she said, holding Cully out for my inspection. The whelp bared its milk fangs and hissed like a startled kitten, clawing the air in my direction.

"Yes. I see." I replied, stepping forward.

"*No!*" Tiffany wailed, pulling her precious bundle tight to her chest. "Who *says* he has to be like them?"

"He's an *ogre*, Tiffany. That's just how ogres *are*."

"But what if I teach him to be a *good* monster?"

Jesus, the kid was really busting my chops.

"Tiffany," I sighed. "That's impossible."

"Why?" she asked, her voice trembling on the verge of tears. "Just because he *is* a monster doesn't mean he has to *be* a monster! *You're* a good monster, aren't you?"

I opened my mouth, but could not find anything to say.

"I *knew* you weren't going to hurt me," Tiffany said. "Fiona thought you wanted to eat me. But I knew you were different. I don't know why, but I just *did*."

I cocked my head and dropped my vision into the occult spectrum. There was a faint glimmer of intuition about the child's head—not enough to qualify as a sixth sense, but enough to be of use in tight situations. I wondered if she had been born with it, or whether her ordeal with Fiona and her demonic brood had forced its development.

I turned and left the bedroom, stepping over Fiona and Garth's cooling bodies, and entered the combination living room and kitchen. Tiffany's father was curled up in the middle of the floor in fetal position, muttering to himself under his breath as he rocked back and forth. He quickly lifted his head upon hearing my footsteps.

"*Fiona—?*" he whispered hoarsely.

I grabbed Tiffany's father by the back of his neck and carried him into the bedroom like a kitten. Upon seeing his second wife splayed in a slowly expanding pool of blood, his entire body began to shake.

"*Thank God,*" he sobbed. "*Thank God, thank God...*"

He staggered as I let go of him. I didn't know how much longer Tiffany's father had, but at least he possessed enough sanity to rejoice over his captor's demise.

"Do you have family elsewhere?"

Tiffany's father nodded weakly. "Back in New Mexico."

I reached into the breast pocket of my jacket and removed a thick fold of hundred dollar bills I keep for emergencies. "Take this. Pack what you can in two suitcases and go. Don't worry about the cops. There's no way in hell the authorities are going to pursue this, believe me. Besides, homicide only applies to human beings. Take Tiffany and the baby and walk away like this never happened. "

Tiffany's father shot a fearful look at Cully, who promptly bared his little milk fangs and growled. He swallowed loudly, and then looked back at me.

"Are you sure?"

I glanced at the snarling ogre whelp, then at Tiffany's tear-stained face.

"Family is family. Whatever else Cully might be, he's still your son. " Having told that lie, , I turned my back on Tiffany, her father and Cully and walked out of the apartment and their lives. I had done what I could; now it was up to them. I have not seen or heard from them since. Nor do I expect to.

Every now and again, though, I wonder whether I made a mistake not destroying the ogre when I had the chance. But then I remember how it smiled and cooed in Tiffany's arms, and how brightly the love in her eyes had shone for the monstrous infant she claimed as kin, and my doubts are set aside.

There is a character from one of the old Oz books called the Hungry Tiger. Like his companion, the Cowardly Lion, he was a most uncommon talking beast. Although the Hungry Tiger longed to eat fat babies, even drooled when he thought about it, his tender heart would not allow him to do such a horrid thing.

There is no telling what role nature plays over nurture in human families, much less those of ogres. If it turns out I made the wrong decision, Tiffany and her father will no doubt pay with their lives, if they have not done so already. But if it turns out I made the right decision... well, the world could stand a few more tender tigers.

vampire king of the goth chicks

—from the journals of Sonja Blue

The Red Raven is a real scum-pit. The only thing marking it as a bar is the vintage Old Crow ad in the front window and a stuttering neon sign that says *lounge*. The johns are always backing up and the place perpetually stinks of piss.

During the week, it's just another neighborhood dive, serving truck drivers and barflies. Not a Bukowski among them. But, since the drinks are cheap and the bartenders never check ID, the Red Raven undergoes a sea change come Friday night. The bar's clientele transforms radically, growing younger and stranger, at least in physical appearance. The usual suspects who occupy the Red Raven's booths and bar stools during the week are replaced by young men and women tricked out in black leather and so many facial piercings they resemble walking tackle boxes. Still not a Bukowski among them.

This Friday night's no different from any other. A knot of Goth kids are already gathered outside on the curb when I arrive, plastic go-cups full of piss-warm Rolling Rock clutched in their hands while they talk among themselves. Amid all the bad Cure haircuts, heavy mascara, dead-white face powder and black lipstick, I hardly warrant a second look.

Normally I don't bother with joints like this, but I've been hearing this persistent rumor that there's a blood cult operating out of the Red Raven. I make it my business to check out such rumors for myself. Most of the time it turns out to be nothing, but occasionally there's something far more sinister at the heart of urban legends.

The interior of the Red Raven is crowded with young men and women, all of whom look far stranger and more menacing than I do.

What with my black motorcycle jacket, ratty jeans, and equally tattered New York Dolls T-shirt, I'm on the conservative end of the dress code.

I wave down the bartender, who doesn't seem to consider it odd I'm sporting sunglasses after dark, and order a beer. It doesn't bother me that the glass he hands me bears visible greasy fingerprints and a smear of lipstick on the rim. After all, it's not like I'm going to drink what's in it.

Now that I have the necessary prop, I settle in and wait. Finding out the lowdown in places like this isn't that hard, really. All I've got to do is be patient and keep my ears open. Over the years I've developed a method for listening to dozens of conversations at once—sifting the meaningless ones aside without even being conscious of it, most of the time, until I find the one I'm looking for. I suspect it's not unlike how a shark can pick out the frenzied splashing of a wounded fish from miles away.

"...told him he could kiss my ass goodbye..."

"...really liked their last album..."

"...bitch acted like I'd done something..."

"...until next payday? I promise you'll get it right back..."

"...the undead. He's the real thing..."

There. That one.

I angle my head in the direction of the voice I've zeroed in on, trying not to look at them directly. There are three of them—one male and two female—in earnest conversation with a third young woman. The first two females are archetypal Goth chicks. They look to be in their late teens, early twenties, dressed in a mixture of black leather and lingerie and wearing way too much eyeliner. One is tall and willowy, her heavily applied makeup doing little to mask the bloom of acne on her cheeks. Judging from the roots of her boot-black hair, she's probably a natural dishwater blonde.

Her companion is considerably shorter and a little too pudgy for the black satin bustier she's shoehorned into. Her face is painted clown white with an ornate tattoo at the corner of her left eye, which I've been told is more in imitation of a popular comic book character than in tribute to the Egyptian gods. She's wearing a man's riding derby draped in a length of black lace that makes her look taller than she really is.

The male member of the group is tall and skinny, outfitted in a leather jacket and a pair of matching pants held up by a monstrously ornate silver belt buckle. He isn't wearing a shirt, and his bare breastbone is hairless and a tad sunken. He's roughly the same age as the girls, perhaps younger, and constantly nodding in agreement with whatever they say, nervously flipping his lank, burgundy-colored hair out of his face. It doesn't take me long to discern that the tall girl is called Sable, the short one in the hat is Tanith, and the boy is Serge. The girl they are talking to has close-cropped Raggedy-Ann-red hair and a nose ring. She is Shawna.

Out of habit, I drop my vision into the Pretender spectrum and scan them for signs of inhuman taint. All four check out clean. Oddly, this piques my interest. I move a little closer to where they are standing huddled so I can filter out the Marilyn Manson blaring from the jukebox.

Shawna shakes her head and smiles nervously, uncertain as to whether she's being goofed on or not. "C'mon—a *real* vampire?"

"We told him about you, Shawna, didn't we, Serge?" Tanith looks to the gawky youth hovering at her elbow. Serge nods his head eagerly, which necessitates him flipping his hair out of his face yet again.

"His name is Rhymer. Lord Rhymer. He's three hundred years old," Sable adds breathlessly, "and he said he wanted to meet you!"

Despite her attempts at post-modern death-chic, Shawna looks like a flattered schoolgirl.

"Really?"

I can tell she's hooked as clean as a six-pound trout and that it won't take much more work on the trio's part to land their catch. The quartet of black-leather clad young rebels quickly leave the Red Raven, scurrying off as fast as their Doc Martens can take them. I give it a couple of beats then set out after them.

As I shadow them from a distance, I can't shake the nagging feeling that something is wrong. I seem to have found what I've come looking for, but something's not quite right about it and I'll be damned (I know— I'm being redundant) if I can say what.

In my experience, most vampires avoid Goths like daylight. While their adolescent fascination with death and decadence might, at first, seem to make them natural choices as servitors, their extravagant fashion sense attracts far too much attention. Vampires prefer their servants far more nondescript and discrete. But perhaps this Lord Rhymer, whoever he may be, is of a more modern temperament than those I've encountered in the past.

I don't know what to make of this trio who seem to be acting as his Judas goats. Judging by their evident enthusiasm, perhaps "converts" is a far more accurate description than servitors. They don't seem to have the predator's gleam in their eyes, nor is there anything resembling a killer's caution in their walks or mannerisms. As they stroll down the darkened streets their chatter is more like that of mischievous children out on a lark—say TP-ing the superintendent's front lawn or soaping the gym teacher's windows. They certainly aren't aware of the extra shadow that attached itself to them the moment they left the Red Raven with their fresh pick-up.

After a ten-minute walk they arrive at their destination—an abandoned church. Of course. It's hardly Carfax Abbey, but I suppose it will do. The church is a two-story wooden structure boasting an old-fashioned spire, stabbing a symbolic finger in the direction of Heaven.

The feeling of ill-ease rises in me again. Vampires dislike such obvious lairs. Hell, these aren't the Middle Ages. They don't have to hang out in ruined monasteries and family mausoleums anymore—not that there are any to be found in the US, anyhow. No, contemporary bloodsuckers prefer to dwell in warehouse lofts or abandoned industrial complexes, even condos. I tracked one dead boy to ground in an inner-city hospital that had been shut down during the Reagan administration. I suspect I'll have to start investigating the various military bases scheduled for shutdown for signs of infestation within a year or two.

As I watch the little group troop inside the church, there is only one thing I know for certain—if I want to know what's going down here, I better get inside. I circle around the building, keeping to the darkest shadows, my senses alert for signs of the usual sentinels that guard a vampire's lair, such as ogres and renfields. Normally vampires prefer to keep their bases covered. Ogres for physical protection, renfields—warped psychics—to protect them against psionic attacks from rival bloodsuckers.

I reach out with my mind as I climb up the side of the church, trying to pick up the garbled snarl of ogre-thought or the tell-tale dead-space of shielded minds accompanying renfields, but all my sonar picks up is the excited heat of the foursome I trailed from the Red Raven and a slightly more complex signal from deeper inside the church. Curiouser and curiouser.

The spire doesn't house a bell—just a rusting Korean War-era public address system dangling from frayed wires. As it is, there is barely enough room for a man to stand, much less ring a bell, but at least the trapdoor isn't locked. It opens with a tight squeal of disused hinges, but nothing stirs in the shadows at the foot of the ladder below. Within seconds I find myself with the best seat in the house, crouched in the rafters spanning the nave.

The interior of the church looks appropriately atmospheric. What pews remain are in disarray, the hymnals tumbled from their racks and spilled across the floor. Saints, apostles, and prophets stare down from the windows, gesturing with upraised shepherd's crooks or hands bent into the sign of benediction. I lift my own mirrored gaze to the mullion window located behind the pulpit. It depicts a snowy lamb kneeling on a field of green, framed against a cloudless sky, in which a shining disc is suspended. The large brass cross just below the sheep-window has been inverted, in keeping with the desecration motif.

The only light comes from a pair of heavy cathedral-style candelabras, each bristling with over a hundred dripping red and black candles, that flank either side of the pulpit. The Goth kids from the Red Raven gather at the chancel rail, their faces turned toward the pulpit situated above the black-velvet-draped altar.

"Where is he?" whispers Shawna, her voice surprisingly loud in the empty church.

"Don't worry," Tanith assures her. "He'll be here."

As if on cue, there is the smell of ozone and a gout of purplish smoke arises from behind the pulpit. Shawna gives a little squeal of surprise despite herself and takes an involuntary step backward, only to find her way blocked by the others.

A deep, highly cultured, masculine voice booms forth. "Good evening, my children. I bid you welcome to my abode that you enter gladly and of your own free will."

The smoke clears, revealing a tall man dressed in tight-fitting black satin pants, a black silk poet's shirt, black leather English riding boots, and a long black opera cape with a red silk lining. His hair is long and dark, pulled back into a loose ponytail by a red satin ribbon. His skin is as white as milk in a saucer, his eyes reflecting red in the dim candlelight. Lord Rhymer has finally elected to make his appearance.

Serge smiles nervously at his demon-lord and steps forward, gesturing to Shawna as Tanith and Sable watch expectantly. "W-we did as you asked, master. We brought you the girl."

Lord Rhymer smiles slightly, his eyes narrowing at the sight of her.

"Ah, *yesss*. The new girl."

Shawna stands there gaping up at the vampire lord as if he were Jim Morrison, Robert Smith and Glenn Danzig all rolled into one. She starts, gasping more in surprise than fright, as Rhymer addresses her directly.

"Your name is Shawna, is it not?"

"Y—yes." Her voice is so tiny it makes her sound like a little girl. But there is nothing childlike about the lust dancing in her eyes.

Lord Rhymer holds out a pale hand to the trembling young woman. His fingernails are long and pointed and lacquered black. He smiles reassuringly, his voice calm and strong, designed to sway those of a weaker nature.

"Come to me, Shawna. Come to me, so that I might kiss you."

A touch of apprehension crosses the girl's face. She hesitates, glancing at the others, who close in about her even tighter than before.

"I... I don't know."

Rhymer narrows his blood-red eyes, intensifying his stare. His voice grows sterner, revealing its cold edge. "*Come* to me, Shawna."

All the tension in her seems to drain away and Shawna's eyes grow even more vacant than before. She moves forward, slowly mounting the stairs to the pulpit. Rhymer holds his arms out to greet her.

"That's it, my dear. Come to me as you have dreamed, so many times before..." Rhymer steps forward to meet her, the cape outstretched between his arms like the wings of a giant bat. His smile widens and his mouth opens, exposing pearly white fangs dripping saliva. His voice is husky with lust. "Come to me, my bride..."

Shawna grimaces in pain and pleasure as Rhymer's fangs penetrate her throat. Even from my shadowy perch above it all I can smell the sharp tang of blood, and feel a dark stirring at the base of my brain, which I quickly push aside. I don't need that kind of trouble—not now. Still, I find it hard to look away from the tableau below me.

Rhymer holds Shawna tight against him. She whimpers as if on the verge of orgasm. The blood rolling down her throat and dripping into the pale swell of her cleavage is as sticky and dark as spilled molasses.

Rhymer draws back, smiling smugly as he wipes the blood off his chin. "It is done. You are now bound to me by blood and the strength of my immortal will."

Shawna's lids flutter and she seems to have trouble focusing her eyes. She touches her bloodied neck and stares at her red-stained finger for a long moment.

"*Wow...*" is all she can say.

She steps back, a dazed, post-orgasmic look on her face. She staggers slightly when she moves to rejoin the others, one hand still clamped over her bruised and bleeding throat. Tanith and Sable eagerly step forward to help their new sister, their hands quickly disappearing up her skirt as they steady her, cooing encouragement in soothing voices.

"Welcome to the family, Shawna," Sable whispers, kissing first her cheek, then tonguing her earlobe.

"You're one of us, now and forever," Tanith purrs, giving Shawna a probing kiss while scooping her breasts free of her blouse. Sable presses even closer, licking at the blood smearing Shawna's neck. Serge stands off to one side, nervously chewing a thumbnail and occasionally brushing his forelock out of his face. Every few seconds his eyes flicker from the girls to Lord Rhymer, who stands in the pulpit, smiling and nodding his approval. After a few more moments of groping and gasping, the three women begin undressing one another in earnest, their moans soon mixed with nervous giggles. Black leather and lace drop away, revealing black fishnet stockings and garter belts and crotchless underwear. At the sight of Shawna's pubic thatch—mousy brown, as opposed to her fluorescent red locks—Serge's eyes widen and his nostrils flare. He looks to Rhymer, who nods and gestures languidly with one taloned hand to signal that the boy has his permission to join the orgy.

Serge fumbles with his ornate silver belt buckle, which hits the wooden floor with a solid *clunk!* I lift an eyebrow in surprise. While Serge is thin to the point of emaciation, I must admit the boy's hung like a stallion. Sable mutters something into Serge's ear that makes him laugh just before he plants his lips against her own blood-smeared mouth. Tanith, her eyes heavy-lidded and her lips pulled into a lascivious grin, reaches around from behind to stroke him to full erection.

Serge breaks free of his embrace with Sable and turns to lift Shawna in his arms, carrying her to the black-draped altar, the other girls quickly joining in. There is much biting and raking of exposed flesh with fingernails. Soon they are a mass of writhing naked flesh, giggling and moaning and grunting, the slap of flesh against flesh filling the silent church. And overseeing it all from his place of power is Lord Rhymer, his crimson eyes twinkling in the candlelight as he watches his followers cavorting below him. To his credit, Serge proves himself tireless, energetically rutting with all three girls in various combinations for hours on end.

It isn't until the stained glass windows of the church begin to lighten with the coming dawn that it finally comes to an end. The moment Rhymer notices the light coming through one of the windows the smile disappears from his face.

"Enough!" he thunders, causing the others to halt in mid-fuck. "The sun will soon be upon me! It is time for you to leave, my children!"

The Goths pull themselves off and out of each other without a word of complaint and begin to struggle back into their clothes. Once they're dressed they waste no time hurrying off, taking pains not to look one another in the eye. It is all I can do to suppress a groan of relief as the last of the blood cultists lurches out of the building. I thought those losers were *never* going to leave!

I check my own watch against the shadows sliding across the floor below me. Now would be a good time to pay a social call on their so-called master. I hope he's in the mood for a little chat before beddy-bye.

Lord Rhymer yawns as he makes his way down the basement stairs. What with the candelabra he's holding and the flowing opera cloak, I'm reminded of Lugosi's Dracula. But then, unlike this guy, Bela Lugosi is dead.

The basement runs the length of the building above it, with a poured concrete floor. Stacks of old hymnals, folding chairs, and moldering choir robes have been pushed into the corners. A rosewood casket with a maroon velvet lining rests atop a pair of sawhorses in the middle of the room. An old-fashioned steamer trunk stands on end nearby.

I watch the vampire lord set the candelabra down and, still yawning, unhook his cape and carefully drape it atop the trunk. If he senses my presence, here in the shadows, he gives no evidence of it in his manner. Smiling crookedly, I deliberately scrape my boot heel against the concrete floor. My smile becomes a grin as he spins around, eyes bugging in fear.

"What—? Who's there?"

He blinks, genuinely surprised to see me standing to one side of the open casket balanced atop the sawhorse. I'd already caught the tell-tale smell when I first entered the basement, but a quick glance into the casket confirms what I already knew. It's lined with earth. I reach inside and lift a handful of dirt, allowing it to spill between my splayed fingers. I look up and meet Rhymer's scarlet gaze.

"Okay, buddy, what the hell are you trying to pull here—?"

Rhymer squares his shoulders and pulls himself up to his full height, hissing and exposing his fangs, hooking his fingers into talons. His red eyes glint in the dim light like those of a cornered animal.

I am not impressed.

"Can the Christopher Lee act, asshole! I'm not some Goth chick tripping her brains out! You're not fooling me for one moment!" I kick the sawhorses out from under the casket, sending it tumbling to the floor, spilling its layer of soil. Rhymer gasps, his eyes darting from the ruined coffin to me and back and again. "Only *humans* think vampires need to sleep on a layer of their home soil!"

Rhymer tries to regain the momentum by pointing a trembling finger at me, doing his best to sound menacing. "You have defiled the resting place of Rhymer, Lord of the Undead! And for that, woman, you will pay with your life!"

"Oh yeah?" I sneer. "Buddy, I *knew* Dracula—and, believe me, you ain't him!"

I move on him so fast it's like blinking. One moment I'm halfway across the room, the next I'm standing over him, his blood dripping from my knuckles. Rhymer's lying on the basement floor, dazed and wiping at his gushing mouth and nose. A set of dentures, complete with fangs, lies on the floor beside him. I nudge the upper plate with the toe of my boot, shaking my head in disgust.

"Just what I thought. Fake fangs! And the eyes are contact lenses, right? I bet the nails are theatrical quality press-ons, too."

Rhymer tries to scuttle away from me like a crab, but he's much too slow. I grab him by the ruff of his poet's shirt, pulling him to his feet with one quick motion that causes him to yelp in alarm.

"What the fuck are you playing at here? Are you running some kind of scam on these Goth kids?"

Rhymer opens his mouth and although his lips are moving there's no sound coming out. At first I think he's so scared he's not able to speak—then I realize he's a serious stutterer when he's not a vampire.

"I'm n-not a c-con m-man, if that's what y-you're thinking. I'm n-not doing it for m-money!"

"If it's not for money—then why?" Not that I haven't known his motivation from the moment I first laid eyes on him. But I want to hear it from his own lips before I make my decision.

"All m-my life I've been an outsider. N-no one ever p-paid any attention to m-me. N-not even m-my own p-parents. N-no one ever took me seriously. I was a j-joke and everyone k-knew it. The only p-place where I could escape from being m-me was at the m-movies. I really admired the v-vampires in the m-movies. They were d-different, too. But n-no one m-made fun of them or ignored them. They were p-powerful and p-people were afraid of them. They c-could m-make w-women do whatever they w-wanted.

"W-when my p-parents died a c-couple of years ago, they left m-me a lot of m-money. So m-much I'd n-never have to work again. An hour after their funeral I w-went to a dentist and had all m-my upper teeth removed and the dentures m-made.

"I always w-wanted to be a v-vampire—and now I had the c-chance to live m-my d-dreams. So I b-bought this old church and s-started hanging out at the Red Raven, looking for the right type of g-girls.

"T-tanith was the first. Then came S-sable. The rest w-was easy. They w-wanted m-me to b-be real so b-badly, I didn't even have to p-pretend that m-much. B-but then things started to g-get out of hand. They w-wanted m-me t-to—you know—p-put my thing in them. B-but m-my thing c-can't get hard. N-not with other p-people. I told them it w-was because I w-was undead. So we f-found S-serge. I-I like to w-watch."

Rhymer fixes one of his rapidly blackening eyes on me. His fear is beginning to give way to curiosity. "B-but w-what difference is any of this to y-you? Are y-you a family m-member? One of S-serge's ex-g-girlfriends?"

I can't help but laugh as I let go of him, careful to place myself between Rhymer and the exit. He staggers backward and quickly, if inelegantly, puts distance between us. He flinches at the sound of my laughter as if it was a physical blow.

"I knew there was something fishy going on when I spotted the belt buckle on the Goth stud-muffin. No self-respecting dead boy in his right mind would let that chunk of silver within a half mile. And all that hocus-pocus with the smoke and the Black Sabbath folderol! All of it a rank amateur's impression of what vampires and vampirism is all about, cobbled together from Hammer films and Anton Levy paperbacks! You really are a pathetic little twisted piece of crap, Rhymer—or whatever the hell your real name is! You surround yourself with the icons of darkness and play at damnation—but you don't recognize the real thing even when it steps forward and bloodies your fuckin' nose!"

Rhymer stands there for a long moment, then his eyes widen and he gasps aloud, like a man who has walked into a room and seen someone alive he has believed long dead. Clearly overcome, he drops to his feet before me, his blood-stained lips quivering even more uncontrollably than before.

"Y-y-y-you're real!"

"Get up," I growl, flashing a glimpse of fang.

Instead of inspiring fear in Rhymer, all this does is cause him to cry out even louder than before. He is now actually groveling, pawing at my boots as he blubbers.

"At last! I k-knew if I w-waited long enough, one of y-you w-would finally c-come!"

"I said *get up*, you little toadeater!" I kick him away, but it does no good. Rhymer crawls back on his belly, as fast as a lizard on a hot rock. I was afraid something like this would happen.

"I'll do anything you w-want—give you anything you n-need!" He grabs the cuffs of my jeans, tugging insistently. "B-bite me! Drink my b-blood! *Pleeease!* M-make me like you!"

As I look down at this wretched human who has lived a life so stunted, his one driving passion is to become a walking dead man, I feel my memory slide back across the years, to the night a foolish young girl, made giddy by the excitement that comes with the pursuit of forbidden pleasures and made stupid by the romance of danger, allowed herself to be lured away from the safety of the herd. I remember how she found herself alone with a blood-eyed monster that hid behind the face of a handsome, smooth-talking stranger. I remember how her nude, blood-smeared body was hurled from the speeding car and tossed in the gutter and left for dead. I remember how she was far from dead. I remember how she was me.

I am trembling like I've got a high-grade fever. My disgust has become anger, and I've never been very good at controlling my anger. And part of me—a dark, dangerous part—has no desire ever to learn.

I try to keep a grip on myself, but it's not easy. In the past when I've been overwhelmed by my anger I've tried to make sure I vent it only at those I consider worthy of such murderous rage, such as vampires. Real ones, that is. But sometimes... well, sometimes I lose it. Like now.

"You want to be like *me*?"

I kick the groveling little turd so hard he flies across the basement floor and collides with the wall. He cries out as his ribs splinter like balsa wood, but it doesn't exactly sound like pain.

"You stupid bastard! *I* don't even want to be like *me*!

I tear the mirrored sunglasses away, and. Rhymer's eyes widen as he sees my own. They look nothing like his scarlet-tinted contact lenses. There is no white, no corona—merely seas of solid blood boasting vertical slits that open and close like those of a snake, depending on the strength of the light. The church basement is very gloomy, so my pupils are dilated wide—like those of a shark rising from the sunless depths to savage a luckless swimmer.

Rhymer lifts a hand to block out the sight as I advance on him, his trembling delight now replaced by genuine, one-hundred-per-cent monkey-brain fear. For the first time he seems to realize that he is in the presence of a monster.

"Please don't hurt me, mistress! Forgive me!" he screams.

I don't know what else he might have said to avoid his fate, because his head came off in my hands right after that.

For a brief second Rhymer's hands still flutter in their futile attempt to beg my favor, then there is a spurt of scarlet from the neck stump, not unlike that from a spitting fountain, as his still-beating heart sends a stream of blood to where the brain would normally be. I quickly sidestep the gruesome spray without letting go of my trophy.

Turning away from Rhymer's still-twitching corpse, I step over the ruins of the antique coffin and its payload. No doubt the dirt had been imported from the Balkans—perhaps Moldavia or even Transylvania. I shake my head in amazement that such old wives' tales are still in circulation.

As I head up the stairs, Rhymer's head tucked under my arm, I pause one last time to survey what is left of the would-be vampire king of the Goth chicks. Man, what a mess. Glad I'm not the one who has to clean it up.

This isn't the first vampire wannabe I've run in to, but I've got to admit, he had the best scam. The Goth chicks wanted the real thing, and he gave them what they thought they wanted, even down to retrofitting the church with theatrical trapdoors and magician's flash pots. And they bought into the bullshit because it made them feel special, it made them feel real, and most importantly, it made them feel *alive*. Poor, stupid bastards. To them it's all black leather, love bites, and tacky chrome jewelry, where everyone is eternally young and beautiful and no one can ever hurt you ever again.

Like hell.

As for Rhymer, he wanted the real thing as badly as the Goths. Perhaps even more so. He'd spent his entire life aspiring to monstrosity, hoping that given time his heartfelt mimicry of the damned would either turn him into that which he longed to be through sympathetic magic, or that his actions would eventually draw the attention of the creatures of the night he worshipped so ardently. As, indeed, it had. I was the real thing all right: big as life and twice as ugly.

But I was hardly the bloodsucking seductress Rhymer had been dreaming of all those years. There was no way he could know that his little trick would lure forth not just a vampire—but a vampire-slayer as well.

My unique and unwanted predicament has denied me many things— the ability to age, to love, to feel life quicken within me. And in retaliation against this unwished for transformation, I've spent decades denying the monster inside me; trying—however futilely—to turn my back on the horror that is the Other who dwells in the dark side of my soul. However, there is one pleasure, and one alone, I allow myself to indulge. And that is killing vampires...

And those who would become them.

Dawn is well underway by the time I re-enter the nave. The white-washed walls are dappled with light dyed blue, green and red by the stained glass. I take a couple of steps backward, then drop-kick Rhymer's head right through the Lamb-of-God window.

The birds are chirping happily away in the trees, greeting the coming day with their morning songs, as I push open the wide double doors of the church. A stray dog with matted fur and slats for ribs is already sniffing Rhymer's ruined head where it has landed in the high weeds. The cur lifts its muzzle and automatically growls, but as I draw closer it flattens its ears and tucks its tail between its legs and quickly scurries off. Dogs are smart. They know what is and isn't of the natural world—even if humans don't.

Last night was a bust, as far as I'm concerned. When I go out hunting, I prefer bringing down actual game, not faux predators. Still, I wish I could hang around and see the look on the faces of Rhymer's groupies when they find out what's happened to their "master." That'd be good for a chuckle or two.

No one can say I don't have a sense of humor about these things.

variations
on a theme

When you keep the hours that I do, you often find yourself in other people's stories.

Sometimes the stories are funny, sometimes they're weird, sometimes they're scary. Mostly, though, they're stupid, violent, or pathetic—often all three. Over the years I've come to see a marked similarity between these stories—as if all human lives were merely variations on a theme.

Occasionally I come in at the very beginning, while in others I make an entrance during the denouement. Every so often I'm a part of the plot, if no more than a peculiar deus ex machina. For the most part, however, my role—if I have one—is to serve as an abbreviated Greek chorus, doomed to observe the human suffering before me yet helpless to change its outcome.

I couldn't begin to tell you how many rapes I've interrupted over the years—be they straight, gay, one on one or gangbang. Ditto the muggings and back-alley bashings. Not that I'm bloody Spiderman or Bat Girl, mind you. If I happen across a bunch of thugs tangling over turf or a couple of no-neck knuckle-draggers laying into each other with pool cues and broken bottles, I sit back and let Darwin sort it out.

On any given night I'm more likely to find a junkie sprawled, cold as clay, in some abandoned warehouse, than I am to save a damsel in distress. When I come across the ODs I feel a twinge of regret, if they're young, but it's difficult to dredge up much actual sympathy for them. I don't understand the urge the living have to live as if they were already dead.

But then, perhaps my take on such things is tempered by my situation.

Still, at least none of the junkies ever seem to have suffered overmuch (at least not from the overdose), before whatever awaited them in their disposable syringe of White Tiger bore them away on the eternal nod. Judging from what I've seen—corpses with their arms tied off, works dangling from clotted veins, vomit crusted on chins and shirts—when death comes in a hot shot, it's sudden, if not exactly clean.

Then there are the babies. I've found enough of them to start a nursery school over the years. Usually in the trash. They fall into two categories. The first are obvious stillbirths and miscarriages, delivered by the homeless women who huddle in desolate squats or doss down under freeway overpasses throughout this land. These, too, share surprising similarities: most are still bloody, their nostrils plugged with mucus, and their tiny, discolored faces compressed into constipated frowns, fists clenched as if outraged by the very idea of being brought, half-unmade, into such a cruel, uncaring world. Usually the stillborns are bundled in newspaper, like day-old fish or a bouquet of faded roses, the only evidence of the women who birthed them a foot or so of raggedly severed umbilical cord.

I feel a small sorrow for the stillborns—the same sorrow I feel when I come across the withered carcasses of tiny fledglings who have attempted flight with unready wings—but part of me knows the poor things are better off having never taken their first breath. Good luck next time, kid—I hope.

Then there are the ones in the plastic bags. The ones who have taken that first breath, cried that first cry and were never given a reason to stop. The ones with the bruises, the broken limbs, the black eyes, the scalding scars, the cigarette burns, the bite marks, the torn vaginas and the ruptured anuses. There's not much I can do for them besides make an anonymous phone call to the cops. I like to think the story doesn't really end there, though. Hopefully there is a coda of sorts. But I've learned never to hope too hard or too long for such things. It only results in another piece of what's left of my heart breaking off, and there's precious little to spare.

Of course, if I happen to *witness* the disposal of the body—well, that's a different matter entirely. Those end with the tiny victim and killer sharing the same dumpster.

Like I said, I usually tend to stroll in after the end credits have run, the fat lady's sung, the groundskeepers have rolled the tarp over the pitching mound—chose whichever metaphor you prefer. As a result, I've tripped over more stiffs during the last twenty-five years than Cherri Vanilla.

Most came to their ends rather messily and involuntarily. Some were killed by the things I hunt, but most have been brought low by their own kind—that little ol' psychopathic naked ape called Man. I often find myself staring at their dead faces, as if I might glimpse a last fading image echoing deep inside the brain's gray folds. Sometimes I even do, if they're freshly dead.

If they're too far gone for me to scope them out telepathically, I usually check the area for signs of occult energy to see if their recently disembodied spirits might be wandering about, gaping at their new surroundings like tourists from Wisconsin. Such shades need a quick but gentle nudge into the afterlife if they don't want to find themselves trapped between worlds for the next decade or two. I feel it's the least I can do, given the circumstances.

I'm telling you all this so you'll understand how rare it is for me to actually witness someone's story from start to finish. But it happens. Take this one, for instance. I didn't realize I was walking in on the opening curtain. In fact, it looked pretty damn final to me.

I was checking out the dark alleys, abandoned buildings and other lonely places where the things I hunt like to take their prey. The thing is, its not just vampires who like desolate, dark locations in order to go about their dirty deeds—the human variety of monster prefers these sites as well.

I found the bodies in a blind alley in an inner-city industrial zone that made Hell's Kitchen look like a Martha Stewart makeover. I don't know how the victims got there, unless they were brought from another location for a leisurely execution, because they certainly weren't the type to wander the neighborhood, especially after dark.

Both were male, although the smaller of the two was so slender and short I mistook him for a woman at first. The slightly built one was an Asian—possibly Japanese, although it was hard to tell, since his face had been reduced to pulp. It looked like someone had literally jumped up and down on him. There was also semen pooled in the coagulated blood that had leaked from his shattered mouth. Whoever had beaten the poor bastard to death—and there had been several of them—had orally raped him first. He was neatly dressed, although his pressed chinos and white linen shirt were now stained by his own blood and his killers' piss. A small *Silence = Death* button, no larger than my thumb, was pinned to his shirt collar.

The second body was of a considerably larger and older person He had been a black man with touches of gray at the temples of his neatly kept, close-cropped natural. While tall and big-boned, he hadn't been overly muscular. My impression was of a college athlete turned teacher.

He wore a black navy-style swing jacket, a black turtleneck sweater and black slacks. Although he hadn't been worked over nearly as badly as the Asian, I counted at least six stab wounds in his upper body. He'd put up a fight—no doubt while trying to protect his friend.

Judging from the bodies' state of decay, I estimated they'd been dead for the better part of a day. It wasn't hard for me to figure out the story that lead to this sad end. These hapless lovers were the victims of the Regent Sides, a lovely collection of human flotsam that espouses white supremacy and homophobia in equal measure. Although, judging from the physical evidence, their hatred of gays didn't prevent them from getting hard-ons.

I shook my head in disgust at the death scene. At times like this, it wasn't hard to understand how vampires justified their clandestine manipulation and culling of human society. My one solace was the knowledge that those responsible for such an act bore as much resemblance to the humans who compose operas and build cathedrals as baboons resembled men.

However, even when confronted by such utter barbarity, there was evidence of that which is good and pure in mankind amid the horror and ruin. My gaze returned to the older victim. Despite overwhelming numbers and the certainty of physical harm, this man had died trying to protect his lover. I had to respect his bravery and devotion, although I had no way of knowing who he had been.

Or did I?

I dropped to one knee beside the body and began searching for some form of identification. It was possible—although far from likely—that during the excitement the Regent Sides might have forgotten to take his wallet. I was right. I found it tucked inside the jacket's breast pocket. I flipped the worn calfskin billfold open and discovered my first guess concerning the dead man's occupation had been on target.

According to the faculty ID, the dead man sprawled before me was a history professor at the university. His name had been Clarence Sadler, and, in life, he'd borne a slight resemblance to Harry Belafonte. "What a fucking waste," I grunted, snapping the wallet shut.

Sadler's eyes flew open. I'd seen dead men open their eyes before. That much didn't surprise me. However, the sitting up part was another story.

Sadler rose up slowly, a dazed and confused look on him. It seemed to take him a long second to realize I was there, although he was staring me right in the face. He wetted his lips with a dry, blackened tongue and said, "I came back."

"Yeah. So I noticed." I was already on my feet, keeping my eye on Sadler as he clumsily regained his footing. If I hadn't seen him come back from the dead, it would be easy to mistake him for a drunk as he staggered and lurched on his newly resurrected legs.

I quickly placed myself outside possible striking distance, my switchblade sliding into my hand as if it had been there all along.

I automatically dropped my vision into the Pretender spectrum, scanning the dead man's aura in order to identify his breed, only to be further baffled. Where the auras of vampires are usually corrupted, resembling pulsing, livid bruises, Sadler's was completely black. It was as if he wore an eclipsed sun as a halo. I'd never seen anything like it before, although it seemed to trigger some distant memory. Whatever revenant he might be, it certainly wasn't a vampire or a ghoul. I wondered what manner of supernatural event could pull a man back from the fields of the dead.

"K-Kiko?" Sadler had spotted the twisted, lifeless form of his partner amid the trash and detritus of the alley. "Kiko—are you all right?" He dropped to his knees beside the body, reaching out with trembling hands to roll it onto its back. I didn't have to read his mind to know Sadler realized his lover was no more. There is no true hope among the living dead.

Sadler gave a throaty sob as he saw what was left of his lover's face and pulled him closer, pressing the ruined pulp against his breast. As he cradled Kiko's body like a broken doll, Sadler's mouth pulled itself into a rictus of grief, so that for a moment his features resembled those of a Greek tragedy mask. A dreadful wail issued forth from deep inside him. It was a horrible, hopeless, despairing noise—the sound made by destroyed love and shattered lives. Sadler folded himself over Kiko's body, as if he could somehow warm it back to life—but his flesh was just as cold.

"Look what they did to your face—your beautiful, beautiful face!" he moaned, when he finally found words.

I drew back, feeling somewhat awkward. I had no place in this man's grief—for I had come to the conclusion that was exactly what he was, not a ghoul , zombie, vampire, or larvae. I knew from personal experience that none of those creatures were capable of such sorrow. He did not warrant extermination, from what I could see. Granted, he was one of the living dead—but then again, so am I.

Just as I was about to leave him to his mourning, Sadler lifted his head and spoke directly to me.

"He didn't deserve this."

"I know."

"He was so beautiful—you can't tell that by—by what they did, but he was the most handsome man I'd ever seen in my life. The moment I first laid eyes on him at the library I knew he was the one—the one I wanted to spend the rest of my life with." Sadler smiled at the memory and I caught a brief, mental glimpse of Kiko, alive and whole, flashing a smile as he reshelved books from a librarian's cart. The memory had that golden glow that comes from being cherished. In the immediate wake of the memory came a wave of grief and love so strong, I found myself raising psychic shields to protect myself from Sadler's pain.

"It was his beauty and love that gave me the courage to finally come out, to my family, my associates, and the school. It was hard—especially with my family—but Kiko stuck by me, and whenever I weakened, he made me strong again. I—I would have died for him. I guess I did—didn't I?" This last part was addressed to me.

"Yes, I'm afraid you did."

"I thought it might have been a dream—no, a nightmare, at first. But now I can see it wasn't. The skinheads grabbing us as we left the Tosca, bringing us here in their van. What they did to Kiko and myself, the bird—the talking skull—that all really happened."

"Uh-huh," I replied , although I had no idea what he was going on about.

Sadler looked me in the eye, his voice surprisingly level, as he tenderly laid Kiko's body to rest. "Am I a vampire?"

"No."

He didn't seem completely satisfied by my answer. "Are you sure?"

"Believe me, I know my suckers, and you ain't one of them," I said, flashing him a smile.

The sight of my fangs threw him for a second—he hadn't been one of the living dead long enough to override a lifetime of human behavior. "O-okay—if I'm not a vampire, then what am I?"

"I'm not sure. You said something about a bird—?"

"A raven or crow of some kind... It talked to me. Told me that I was being given a chance to right the scales... There was a woman, too. At least, I think it was a woman. She had a skull instead of a face. She took her head from her shoulders and held it like a bowl. There was something... wine?... blood?... inside it. She offered the skull to me and told me to drink. Does this make any sense?"

I nodded slowly, chewing on a thumbnail. "Sorta. At least I have an idea what kind of walking dead man you are. If the stories I've heard are anything to go by, you're an Avenger. You were reanimated by a force far more ancient than any name human religion has ever given it—be it Sekhmet, Kali, Fury or Nemesis.

"It is a thing that might have been a goddess—or perhaps still is. In any case, she is a being steeped in blood, without mercy or respite. Yet she is not a demon, as the Christians have come to define the term. She is not the handmaiden of Chaos, but a shadow of Order. She is the Angel of the Pit, the Punishing Mother, the Divine Scourge. Hers is the face of dark justice—and her power is that of righteous indignation and holy rage. And you—Clarence Sadler—have been made her anointed champion. You've been sent back from the land of the dead to bring those guilty of the crimes against you and your beloved to immortal judgment. You are an Avenging Spirit, given one last chance to set right the scales of justice."

Sadler nodded his head as I spoke, as if the words were a key that had turned a lock within him. "Yes," he whispered. *"Judgment."* He looked up at me, and for a brief moment I saw something very old and very, very dangerous staring out at me through his eyes. He smiled then—or should I say *it* smiled for him, spun on his heel, and sprinted off into the darkness.

"Hey! You're going the wrong way!" I shouted.

When he didn't reply, I started after him, although I was uncertain I really wanted to spend any more time in the revenant's company. That smile—it was not unlike that of someone who realizes that even its closest compatriot has not recognized his true identity. When I reached the end of the blind alley, Sadler was nowhere to be found, although he couldn't have had more than a two-second start on me.

"Damn," I muttered under my breath. "So *that's* how it feels."

As I stood there scratching my head, I caught a glimpse of what appeared to be a raven silhouetted against the night sky, although they rarely, if ever, fly after dark.

I didn't see Sadler again for a couple of days.

Bear in mind, I wasn't exactly looking for him. Since I'd determined he wasn't the kind of living dead that required my special attention, my attitude was more "live and let live." So to speak.

Still, even in a city of this size, it's only natural—so to speak—that we'd eventually cross paths again.

I was doing my rounds of the scummier dives and rougher clubs that night when I caught up with him again. Vampires tend to prey on those who dwell on the fringes of human society; those who, should they turn up missing or mysteriously dead, aren't likely to cause anyone to go out of their way to solve the crime—or even recognize it as such. Prostitutes, drug dealers, tranny hookers, hustlers, junkies, crackheads and barflies tend to make up the most reliable prey categories, so it pays for me to keep tabs on the local scene.

I had just finished checking out the Backstabber Lounge—an after-hours joint popular with Black and Latino drag queens—when I heard what sounded like screams and gunshots coming from up the street. I smartened my pace and arrived just in time to see an exodus of extremely panicked bar girls fleeing Rackham's, a combination bar and pool hall that was a favorite with the various White Power gangs in the area. A second later a body came flying through the establishment's plate glass window and hit the sidewalk, coming to rest inches from my feet.

Since the corpse was lying face down, I had a clear view of the Regent Side insignia—a pink triangle with a knife stuck in it—on the back of his jacket, so it didn't take a rocket scientist to figure out who was responsible for propelling this human spitball.

Sadler came climbing through what was left of the window as calmly as you please, oblivious to the jagged glass slicing his legs and hands. The first thing I noticed was that he'd acquired both a new wardrobe and substantial armament since we'd last met. His jacket, slacks and turtleneck had been discarded in favor of khaki combat pants, midcalf army boots, and a jungle-issue flak jacket that fairly bristled with small firearms, grenades, knives and ammo. He carried a semiauto pump shotgun and there was an AK-47 slung over his shoulder. At first I thought he'd smeared cammo-stick across his face, but as he drew closer I realized it wasn't lamp-black I was looking at. Sadler might be a revenant, but his mortal form was still susceptible to decay.

He glowered for a moment, then seemed to recognize me, nodding a curt hello.

"So—You were the one who knocked over the Army-Navy Surplus the night we met," I said. "I wondered if it wasn't you when I heard the security door was torn off its hinges. And I suppose you're also the one that ventilated that van full of Regent Sides lurking behind the Tosca last night." I pointed to the weapons jutting from every part of his anatomy. "You, uh, know how to use all that stuff, Prof?"

Sadler lifted his left arm in way of answer, exposing very nasty, very old scar tissue from where shrapnel had torn its way through flesh and muscle. "That's how I got the money to go to college in the first place." His voice sounded strangely thick, then I realized his larynx was rotting along with the rest of him.

Sadler bent over and grabbed the Regent Side by the jacket collar and peeled him off the sidewalk. The basher had the same general "look" favored by his gang—pegged pants, Doc Martens with white shoelaces, a white T-shirt and red suspenders. His extremely short crew cut made him look even younger than he already was. In any case, the kid wasn't getting any older, thanks to the piece of broken glass wedged in his throat.

"Damn!" Sadler spat, letting the dead skinhead drop like a sack of wet laundry. "I was planning on using this one to find out where their leader is hiding!"

"Is that all? Hell, *I* can tell you that!"

"You know where the Regent Sides are?"

"I make it a point to know where *all* the scumbags in this part of town go to ground." The sound of approaching police sirens caused me to step back, casting my gaze skyward. "I'll take you to their hideout, if that's what you want. But there's no way we'll be able to approach them from the ground with you tricked out like Rambo."

"What do you suggest we do, then?"

"Follow me."

I ducked down a nearby alley, Sadler at my heels. I motioned to the metal fire escape a story above out heads. Sadler nodded his understanding, sliding his shotgun into a holster strapped across his back. I jumped up and snagged the railing, boosting myself onto the landing. Sadler was right behind me, showing a great deal of grace for a man I knew had to be feeling the effects of being three days dead.

By the time the police cars fish-tailed to a halt outside Rackham's, Sadler and I were three buildings away, headed in the direction of the Regent Sides' headquarters. Once I was certain we had not been spotted from the ground, I gestured for a halt. I leaned out over the top of the tenement's Victorian facade and looked back up the street at the flashing lights from the assembled squad cars. The cops were standing around scratching their heads, talking to a few shaken pool players, and examining the dead Regent Sides. I cast a glance over my shoulder at Sadler, who was standing behind me, as silent and solemn as a shadow.

"You realize you've stirred up all different colors of shit, don't you?" I asked. "When you whacked that van full of no-necks, the Regent Sides assumed Los Locos did it. So they hit 'em back. Took out most the gang while they were hanging out at Taco Mundo. Now there's all kinds of payback going down. And a lot of the other gangs are fighting for the territory that's opened up."

"My heart bleeds piss for them."

"Yeah, that's what I figured you'd say. Can't say my attitude's any different. I'm just letting you know what kind of fresh hell's going on." I nodded in the direction of the gang's hideout. "Just bear in mind, the Regent Sides might not be expecting *you*, but they're gonna be expecting *someone*. A whole *lot* of someone, to be exact. And they're gonna be armed."

Sadler shrugged, his lips pulled into a bitter smile. "What's the worst they can they do? *Kill* me?"

I laughed and shook my head. For a dead guy, I had to admit Sadler was okay. I could tell he was studying me in return. After a long moment he asked what they always do.

"Are all vampires like you?"

It was my turn to smile bitterly now. "No. Afraid not. I'm something of a fluke. I don't prey on humans—at least, I try not to. Not the innocent ones, anyhow. I hunt vampires."

"Why?"

"Why do you feel compelled to destroy the Regent Sides?"

"They took everything from me: my future, my life, everything and everyone I loved. I can never have or enjoy those things again."

"Bingo."

Sadler met my gaze, hidden behind the sunglasses I wear, and once again I saw the familiar darkness in his eyes looking back at me, only now I knew better than to fear it. There was a long moment of silence between us which I finally ended by moving away from the front of the building.

"C'mon," I said, clearing my throat. "Let's get going. The Regent Sides' crib is six blocks east of here."

Two blocks from our destination, something caught my eye in the alley below. It was little more than a furtive motion in the shadows, as if a prey animal had caught wind of a predator and quickly taken cover. I paused, scanning the alley below in search of Pretender spoor. Sadler turned to scowl at me.

"What's wrong?"

"Not sure—maybe nothing."

I spotted a flash of pallid flesh in the darkness, a look of panicked fear glittering in ruby colored eyes set in a milk-white face. The hairs on the back of my neck prickled and a low growl began to rumble deep in my chest. I could feel the kill-urge coming up, making my body tremble like a junkie needing a fix. I turned to speak to Sadler, all the while keeping my eyes on my prey below.

"Go on ahead without me. I'll catch up with you. The address is 605 Water Street. Corner of Regent. You'll find them there."

Sadler was gone before I'd finished the sentence, leaving me to my work.

It couldn't have possibly taken more than ten minutes for me to finish off the dead boy cowering in the alley, then shag it over to Water Street. I could smell the blood from two blocks away and glimpsed the flames a block later. The bastard sure worked fast.

The decrepit row house where the Regent Sides had their so-called headquarters was little more than a squat with plumbing and electricity, full to overflowing with junked furniture and empty pizza boxes, which probably had a lot to do with the speed at which the flames were devouring it.

There were bodies scattered along the sidewalk leading to the burning building that looked like they'd gotten up close and personal with the business end of Sadler's shotgun. I shook my head in silent admiration. Sadler was definitely a class act in the mayhem department. I glanced around, looking for a sign of the walking dead man, but didn't spot him. Then I heard the screams coming from inside 605 Water.

At first all I saw was a beautiful and deadly curtain of orange and yellow flame, then the figure of a man emerged from the inferno's heart. Although the screams were growing louder and closer, the figure moved with an unhurried yet purposeful stride. As Sadler exited the burning building and headed down the steps to the street, I saw the source of the screams was the man he was dragging behind him by a pair of blood-red suspenders.

Less than fifteen minutes earlier, the leader of the Regent Sides had been a relatively decent-looking young man. Now he looked like 180 pounds of barbecued kielbasa. Except that Polish sausages usually don't scream at the top of their lungs.

Once he cleared the fire, it was clear that Sadler was in even worse shape than the pathetic little neo-Nazi he was towing behind him like a demented pull-toy. Big chunks of flesh were missing from his face, chest, and arms. What I first mistook for sweat running down his forehead and dripping from his face was actually liquefied fat, and his hair was burned right down to his skull. The intense heat had caused his gums to shrivel, exposing the teeth in his mouth all the way to the root and giving him a death's head appearance when he smiled in my direction.

"Looks like you've got things in hand here," I observed, nudging one of the Regent Sides splattered across the pavement. "So—is it over?"

"Not yet," he replied, a burp of smoke escaping his lips as he spoke. Sadler hurled the horribly burned skinhead into the gutter. The Regent Side's leader looked like a giant blister in a sooty white T-shirt and red suspenders. He lifted his seared hands, whether to beg forgiveness or block out the sight of his nemesis was unclear. His eyes flicked to where I stood— although now without lashes or brows they were still startlingly blue, especially in contrast to the lobster-red ruin of what was once his face.

"Help me, lady," he pleaded. "This nigger's a fucking monster!"

I had to chuckle at that one. The look of horror on the skinhead's face when he saw my teeth made me laugh even harder. He began to shriek again—only this time out of fear, not pain. It was the scream of a man who's finally realized that he's dead, even though he's still breathing.

"You stole our lives, scum." Sadler's voice was almost unrecognizable now. It sounded more like the very pits themselves had been given voice. "And now I'm going to send you to hell for the heartless bastard you are."

Sadler pulled a six-inch serrated combat knife from a sheath strapped to his calf and plunged it into the Regent Side's chest, causing blood to erupt from the skinhead's nose and mouth in a crimson gout. Despite the gravity of his wounds, it took the punk a good two minutes to die. The last thing he saw was Sadler removing his still-beating heart from its cage of bone.

As the life, if not the horror, in the skinhead's eyes drained away, Sadler blinked and staggered slightly, like a man coming out from under hypnosis. When he saw the bloody hunk of muscle in his hand, he gave a short cough of disgust and hurled it into the gutter, alongside its rightful owner. He lifted a trembling, crimson hand to his ruined face, grimacing as his fingers encountered exposed bone.

I gently touched his shoulder and he jerked like a startled sleepwalker. He stared at me for a long moment before finally recognizing me.

"What next?" I asked.

He frowned as if I'd spoken to him in Mongolian. "Next? There is no next. It's over."

"Uh-huh. I figured as much. So now what?"

Sadler shook his head, pulling a pistol out of his pocket as he straightened up. "It's *over*." He said it as if I should have understood what it meant. And maybe I did, but I didn't want to. I'd come to enjoy his company.

"Sadler... Clarence..."

"Have they found him?"

"Yeah. I called the cops after you disappeared. His body's at the morgue."

Sadler nodded. The information seemed to put him at ease. "Thank you—" He paused, frowning. "I'm sorry. I don't even know your name."

"Sonja."

"Thank you, Sonja." He smiled, took a giant step backward and brought the gun up to his head. Then he said "Kiko" and pulled the trigger, spraying congealed blood and putrefying brains onto the sidewalk.

And his story ended just like that—as suddenly as it had begun.

I stared at his lifeless body for a long moment before leaving. When I turned away, I caught sight of a large crow perched atop a nearby streetlight, watching me with that same, dark, familiar intelligence I had glimpsed in the dead man's eyes.

I envied Sadler the simplicity of his vengeance. All he had to do was avenge Kiko and himself against a finite, mortal enemy. And when the time came, he knew his job was well and truly finished. In those last moments Sadler had known no lingering rage, no doubt, and most of all, no fear of whatever awaits on the other side.

I wondered what it would be like to surrender the cold thrill of vendetta, to be at one not only with myself but with what I had become, in order to succumb to that final, unending peace. Perhaps that day will eventually come. But I know one thing—it is not coming soon.

As I said before, most of the stories I find myself entangled in prove to be no more than variations on a theme.

Including my own.

some
velvet
morning

She was the most attractive woman he'd ever seen outside a movie theater. She was not just pretty—she was beautiful, the way models and starlets are. Her skin was creamy, as translucent as pearl, with long, wavy hair the color of raw honey. Her fire-engine-red lips matched her low-cut one-piece with spaghetti straps and revealing side-slit. She was wearing black patent leather open-toed shoes with four-inch heels, which revealed toenails painted the exact same shade as her lips. And she was smiling at him from across the hotel bar.

He had to double check to make sure there wasn't another, younger man sitting directly behind him before he dared respond. No. There wasn't anyone else she could possibly be paying attention to. It had to be him.

"Hey, buddy," he said, pushing a ten across the damp bar top. "I'd like to buy that lady a drink."

The bartender nodded and palmed the bill without saying a word. A couple of minutes later a fresh Bloody Mary was placed in front of the woman in red.

She lifted the drink in a half toast and smiled at him. And this time there was no mistaking it: She was smiling one hundred percent at him.

He nervously slicked back his thinning hair and coughed lightly into his fist, surreptitiously sniffing it to make sure his breath was passable. Satisfied, he slid off the barstool and tried to look nonchalant as he strolled to the end of the bar.

"I couldn't help noticing you were alone," he said, trying not to sound nervous. "Would you mind terribly much if I joined you for a drink?'

"Why should I mind?" she said, flashing yet another one of those smiles. "After all, you were the one kind enough to buy it for me."

He moved to sit next to her, then stopped and looked around the bar. He was a thousand miles away from home, his wife, and their friends and associates, but old habits were hard to break.

"Would you mind if we sat somewhere a little more... private?" he said, gesturing to a booth in one of the shadowy corners.

"Whatever you like—?" She paused, waiting for him to supply his name.

"John," he said, his cheeks coloring slightly. "My name is John."

"Of course it is," she replied, no hint of irony in her honeyed voice. "My name is Phaedra."

"That's an unusual name," he said as he slid into the booth beside her.

"It's from the classics. Phaedra was a queen who was possessed by unnatural desires."

"How fascinating," he said, feigning interest. He suspected Phaedra was as much her name as John was his. It sounded too deliberate to be real.

Once they were safely in the booth, he went into the same little song and dance he always did on business trips. He inflated his importance at the firm while avoiding telling her the exact company he worked for and what it was it was he really did for a living, and when she asked him where he was from, he gave her the correct state but lied about the city. And some time during the small talk he let his hand fall on Phaedra's leg, just above the knee. To his relief, she did not shift about uncomfortably or demand that he remove his hand. Her dress was silky smooth under his palm, and beneath its flimsiness he could feel warm flesh and taut muscle. It had been years since his wife's thigh had felt like anything besides a bag of suet.

He had to fight to keep from choking on his drink when she shifted her leg so that his hand slid further up her thigh, toward the heat between her legs. His suspicions were confirmed: She wasn't wearing panties. He began to sweat, his scalp itching under his thinning hair. His crotch throbbed like a high school freshman with a case of blue balls.

"I, uh, have a room here at the hotel..." he stammered clumsily.

She shook her head and wrinkled her nose in disgust. "I detest hotel rooms. They're so impersonal. Why don't we go to my place, instead?"

"Sure. Whatever you want, baby."

As he heard himself saying those words, he wondered what the hell he thought he was doing. He had to catch a flight first thing in the morning, not to mention turn the rental car back in at the airport. He didn't have the time to waste going to some hottie's apartment out in the 'burbs. But when he looked into Phaedra's eyes, he knew he would do whatever it took to get her in bed, even if it meant flying standby.

As he signed for the drinks, she slid out of the booth and motioned for him to follow.

"Let's go in my car," she said, holding up a key ring attached to a pair of red plastic dice.

He knew he should protest. The last thing he needed was to get stranded out in the middle of nowhere, unable to get back to the hotel in time to pick up his bags and make his flight home. There was something about the arrangement that set off an alarm in the back of his head, but it was quickly muffled by the lust rising from below decks.

Phaedra led him out the side door of the hotel bar to the parking lot outside. She walked ahead of him with quick, purposeful strides, which made her jiggle in all the right places.

"Here's my car," she said, gesturing to a little convertible, painted the same color red as her lips and nails. "Hop in, John."

He opened the passenger door halfway, then paused, indecision flickering across his brow.

"I don't know... maybe I should follow you..."

"You can do that, if you like," she said, with a shrug. "I live out on the lake. It's not that far, but it's easy to get lost if you don't know where you're going."

He suddenly had a vivid mental picture of himself driving around unfamiliar suburbs in the dark, a raging hard-on in his pants, and with no clear idea of how to get back to the hotel.

"Okay," he said with a resigned sigh. "I'll ride with you."

He wasn't sure if Phaedra was driving particularly fast, or if merely riding in an open convertible in the dead of night made it seem that way. The wind tore at him, turning his tie into a windsock and exposing his comb-over for the lie it was.

As they sped through the night, she rubbed his thigh gently, moving her hand closer and closer to his groin. He licked his lips and coughed nervously into his fist. The lights of the strip malls and main boulevard had long since disappeared, plunging them into an inky darkness that was relieved only by the glow from the dashboard and the beams of the headlights on the road ahead.

"Where is it you said you live?" he shouted over the roar of the wind and the engine.

"Red Velvet Manor!" she shouted back.

"Is that some kind of subdivision?"

"Lord, no!" she laughed. "That's what it was called a hundred years ago! It's something of an unofficial landmark around here. It used to be a brothel for the super-rich. All the rooms had red velvet wallpaper— that's where it got its name. Now it's a private residence. I live there."

"All by yourself?"

"No."

Before he could ask another question, the car rounded a turn in the road and he saw their final destination. It was an impressive late-Victorian pile, with turrets and huge picture windows that glowed like the eyes of a jack-o'-lantern, situated on an outcropping that overlooked the lake. Judging from the utter darkness surrounding the estate, the nearest neighbors had to be at least a mile away.

Phaedra steered the car up the lengthy drive that lead to the old-fashioned covered carriage port located on the side of the house, the gravel crunching loudly under the wheels.

"Wow, this place really is something," he said, leaning back in his seat to ogle the building. "How much does a house like this go for, nowadays?"

Phaedra shrugged indifferently. It was clear that the subject did not interest her in the slightest. "A million, maybe two, if you count the lakefront that's attached to it. The Contessa says it's been in the family for generations, and that's probably where it's going to stay."

She switched the car off and turned to face him. She moved quickly, leaning in to plant a deep, passionate kiss on his mouth. His thoughts of money and real estate disappeared entirely, turned to steam by the heat growing within his belly. He took her in his arms, holding her body tight against his own. In twelve years of marriage, he had never experienced anything as sensuous as Phaedra's lips moving against his own.

Phaedra broke away from the kiss, studying him with hooded eyes, a sly smile on her lips. "You're shivering," she said. "How sweet."

"I don't know what to say. This is all so new to me," he lied.

"I think we better go inside before you cum outside," she said with a wink.

"Uh, yeah," he grunted.

The interior of the house was as impressive as its exterior. The first thing he saw was a grand foyer with an elaborate parquet floor and a grand staircase that split on the second floor into two separate wings. An antique chandelier swayed in the air above their heads like a giant gold and crystal wind chime. The walls of the reception hall were paneled in the finest cherry wood, burnished to a healthy glow by decades of care. Marble hamadryads sported with marble fauns while a massive grandfather's clock with a zodiac face counted out the time nearby. Twin mirrors in gilt rococo frames, each the size of a door, made the foyer seem even larger than it already was.

"Man, this must have really been something, back in the day," John marveled aloud, his voice echoing in the hall.

"You have no idea how grand it was, young man. No idea at all."

There was a buzzing sound and an electric wheelchair emerged from the parlor off the foyer. The rider was an old woman dressed in a velvet housecoat the color of oxblood, a woolen throw draped across her lap for extra warmth. Her face was as wrinkled as an apple-doll's, her swan-white hair bound in a long braid that coiled about her fragile shoulders like an albino python. The old woman's hands were as gnarled and twisted as the claws of a vulture, the nails long and yellowish.

None of this was unusual, given her obviously great age. However, what he was unprepared for was the sight of metal legs that resembled a cross between stilts and pogo sticks emerging from underneath the fringe of the blanket covering the old lady's lap. Upon noticing his stare, the elderly woman hastily rearranged the throw, screening the prostheses from view.

"Contessa! What are you doing up at this hour?" Phaedra said mock-reproachfully, bending to kiss her benefactor's' withered cheek.

"It's these bones of mine. The older they get, the harder it is to sleep the night through. I did not mean to startle your gentleman friend, my dear."

"Allow me to introduce you. Contessa, this is... John."

The Contessa offered her gnarled hand to him. There was a ring with a diamond the size of a man's thumb glinting on one arthritic finger.

"*Enchanted*, my dear," she said.

"My pleasure, ma'am."

"I have do doubt it will be," the old woman said, a sly grin on her face.

"Uh. Right." The man smiled awkwardly and pulled away, unsure of how to react.

"Can I get you anything, Contessa?" Phaedra asked, apparently unfazed by the old woman's behavior toward her guest.

"No, my dear. Do not mind me," she said, toggling the joystick so that the chair went back the way it came. "You two have fun," she said over her shoulder. "That is what youth is for, after all!" Something about what she had just said must have struck the old woman as funny, because she began to laugh. It was a wild sound, like the call of a screech owl.

Phaedra took his hand and led him toward the stairs. He paused to look back at the parlor, where the Contessa sat chuckling to herself.

"She doesn't mind you bringing men home?"

"Mind? Why should she mind?" Phaedra snorted. "Remember what I told you about Red Velvet Manor? She used to run the joint."

A leer spread across his face. "You mean she was a—?"

"Yes. But not since they closed the place back in '44. She married an expatriate Romanian nobleman who didn't have anything but a title. But that's okay, because that's all she wanted from him."

"What happened to her, uh, you know…?"

"Her legs were amputated a few years ago, due to complications from diabetes. That's when I began working for her."

"You're her nurse?"

"She prefers the title 'companion.' So do I. I've accompanied her on numerous trips around the world. It's only recently that her condition forced her to return here."

"Real jetsetter, eh?"

"She knew them all: Rita and Ali, Liz and Dick, Rainier and Grace, Coward, Capote, Warhol…" She turned suddenly to fix him with her gaze. "But that's enough about the Contessa. We've got better things to do. Don't you agree?"

He tried to answer, but something in the way she looked at him made it hard for him to formulate a coherent sentence, so he contented himself with nodding his head. As she resumed her climb, he lagged behind a few steps, watching her perfectly formed ass. This was all too good to be true. She had to be a pro. He'd been around enough to know the difference between a call girl and a bored housewife on the prowl. Her mentioning the old lady's former profession had to be a tip-off. No doubt once the credit card clicker finally made its appearance, she'd be charging for her services, but something told him it would be well worth the expense. He'd had his share of paid women before, but none of them had this amount of style or heat.

She paused in front of an elaborately carved wooden door at the end of the second floor hallway. "This is my room," she said with a smile. "Come on in." She opened the door and stepped inside, motioning for him to follow.

He followed, moving cautiously into the darkened room.

"Hey... where did you go?" he said with a nervous laugh. All of a sudden he was aware of the fact that nobody knew he was miles from the city, in an isolated house occupied by strangers whose last names he didn't know.

"Wait a second—I'll get the lights." Phaedra's voice came out of the darkness, behind and to one side of where he stood.

The lights came on with a sudden flash of brilliance, enough to make him wince. The first thing he noticed was that the walls were the color of spilled blood. The second thing he noticed was the huge mirror mounted on the ceiling, which reflected plush carpeting a shade lighter than the walls. The overhead light fixtures and wall sconces were shaped like gilded cherubs armed with cornucopias. In the middle of the room was a king-size circular bed outfitted with red satin sheets. Heavy crimson velvet curtains covered the windows.

"We can do whatever we like without disturbing anyone," Phaedra said. She was still behind him, near the light switch. "All the bedrooms are soundproofed."

He turned to face her, but whatever he was planning to say never found its way past his lips. Phaedra was leaning against the blood red wall, stark naked except for her shoes. Her dress lay in a pool at her feet, as if it had melted off her body.

"You like?" she smiled.

Unable to find his voice, he nodded vigorously.

She gave a little chuckle and did something with the light switch, and the room abruptly dimmed. "That's better," she said, stepping toward him.

He began to remove his own clothes, but his fingers kept fumbling because he couldn't take his eyes off her. Her skin was as white and flawless as an alabaster statue, her hips shapely and inviting, without a hint of cellulite. Her belly was flat and her pubic hair carefully trimmed. She smelled of sex and expensive perfume and did not want to discuss children, in-laws, bank balances, mortgage payments, or any of the things that defined the confines of his life. She was young and desirable and available. And the knowledge that he was none of these things made his penis so painfully rigid it vibrated like a tuning fork.

He was breathing fast and his mouth was open as Phaedra approached him. She stood facing him, close enough that he could feel the heat from her body. She looked into his eyes, then down at his penis, jutting forward from underneath the swell of his middle-management paunch.

As Phaedra's hand wrapped around his erection, his wife's face shimmered across the back of his eyes like a summer haze, then was gone. Phaedra began to rub his cock up and down with sure, practiced strokes.

He gave a choked little cry and placed his hand atop her own, staying the movements.

"That feels too good," he whispered hoarsely.

"But I *want* you to feel good," she purred. "I want you feel better than you *ever* have... or ever will again." She pressed herself tightly against his body, rubbing her breasts against the naked expanse of his chest. "That's why you're here, isn't it? To make yourself feel good?"

With a sly smile, she gracefully dropped to her knees before him. He gave a groan of approval and tilted his head back, staring up at his reflection in the mirrored ceiling.

As his cock slid into her ready mouth, his vision grew blurry around the edges and a groan of intense pleasure escaped him. Phaedra's lips glided over the shaft, her tongue exploring every inch of him. He'd never felt anything so incredible in his life, neither with his wife nor with any of the coworkers or call girls he had used over the years. At first her movements were slow, but quickly picked up speed and intensity. He could feel her fingernails dig into his ass cheeks, urging him onward.

That was all the encouragement he needed to surrender to the urge that had been gnawing at his loins all night. He dug his fingers tight into the hair at the back of Phaedra's head and began fiercely pumping in and out of her mouth. Even if she had wanted to stop, there was no way he was going to let her. He wanted—no, *needed*—to cum in her mouth more than anything in his life. He needed it more than a promotion, more than food and shelter. Somehow, everything that was wrong and dull and empty in his life would be set right, if only he could reach orgasm with this woman. And at that moment he was willing to sacrifice everything he had ever held dear—his wife, his children, his career—if it meant he could empty himself between her blood-red lips.

A sweat broke out all over his body as his balls jerked up to the sides of his cock, flooding her mouth with their warm, bitter cream. His head dropped back, his mouth open, as his hips continued to thrust blindly forward. A deep groan escaped him, and then his hands let go of her head as he stepped back on numbed legs, his wilted penis sliding free of her lips. He was lightheaded and rubber-kneed, as weak and vulnerable as a freshly foaled colt.

Phaedra was still kneeling before him, wiping spittle and sperm from her lower lip with the back of her hand. There was a distance in her eyes he had not seen before, or at least had not allowed himself to notice. Although less than five seconds before they had been as intimate as two humans could possibly be, it was as if she were miles away.

"I- I need to pee," he stammered.

Phaedra pointed silently in the direction of the bathroom door. He staggered away from her, glad to be free of her thousand-yard stare. She was probably thinking he was a jerk for coming so soon. He meant to apologize, say something about her being so sexy he couldn't hold back, but he couldn't work up the energy to bother with it. Besides, she didn't seem so much disappointed as kind of dazed. Maybe those Bloody Marys were finally catching up with her, after all.

The bathroom, in keeping with the rest of the house, was much larger and far grander than anything he'd ever seen in a private residence. It looked like something you might expect to see in an old-fashioned movie star's home... or at a high-class knocking shop.

The walls were mirrored, casting myriad images of his nakedness into infinity. The floor was ceramic tile, embossed with starfish and crustaceans painted in Mediterranean blue. The oceanic theme continued in a wash basin fashioned from a gigantic conch shell and solid gold fixtures shaped like medieval dolphins. As impressive as those features were, the piece de resistance was the huge, oval-shaped marble tub that sat atop its own a dais in the middle of the room. He climbed up the steps that led to the tub and gazed down at it. It was easily the width of a child's swimming pool, and twice as deep. The sides were worn smooth from use and sloped steeply toward the drain, which looked somewhat rusty and was set squarely in the bottom of the tub. Still, he couldn't help but feel that there was something not quite right. Then he realized there was no faucet anywhere in sight. Perplexed, he looked upward, thinking there might be a showerhead set into the ceiling.

There was something hanging overhead, but it wasn't plumbing. As he stood gaping up at the ceiling, he was dimly aware of Phaedra having joined him in the bathroom.

"What the fuck is that doing up there?" he asked, pointing at the old fashioned block-and-tackle suspended over the tub.

Phaedra's answer came in the form of a baseball bat connecting with the side of his head.

The first thing he felt upon regaining consciousness was the congestive pressure of his own blood in his ears. The second thing he felt was pain from his broken jaw. He tried to open his eyes, but his right one was swollen shut. Still, he didn't need both eyes to know that he was hanging upside down by his heels over the marble tub.

"That didn't take long."

He recognized the voice as the Contessa's. He caught a glimpse of her in one of the mirrors, her wheelchair parked in the open door of the bathroom.

"Thank God for small favors. And I *do* mean small," Phaedra sneered. She was seated on the toilet, smoking a cigarette. "I prefer it when they cum in my mouth. I hate it when they stick it in me." She shivered in revulsion at the very thought.

"Yes, my dear. I understand all too well," The Contessa said sympathetically. "The penis is such a *transgressive* organ."

He tried to open his mouth and demand that they let him go, but the pain from his shattered jaw turned his shout into an agonized moan. The two women glanced up at him as if he was nothing more than a chiming clock.

"He's awake," Phaedra said, flicking the cigarette into the conch-shaped wash basin.

"Good," The Contessa replied, tossing aside her lap blanket and levering herself out of the wheelchair. "Let's get this over with."

Compared to the rest of her body, the tubular metal and carbon filaments of her prosthetic limbs were frighteningly sturdy. She wavered like a young tree in a stiff wind, then took a step forward, the hydraulic knees and tendons hissing and popping like steam-driven pogo sticks.

Phaedra moved to meet the Contessa, helping the older woman to remove her garment. Her body was so wrinkled it was almost impossible to tell what sex she was, her dried-up dugs hanging flat against her chest like deflated wineskins. With trembling, gnarled fingers, the Contessa loosened her hair, allowing it to spill down upon her shoulders like a fall of snow.

The old woman nodded to the younger one, and Phaedra began to methodically unfasten the elaborate suspension gear—half corset, half truss—that held the Contessa's artificial legs in place. When the last strap was finished with, the Contessa linked her arms around Phaedra's neck as her companion lifted her free of the legs. The prostheses, empty of their operator, dropped to the tiled floor with a loud clatter.

Phaedra carried her mistress easily up the steps of the dais and carefully balanced her on its worn lip. Using her arms to propel herself, the Contessa scuttled down the side of the tub like a pallid crab.

The man who said his name was John was finally beginning to figure out that whatever plans Phaedra and the Contessa had for him, they were not sexual. At least not as he understood the term. His initial indignation and anger turned to fear, then panic. He tried to call out Phaedra's name, but the best he could manage was a cry of animal-like pain. Phaedra was standing at the edge of the tub. Even though he was disoriented from the blow and able to see out of only one eye, he was still able to glimpse the knife she held in her hand. His mind was racing so fast it was standing still, unable to gain the traction necessary to escape, as Phaedra grabbed his hair and yanked backwards, exposing his Adam's apple. He didn't have enough spirituality to find comfort in faith, but he *had* watched enough TV to delude himself into thinking that someone—Kojak, maybe, or Jim Rockford—would kick open the door, right in the nick of time.

He was still waiting on the cops to make their last-minute appearance when Phaedra slit his throat from ear to ear.

The last thing he saw before escaping into unconsciousness, then death, was the sight of his life's blood jetting forth from his severed jugular veins and carotid arteries, like wine from a newly tapped keg. His body involuntarily jerked with the release, much as it had during his orgasm.

The red splashed against the smooth marble surface with a thick, wet sound, like rain gushing from a choked gutter. The Contessa thrust herself under the grisly downpour, eagerly massaging it into her thirsty flesh with obscene abandon. The stolen blood did not smear or clot upon her skin, but was absorbed, like rain falling on a sun-baked riverbed. The Contessa's withered flesh grew firm and taut, smoothing out the creases and wrinkles that crosshatched her face from within. Like ink dropped into a glass of milk, darkness reclaimed her hair. Her eyes shed their clouds to burn as brightly as twin goblets of fine claret held before a fire. She smiled up at her companion, who knelt on the lip of the tub, watching her with the keen attention of a surgeon overseeing an operation.

"You shouldn't frown so, my dear," the Contessa said, clucking her tongue. "It leaves wrinkles. Don't just stand there—help me out."

Phaedra leaned forward and gathered her mistress into her arms, lifting her free of the gore-streaked tub. The Contessa's head lolled against her shoulder like that of a newborn child's. Rejuvenation always left her torpid. The languor would pass after a few minutes, but until then she needed to be guarded and protected.

Phaedra carried the Contessa out of the bathroom and placed her on the circular bed, carefully arranging the red velvet bolster and satin pillows against the headboard.

"The night," the Contessa said with a breathy sigh. "I want to see the night."

Phaedra nodded and picked up a remote control from atop the bedside table and pointed it at the heavy velvet drapes. She pressed a button and the curtains parted, revealing a picture window that filled the entire wall. Phaedra assumed that during the day the view was spectacular, but now it was dark as only night on the water can be. The sky was clear, undimmed by the glare from city lights and suburban development, and the millions of stars that filled the night sky were twinned in the inky surface of the lake. The Contessa loved to stare out at the lake for hours on end, although nothing moved except the twinkling of the stars and the gentle motion of the lake's surface. At least nothing Phaedra's mortal eyes could see.

"So beautiful," the Contessa said, slurring the words slightly. She patted the coverlet beside her. "Come. Sit by me, child."

Phaedra sat beside her, her naked body pressed close to the Contessa's own. The older woman looked at her for a long moment, then motioned to Phaedra's hair.

"Take that dreadful thing off."

Phaedra nodded and tossed the blonde wig to the foot of the bed.

The Contessa stroked Phaedra's close-cropped, mousy hair as she would the fur of a cat. "That's better," she said. "You must be tired after all that. Come child, rest your head."

With a grateful sigh, Phaedra pillowed her cheek against the smooth curve of her mistress's right stump. The Contessa's hands, no longer twisted by arthritis, continued to play with her hair.

"Contessa—?" Phaedra's voice was high and sweet, like that of a little girl.

"Yes, my pet?"

"Tell me a story."

"Very well, my dear. Which story would you like to hear? How about the one about the Secret Princess?"

"No. The other one."

The Contessa smiled and nodded her understanding. "Ah, yes. *That* one. Very well. As you wish, my precious. Now, how does that one begin...?"

"'Once upon a time, long, long ago, there was a beautiful young girl named Elizabeth'..." Phaedra prompted.

"Of course!" The Contessa chuckled. "*Now* I remember! Once upon a time, long, long ago, there was a beautiful young girl named Elizabeth, who lived in a land far, far away. This faraway land was very beautiful, and because it was so beautiful, everyone wanted to own it. So there was constant war for control of the land. Life was very hard for the peasants and commoners who lived in the battle-torn land, as there was little money and rarely enough food.

"But since Elizabeth's family was very rich and very powerful, none of this concerned her, for she always had plenty of food to eat and nice clothes to wear and servants to wait on her, hand and foot, day in and out, from the moment she was born until the day she died. Elizabeth was a very pretty little girl, and everyone adored her because she was so beautiful. As she grew to womanhood, she quickly learned that because one cousin was the Prime Minister, another was the ruler of an allied kingdom, and her great-uncle was a cardinal in the Church, there was nothing she could do that would not be overlooked or forgiven.

"When Elizabeth was but fifteen years old, her family married her to the Black Count, who was eleven years her senior. The Black Count was not as politically important as Elizabeth's family, but he had a great deal of money and possessed considerable property, and the marriage was deemed a good one. So Elizabeth was sent away, against her wishes, to live in her new husband's castle, which was in the farthest reaches of the land.

"Things did not go well from the very start. Although the Black Count was not unhandsome, he was always going off to some battle or another, leaving his young bride alone with only his mother and castle retainers for company.

"The wicked mother-in-law was a horrible woman, with a shrewish tongue and narrow mind. All the wicked mother-in-law did day in and day out was pray to God and berate poor Elizabeth for not being perfect. There was nothing Elizabeth could do that the wicked mother-in-law approved of. If Elizabeth had the servants put more logs on the fire, the wicked mother-in-law accused her of being a spendthrift. If Elizabeth did not order the servants to light a fire, the wicked mother-in-law accused her of stinginess. But what the wicked mother-in-law complained the most about was how Elizabeth had failed to produce an heir.

"The wicked mother-in-law was most eager to have the marriage annulled, so that the Black Count might take a more 'suitable' wife, one who would give him children—and plenty of them. It did not matter that her son was rarely home long enough to change his clothes, much less impregnate his wife. The fault, it was clear, lay with Elizabeth.

"As much as she resented being married to the Black Count, Elizabeth knew that to be sent back to her family as a failed wife would be her undoing. Determined to secure her place as lady of the castle, Elizabeth began to scheme on how to beget a child. When the folk remedies and old wives tales proved useless, she took as lovers men similar in build and appearance to the Black Count, so that any child sired by such a union could be easily mistaken as her husband's. But nothing came of those liaisons, either.

"Despairing, she begged her old nurse to help her. The loyal servant introduced her mistress to a witch, who claimed she could use her dark arts to place a child within Elizabeth' womb. So, during the dark of the moon, the witch smuggled Elizabeth out of the castle and into to the surrounding forest, to a magic grove used by her kind since the days of Rome.

"The witch had Elizabeth strip naked and anointed her body with an unguent made from the fat of unbaptised babies. Then she poured the blood of a black goat upon the ground and called upon her master: 'With this blood I summon thee, He Who Makes Shadows! With my will I bring thee forth, He Who Makes War! With these words I beseech thee, He Who Makes Dreams! Come forth from your world into this!'

"A cold wind blew down from the mountain tops, and the shadows in the darkness shaped themselves into the semblance of a tall, dark man with the legs of a goat, eyes of flame, and six fingers on each hand. 'Who calls me forth upon this plane?' asked the dark man, his voice echoing like thunder through the mountains. 'Who would summon He Who Makes?'

"The witch bowed before her master and said, 'I call you forth, master, in the name of this woman.'

"He Who Makes looked upon Elizabeth, who stood before him, naked and shivering. 'Daughter of Eve,' said he. 'What would thou have me Make for thee this night?'

"The very sound of the demon lord's voice was enough to cause Elizabeth's breath to freeze in her mouth. But although she was sorely frightened by the thing that stood before her, she was even more fearful of being sent back to her people in disgrace. 'I would make a child, my lord.'

"He Who Makes looked at Elizabeth's naked belly as if it was glass and shook his head. 'No seed sown by a human husband can ever take root in such rocky soil as yours, little sister.'

"'Then I have no choice but to take an inhuman husband, lord,' she replied.

"The flames within the demon lord's eyes leapt like burning bonfires as Elizabeth knelt before him. With a fearsome roar, he took her under the moonless sky like a beast of the field, his member as hard as horn and as cold as ice, never once growing warm within her. Elizabeth cried out as her demon lover loosed his seed, which burned like oil of peppermint poured upon an open wound. Once he was finished with her, the dark man returned to the shadows from which he had emerged, leaving Elizabeth collapsed upon the ground, clutching her belly as if she had been stabbed in the vitals.

"The witch quickly re-dressed Elizabeth and hurried her back to the castle before any of the courtiers noticed she was gone. For several days Elizabeth lay abed, wracked by fever, tended by none but her loyal nurse. When she awoke from her delirium, she could feel the seed He Who Makes had planted within her womb.

"That night she crept into her husband's bedchamber and made herself available to him. But as the Black Count placed his member inside her, he cried out in alarm, for she was cold as ice. It was then Elizabeth realized that He Who Makes had placed his mark upon her, assuring that no mortal man would ever again know her as Adam had known Eve. In her own way, she was bound to her demon lover in unholy chastity as surely as the Brides of Christ were wed to their resurrected lord.

"Despite this change to their marriage bed, if the Black Count suspected that the child belonged to any but himself, he showed no sign of it. The impending arrival of an heir appeased, somewhat, the wicked mother-in-law, and her scolding grew less frequent, although it did not stop, for there was still plenty of other things for her to find fault with in her son's wife.

"As time passed, Elizabeth's belly grew, and she took to lying in, attended by her loyal nurse, the witch, and her majordomo. Then, seven months into her maternity, she fell into heavy labor, her body struggling to bring forth the thing within her.

"What emerged from Elizabeth's womb resembled something dragged from the bowels of the sea, for it was without bones or limbs. Its skin was the color and consistency of fresh pitch, broken only by patches of hair, a lipless mouth ringed with tiny, razorlike teeth, and a single red eye. The witch screeched and wailed and called it a name unspoken in a thousand years. Then, as the nurse and the majordomo whispered among themselves as to whether or not to slay the wretched thing as it lay shivering on the counterpane, it gave a solitary cry and surrendered its breath.

"Elizabeth gnashed her teeth and cursed herself for not having been more specific when she bargained with the demon. She had asked for a child, but did not say she wanted a human one or that it should be born alive and healthy. She was ruined for childbirth, her womb having been rendered as icy as a tombstone in the dead of winter.

"The thing that she delivered forth was not given a name, nor was it buried in holy ground. Instead, the witch placed it in a bag and left with it hidden under her cloak, no doubt with intentions of rendering it for its unbaptised fat. To allay suspicions, Elizabeth's loyal nurse bought the corpse of a newborn from a midwife, who specialized in the disposal of unwanted children, and presented it to the Black Count as his stillborn son and heir.

"The Black Count, who was more interested in warfare than posterity, seemed slightly grieved by the loss, while the wicked mother-in-law was visibly relieved she no longer had to be civil to Elizabeth. However, with the entombment of the infant impostor in the family vault, the subject of annulment was no longer whispered in the castle hallways.

"As the wicked mother-in-law grew older and more and more feeble, Elizabeth's power within the castle strengthened. The years passed and became decades, and the wicked mother-in-law's sharp tongue became blunted, for fear of Elizabeth and her allies within the court. As the old woman's reign as the lady of the castle neared its end, she kept more and more to her chambers, until she was little more than a memory. Then, one day, a courier came bearing news of the Black Count's death on the field of battle.

"Upon her husband's passing, Elizabeth assumed the title and power of Countess and lost no time in banishing the wicked mother-in-law to a small hunting lodge atop a distant mountain. There the elderly woman was forced to chop her own firewood, draw her own water, and subsist on nothing but black bread and stone soup. Needless to say, the wicked mother-in-law quickly joined her son in the grave.

"For the first time in her life, Elizabeth was free from her husband and the control his family had exerted over her. She was the most powerful and wealthy woman in the land. None could compare to her when it came to her riches, station and comeliness.

"But of these three attributes, it was her beauty that Elizabeth treasured most. Although she had long since lost interest in the love of men, Elizabeth was proud of her physical appearance. It pleased her that men would be moved to unthinking lust by the sight of her. For, as she had long ago learned, men possessed by lust have their uses in the political arena.

"Since she no longer enjoyed the embraces of men, she developed a taste for the pleasure of others, and orchestrated orgies for her amusement. As the years passed, the orgies became more and more extreme in nature, involving erotic circuses complete with acrobats, trained animal acts and assorted freaks of nature. Black Sabbaths were held within the castle's chapel, where highborn guests ritually desecrated the altar and baptismal font in honor of He Who Makes.

"There were whispers of the goings on at the castle among the villagers, but the rumors rarely made it to the royal court. And even if they did, what did it matter? The Countess was a blood cousin of the vice-chamberlain. Who would dare lift a hand against her? Any outraged guest or disgruntled servant who threatened to expose her was quickly disposed of by her manservant, their corpses harvested for those parts useful in the casting of spells by the witch, then sealed behind the castle walls.

"And so it went for several years. But as roses fade and silver tarnishes, as the sun will, one day, lose it fire, Elizabeth's great beauty finally began to dim. She was in her fourth decade and lines had etched themselves into the corners of her mouth and the folds of her eyes. Her breasts were no longer firm like apples, but more like ripened plums. Her buttocks and belly were starting to sag, victims of gravity's toll. Silver threads were now woven throughout her dark hair, and her hands resembled more the claws of crows than the wings of doves.

"For a woman such as Elizabeth, the effects of aging were no more to be suffered than the stare of an insolent peasant. She became determined to restore her rapidly disintegrating beauty and youth, no matter what the cost. She instructed the witch to find a rejuvenation spell or she would put her to death.

"The witch pored through her collection of spells and incantations, until she came upon a ritual described within the pages of an ancient tome known as *The Aegrisomnia*. The spell promised the restoration of youth and vigor and, eventually, the gift of immortality, but only by bathing in the freshly shed blood of young virgins. Elizabeth decided that if Cleopatra became one of the great beauties of the civilized world with the help of ass's milk, then she would have her bath of blood.

"The majordomo, in collaboration with the witch, butchered one of the servant girls and bled her into a large cauldron, in which Elizabeth steeped herself. From that day on, the ravages of age held no sway over her.

"For ten years Elizabeth's loyal inner circle scoured the countryside in search of suitable young girls, free of sin and untainted by illness, which, in those days, was not as easy as it sounds. Numerous peasant girls, born into ignorance and poverty, were offered a chance of a lifetime: positions as chambermaids and scullery servants in the comparative grandeur of the castle.

"The moment the new serving girls arrived at the castle, they were drugged, bound and butchered like sheep. Like the slaves who toiled and died to build the Great Pyramids, these nameless peasant girls transcended their insignificance by serving to restore one of the living wonders of the world to her full glory. Over those ten years more than forty young girls were fed to Elizabeth's beauty. And it would have continued for another decade, possibly a third, if a fatal case of mistaken identity had not been made.

"When the young daughter of the Archduke arrived at the castle for an unannounced visit after a particularly long and arduous journey, she was mistaken for the most recent recruit and summarily drugged and bled out before anyone realized whom she was.

"The Archduke became concerned when his favorite daughter did not return from her trip. He wrote several letters to Elizabeth, asking what had become of his child. At first Elizabeth assured the Archduke that the girl was fine and had merely decided to extend her stay. But when he still did not hear from his daughter, the Archduke became more insistent. Elizabeth then claimed that the young girl had contracted a fever and could not be moved. This news upset the Archduke greatly, and he promptly sent a messenger to the castle to inform Elizabeth that he would be leaving his palace to personally attend his ailing daughter.

Halfway to the castle, the Archduke was met by one of Elizabeth's retainers, who said the Archduke's daughter had died of the plague and that the castle was under quarantine. The Countess had been forced to burn the body of his daughter, for fear of contamination.

"This last piece of news was more than the Archduke could bear. He had heard rumors of the goings on at the castle but had not given them credence. He knew his child was dead, but he suspected her end had come by mortal hands. He petitioned the king for an investigation into the goings on at the castle. Elizabeth's cousin, the vice-chamberlain, tried to block the request, but since the king was himself a cousin of the Archduke, he was unable to stop it being approved.

"A division of the king's army, lead by the Archduke and accompanied by Church inquisitors, stormed the castle. They found the Archduke's dear, departed daughter moldering in the dungeon, her highborn corpse alongside the daughters of swineherds and hodcarriers.

"The lowborn accomplices who had served Elizabeth so loyally and so well over the years were put to the question and quickly gave evidence against their mistress. For collaborating with the Crown, the witnesses privy to the secret of Elizabeth's unique beauty treatments were rewarded by having their fingernails pulled out with pliers, their kneecaps broken, and then they were hanged and dismembered in the public square. The witch, for the additional crime of blasphemy, was broken on the wheel and then burned at the stake.

"There was a great deal of excitement about the case, and thousands of people came from far and wide to see the accomplices to the Countess put to death. Those unable to attend the executions read about them in widely distributed broad sheets, which recounted the story in gruesome detail, and, for those unable to read, featured numerous graphic woodcuts of the crimes committed and the punishment meted out.

"Because of her high station, Elizabeth was not put to death. Indeed, she was not even placed on trial. Instead, it was decreed that she would spend the rest of her natural life under house arrest. And to make sure that her sentence would be as short as possible, her jailer was the Archduke.

"The day after sentence was passed on Elizabeth, the Archduke arrived at her castle and ordered all the fixtures removed. The beds, chairs, tables, tapestries, even the chamber pots, were taken from the castle and distributed among the families of those who had lost their daughters to the blood bath. Once the interior of the castle was as bleak and bare as its exterior, the Archduke ordered what few servants remained to leave the premises. By the end of the second day, all that was left inside the once grand castle was a pallet of dirty straw, a crooked foot stool, a rough-hewn table, and Elizabeth.

"The Archduke then summoned his master mason and ordered him to brick up every door and window in the castle, save for one. The sole egress into the castle was a small window in Elizabeth's bedchamber, accessible only via a long ladder. It was through this narrow portal that Elizabeth's jailers pushed her daily meal of black bread and stone soup.

"Elizabeth's isolation from the world was total, as she was forbidden pen and paper to pass her days, candles or fire to illuminate the darkness or warm herself, and her keepers were forbidden to speak even one word to her, under pain of death.

"She spent four years sealed away from the light of day. Four years spent shitting in the ballroom fireplace. Four years spent prowling the dark for rats and mice to supplement her diet. Four years spent licking condensation off the walls to quench her thirst. Four years spent freezing in the winter and sweltering in the summer.

"Her only clothes were those upon her back the day the master mason sealed her away. Her only blanket was a tattered piece of tapestry the Archduke's men had overlooked the day they emptied the castle. Although her family had been spared the shame of Elizabeth being put to death in the public square, in truth it would have been far less cruel if she had been broken on the rack and burned alive as a witch than left to dwell in filth and darkness, perpetually on the edge of starvation.

"Finally, after years of such ill treatment, Elizabeth collapsed in her bed chamber, too weak to rise. As she lay dying on the hard, chill floor, the shadows in the corner of the room took a form familiar to her. It knelt beside her, its eyes flickering in the eternal gloom.

"'Thou breathest thy last, fair Elizabeth, but despair not. In life thou embraced monstrosity, and, in doing so, secured for thyself unlife neverending. In three days time thou shalt rise and walk the earth once more, as one Made in mine own image.'

"When the guard next climbed the ladder to pass Elizabeth her meal of black bread and stone soup through the window, she was not waiting for him. He glanced into the room and saw a woman's body sprawled, motionless, on the floor.

"The guard informed the Archduke, who had one of the castle doors unsealed. They found the body of Elizabeth, reduced to little more than a skeleton, covered in filth and open sores. Although the Archduke would have gladly thrown her corpse on the dung heap for the dogs to tear apart, he had no desire to offend her powerful relatives. So he had Elizabeth's body placed in the family tomb, without the benefit of clergy, alongside her long-dead husband. And so ended the story of the Black Countess, as far as most people were concerned.

"Except that the night following her entombment, Elizabeth rose from her resting place and walked out into the darkness, never to return to her native land. For He Who Makes was as good as his word; although dead, she did still move upon the earth. She was now one of the Unliving, who walk by night and feed upon the blood of mortals.

"But Elizabeth was different, in many ways, from those creatures whom humans know as vampires. She did not have fangs to bite her victims, but instead absorbed their blood directly through her skin. And now that she was undead, she no longer had to worry about the blood being that of a male or a female, virgin or sinner.

"So Elizabeth wandered the world, eager to quench her thirst and continue the existence she had once known. She soon learned that the best cover for her operations was that of the brothel. Men, as a rule, were far easier to entice to their deaths, and much less likely to be missed than virginal young maidens.

"Over the centuries she went from country to country, city to city, establishing a series of bordellos notorious for their willingness to cater to the most perverse—and wealthiest—patrons. She knew them all, and they knew her—under a dozen different names, but always the same title: Countess.

"Empires rose and fell. Religions were founded and destroyed. The ancestral line of which she was once so proud grew anemic and fell into decline. To her eyes, human society was like a castle made of sand, constantly being washed away and rebuilt. The one thing that remained unchanged was her beauty... and the blood that fed it.

"And so things would have remained until the world's end, except for the Blue Monster.

"The Blue Monster was a fearsome creature that hated all things inhuman. It had mirrors for eyes, a leathery black skin, and a single, deadly silver tooth, which it plunged into the hearts of its hapless victims. It scoured the world in search of vampires and other nonhumans, stalking its prey without mercy.

"One night, not too long ago, while returning from an exclusive sex club in Monte Carlo, Elizabeth was accosted by the Blue Monster. The creature attacked without warning or provocation, slicing Elizabeth with its horrible silver tooth. It took all of her strength to escape the dreadful beast.

"Although Elizabeth had avoided true death at the hands of her enemy, the Blue Monster's silver tooth had done its damage, turning her legs gangrenous. To keep the rot from spreading, Elizabeth had no other choice but to have her legs removed. Although the surgery was successful, her existence was forever changed. As all vampires know, wounds dealt by silver weapons never truly heal, and limbs lost to silver never regenerate.

"For the first time in centuries, Elizabeth was unable to feed her beauty, and without the blood of her admirers, the full weight of her years began to bear down on her brittle bones. Elizabeth needed a companion to help restore her youth and beauty; a companion who would do her bidding without question or qualm; a companion who would deceive, seduce and kill for her. Most of all, she needed a companion who would protect her from the Blue Monster.

"Elizabeth looked in penthouses and boxcars, prep schools and prisons for such a companion. Then, one night, while at an interstate travel plaza, she noticed a young girl dressed in a tank top and cut-off jeans going from rig to rig, soliciting the truckers for sex. She watched as the girl climbed into one of the cabs, then exited ten minutes later, her hands stained with blood and clutching a large roll of paper currency. It was then that Elizabeth knew she had found her companion.

"Elizabeth took the girl away from the truck stops and rest areas that had been her world and gave her nice clothes, money, expensive cars, and took her traveling around the globe. And in exchange, all the companion—who was, in reality, a Secret Princess—had to do was keep

Elizabeth's beauty fed with fresh blood. Which proved very, very easy to do. The End."

"But you didn't say if Elizabeth and the Secret Princess lived happily ever after,"

"How remiss of me! And Elizabeth and the Secret Princess lived happily ever after forever and ever. The End."

"I like it when you do the voices," Phaedra said, her voice drowsy.

The next john whose name wasn't John was a Japanese business executive with an Osaka electronics concern. Phaedra picked him up at a gentleman's club while wearing the red wig and driving the Lamborghini. He had insisted on vaginal intercourse, but didn't last three minutes. Not that it mattered. In the end he met the same fate as all the other nameless johns she had slaughtered in the service of the Contessa's beauty.

Still, she was beginning to worry. They had been in one place far too long. And the cycles between baths were becoming disturbingly short. When Phaedra first began working for her, the Contessa required only one bath a week. Now it was two, sometimes three. The local police would eventually tie the various disappearances together, despite her care in changing her appearance and making sure she didn't trawl in a discernible pattern.

Even if the cops were slow on the uptake, there was no guarantee the papers wouldn't smell a story and start writing about the sudden spate of missing midlevel executives. Neither the cops nor reporters really concerned Phaedra overmuch. She was used to dodging both. But what she was afraid of was the story getting picked up by the wire services. That meant the Blue Monster would be headed their way.

Phaedra felt much safer in Europe than the States. Part of that was personal. After all, nothing bad had ever happened to her on the Continent. She had repeatedly begged her mistress to leave the country, but the Contessa remained adamant about staying put. Phaedra feared her mistress's frequent aging cycles had somehow affected her mind. Sometimes she seemed distant and disjointed, as if centuries of memory were playing inside her head at the same time. On occasion she called Phaedra by different names and spoke to her in foreign languages.

There were other changes, too. The torpor that followed her rejuvenation now lasted hours. All the Contessa seemed interested in doing was sitting on her bed and staring out at the night, watching the moon's reflection on the lake's liquid surface. The only thing that seemed to interest the Contessa, besides watching the night, were the fairy tales.

Phaedra liked lying with her head in her mistress's truncated lap while the Contessa absently stroked her hair and told her bedtime stories. It was something her mother had never done for her as a child. Her stepfather used to come into her room and put her head in his lap, but that was different.

If there was one thing Phaedra had learned in her short life, it was that love was not to be trusted. Need was better than love, safer than want, more reliable than lust. The Contessa needed her more than anyone else ever had. She needed her like Phaedra needed to eat and breathe. That, more than the money, was what kept her bound to the old woman.

The Contessa had done more for her than any other person on the face of the earth, including her mother. All that bitch ever did was give birth to her. The Contessa, on the other hand, had lifted her up from the gutter, taught her how to act and dress and talk to attract a more affluent john. It was the Contessa who exposed her to the world beyond the grim, gray confines of truck stop plazas, trailer parks, and cheap motels.

It was the Contessa who taught her how best to butcher a human being and disassemble them with a hacksaw and a cleaver;. It was she who showed her how to dispose of a body without attracting attention. When they first met, Phaedra was a callow young girl with a lot of anger and a straight razor; the Contessa had turned her into a sophisticated femme fatale and a world-class serial killer.

The Contessa had given her a life where before there was nothing but day-to-day existence. Phaedra owed it to her mistress to protect her and make her safe from her enemies. But there was only so much she could do for her lady. Why the Contessa chose to come back to this place, she was not certain.

Phaedra knew the Contessa had lived in Red Velvet Manor far longer than any other place in the four hundred years of her existence. Then again, perhaps the old woman's reasons for returning were more practical than sentimental. After all, Red Velvet Manor was already outfitted for her special needs.

It was Phaedra's job to protect her mistress, and that meant making sure their camouflage within the community remained intact. The best way to do that was to maintain a low profile, make sure the curious stayed at arm's length, and keep moving. The longer they stayed at Red Velvet

Manor, the more likely it was that the Blue Monster would sniff them out. Phaedra had never seen the Blue Monster, but she did not doubt it existed. The Contessa's legs were proof enough of that.

In the years spent making sure the Contessa was one step ahead of her nemesis, Phaedra had come to realize that the Blue Monster was as smart as it was tenacious. While Red Velvet Manor was isolated, it did have a historical connection to the Contessa, one that was easily accessible to anyone with an Internet connection and knowledge of the Contessa's various pseudonyms.

If her lady wished to remain at Red Velvet Manor, then they would stay put. But Phaedra could not shake the sensation that things were about to go bad. It was the same feeling she used to get when she stood on the concrete block that had served as the trailer's front stoop, sniffing the summer wind while cicadas sang in the trees. On the surface everything seemed safe, but there was always an edge of potential disaster in the rising wind. There was a storm coming. But would it be just another summer squall or a twister? Do you run for cover or stand your ground? Do you batten down the hatches or flee for your life? There was no way of knowing, really, until the storm was upon you. And by then it was too late to do anything but ride it out.

"Have you seen this woman?"

"Nope," the bartender grunted, barely glancing in the direction of the photo on the top of the bar.

A fresh twenty suddenly appeared atop the photograph.

"You sure about that?"

The bartender stopped cleaning the highball glass and glanced up, for the first time, at the woman standing opposite him. His eyebrow went up even higher. Hotel Orso was a four-star establishment, catering to wealthy business executives. It rarely saw young women tricked out in leather motorcycle jackets, mirrored sunglasses, and tattered Black Flag T-shirts, even when rock stars were staying in the hotel.

The bartender palmed the twenty and picked up the photo, knitting his brows as he frowned. It was a candid surveillance shot, taken with a telephoto lens.

"Which one you mean? The old lady?"

"No. The blonde pushing the wheelchair," the woman in the leather jacket said, tapping the picture.

The bartender shook his head and tossed the photograph back onto the counter. "Naw. Can't say I recognize her. Sorry."

"How about this one?" She flipped another photo out of a small deck held in a fan like playing cards.

The second photograph was in better focus, although taken under the same conditions as the first. It was of a sexy brunette in a red cocktail dress being helped into a sports car by a slightly balding middle-aged man in evening clothes. The bartender's eyes narrowed.

"Now this one looks familiar. She wears her hair different, but I'm pretty sure it's her. She comes in from time to time. Checks out the bar. Working girl, from what I've seen of her."

"She ever talk to you?"

The bartender shook his head. "Just to order drinks. Virgin Marys. Keeps to herself, unless she hooks a john."

"When's the last time you saw her?"

"Couple of weeks ago, I guess. She left with some suit." He tilted his head to one side. "Are you a cop, lady?"

"Do I look like a cop?"

"Hell no!" the bartender snorted. "The reason I asked, see... That suit she walked out with turned up missing a couple of days later."

"You don't say?"

"Cops were all over this place, asking questions. I guess he was some kind of business bigwig," he said, turning to slide one of the long-stems into its overhead rack. "The cops seemed to think the bastard high-tailed it to Rio with company funds. The way I see it..."

When the bartender turned back in her direction, he found himself addressing empty space. He shrugged and resumed polishing the highball glasses. Fucking tourists.

Sonja strode purposefully across the Hotel Orso lobby, oblivious to the stares from the staff and guests. She had more important things on her mind. The blood witch was in the area. There was no doubt the Contessa's renfield was out and about, doing her mistress's work.

She had spent the better part of two years tracking down the old bitch. She had come close to killing her back in Vienna, only to have the hag escape. Now it was up to her to track the Contessa down and finish her off, much like a master hunter would a wounded deer.

Vampires as ancient as the Contessa were never easy prey. You didn't get to be hundreds of years old without being able to go to ground. If one identity got too hot for them, they switched to another as easily as changing socks. This made her quarry especially difficult to track. However, since ancients such as the Contessa rarely had to worry about being recognized from one generation to the next, they tended to use the same identities over and over again. Another thing in her favor was the inherent difficulty the old ones seemed to have in regard to understanding the importance of technology. This led to her commissioning a computer database, based on her own design, that could access and cross-reference real estate records, land titles, newspaper reports, census information, birth and death certificates, scanning them for known identities and pseudonyms of the so-called ruling class. As an afterthought, she had an anagram generator incorporated into the system, just in case someone decided to get cute.

A search on "The Contessa" pulled up newspaper reports dating from the Depression of a notorious high-class house of ill repute called Red Velvet Manor. Its madam was one Eliza Bayroth, who was rumored to have catered to the more outré tastes of captains of industry, Supreme Court justices, and the occasional American president. After the start of the Second World War, rumors began to circulate of occult rituals, which may or may not have been a cover for Fifth Columnist activities.

The brothel shut down shortly after a newspaperman famous for underworld reportage announced his intention of publishing an expose of Red Velvet Manor. The reporter disappeared off the face of the earth not long after that. A year later, a badly decomposed body, believed to be that of the missing journalist, was found in a nearby landfill. It was assumed to be a gangland killing. By the time the body was uncovered, Madame Bayroth had married a dissolute Romanian nobleman and set sail for the Continent, where, from there on in, she was known simply as the Contessa.

This information dovetailed into what Sonja herself had uncovered from her European sources and microfiche issues of *Le Figaro*, *Paris-Match*, and *Der Spiegel*. Studied in its totality, the data answered several nagging questions she had concerning her quarry.

She had been hunting vampires for almost thirty years. Her knowledge of their strengths and weaknesses, their abilities and limits, did not come from reading books or watching movies, but from hands-on experience. But, for all her familiarity with the world and ways of the undead, the Contessa had baffled her. For one, the bitch did not seem to possess the telltale fangs, nor did she surround herself with lesser vampires of her own making. And, most importantly, she had survived an attack with a silver weapon, albeit as a double amputee.

Sonja realized now that she had made a grave mistake in classifying the Contessa as a garden-variety vampire. From what she had since learned from various sources and her own research, the Contessa was not a true vampire, but a *strega*—those who transform themselves into the undead through the use of black magic. Such creatures were rare, but those that existed were crafty and possessed different strengths and weaknesses than "typical" vampires.

While the Contessa's means of feeding on her victims did not spread the taint, that didn't make her any less dangerous. Like all vampires, she was a corrupting force on any human who fell into her sphere of influence. To allow such a monster to continue to exist was anathema to Sonja.

After all, it was one such monster that had attacked her, over thirty years ago... and made her one of them.

Phaedra was wearing the short red wig and the black silk sheath that night. It hadn't taken her very long to reel in the next john whose name wasn't John. As they headed for the Boxter, he began to drag his heels. She turned to look at him.

"Is there something wrong, sugar?"

"Look, lady..." he said, his face coloring. "I thought I could go through with this—"

"What do you mean?" she asked, genuinely baffled.

"It's not you—!" he said with a nervous laugh. "God knows, you're one of the most beautiful woman I've ever met! It's just that—well, I keep thinking of my wife and the kids. And, well, I'm sure you're a *great* person and all that... but I just can't go through with this. I'm sorry if I lead you on back at the bar."

Phaedra blinked and shifted around uncomfortably, uncertain of what she should do. She had never had a john throw the hook before. The one or two who had gotten away in the past had done so simply because someone who would have been able to give a description to the local authorities or remember a license plate number had walked up at an inopportune moment. But nothing like actual rejection had ever happened to her before. It had never once crossed her mind that a man might be capable of passing up sex. In her experience, given the chance, men fucked anything that was willing, and much that was not.

"I feel like I haven't been honest with you or myself. My name isn't John, it's Frank. Frank Hensley," he said, an abashed look on his face. "Believe me, I would love to spend the night with you..."

"Get in the car," she said.

"Beg pardon?" Hensley blinked, uncertain he'd heard her correctly.

"Get in the car, damn you!"

Hensley's eyes widened at the sight of the gun aimed at his midsection. "Whoa, lady!" he said, automatically raising his hands. "Don't you think you're overreacting?"

Bartenders, like cops, develop a sixth sense for trouble. And the chick in the leather jacket was definitely that. Over the years he learned never to trust anyone who wore sunglasses after the sun went down, since it usually meant they were strung out on something. Still, potential trouble or not, it was his job to serve her, just as he would any other customer who happened to stroll into the Embers Lounge.

"What'll it be, ma'am?"

"I don't want a drink, just information. Have you seen this woman?" she asked, pushing a snapshot wrapped in a twenty toward him.

"What's the deal?" he said, eyeing her suspiciously. "She owe you money or something?"

The woman in the sunglasses smiled crookedly without showing her teeth. "Far from it. In fact, *I'm* the one who owes *her.* I'm just trying to track her down so I can pay her back."

The bartender hesitated for a moment, but the twenty was too tempting to ignore. He picked up the photo and frowned at it for a moment.

"Yeah, I recognize her."

The stranger in the leather jacket and mirrored shades grew attentive. "When was the last time you saw her?"

"Just a few minutes ago." He nodded in the direction of the side door. "She just left with some suit."

To his surprise, the stranger bared her teeth in a snarl and headed in the direction of the exit as if the joint had suddenly caught fire. The bartender wasn't certain, but he could have sworn he'd seen fangs. He shook his head, doing his best to forget what he had just witnessed as he pocketed the twenty.

Yeah, she was trouble all right. But not his, thank God.

"Shut up and get in the car!" Phaedra said, jerking open the passenger door.

Hensley stared at the gun, then at Phaedra. What he saw in her eyes was enough to turn him on his heel and send him sprinting back in the direction of the motel. He managed to get halfway across the parking lot before she dropped him with a single shot to the right leg. He lay on the asphalt, writhing in pain as he clutched what remained of his kneecap.

Phaedra hurried to claim her prize, removing the handcuffs she kept in her purse as she crossed the lot with brisk, purposeful strides. Frank cringed in fear, lifting his bloodied hands to shield his face, as she loomed over him.

"Take my wallet, if that's what you want! I don't care! Just don't kill me—! Please! I've got a wife and kids!"

Phaedra cursed under her breath and quickly scanned the parking lot for witnesses. The bastard was making too much noise. She would be better off popping him here-and-now and fleeing the scene, then starting from scratch in one of the gentlemen's clubs across town. Phaedra returned the handcuffs to her purse and raised the gun. Frank began to alternately pray and sob.

Before Phaedra could squeeze the trigger, the side door of the bar banged open, causing her to swing the gun in the direction of the noise. She saw a woman standing framed in the doorway. The stranger was dressed in a black leather motorcycle jacket and wearing a pair of mirrored sunglasses, even though it was the dead of night.

The woman did not seem surprised by the sight of a man wallowing on the asphalt, nor was she frightened by the gun pointed in her direction. Instead of turning and running back into the building, the stranger let the door close behind her and gave her right wrist a small, sharp snap. A silver blade in the shape of a frozen flame sprouted from her hand as if by magic. Phaedra gasped in recognition, even though she had never seen the woman before.

The Blue Monster fixed Phaedra with its horrible mirrored eyes and moved toward her with determined, measured steps, its hideous silver fang reflecting the glow from the streetlights.

Phaedra squeezed the trigger of the gun, firing on her enemy. The Blue Monster moved with the fluid grace of underwater ballet, twisting its upper torso to allow the bullet to pass by. The second bullet, however, caught it in the upper shoulder, knocking it to the ground.

Phaedra looked down at Frank, still cowering at her feet, then at the Blue Monster, who was already picking itself up off the ground. With a scream of angry frustration, Phaedra fled to the waiting Boxter, and left in her wake six feet of smoking rubber.

Sonja sat up and grimaced at the pain radiating from her shoulder. She bit her lower lip, her fangs inadvertently drawing more blood. It felt like the renfield had broken her damn collarbone. Then again, she'd taken slugs to the heart and lungs without much to show for it except some scars. She grunted as she got to her feet, pushing the throbbing in her shoulder to the back of her mind.

She walked over to where the renfield's intended victim lay huddled on the asphalt. He was alive, although his face was starting to go gray from shock. He flinched as she leaned over him.

"Don't shoot me," he whispered.

"I'm not her."

The side door opened and the bartender stuck his head outside. "What the fuck's going on out here?"

"This man's been shot! Call 911!" she shouted in reply.

The bartender nodded and disappeared back inside the Embers.

Hensley shook his head, a look of baffled pain on his face. "Why'd she shoot me?"

"You must have broken the script. You did something she was unprepared for."

The wounded man laughed without humor. "All I said was that I didn't want to go home with her." His laughter turned into a moan, causing him to close his eyes. When he opened them again, the woman with the mirrored sunglasses was gone. Which suited him just fine. There was something about the way she stared at his bloodied leg that scared him even more than being shot.

The sound of the front door slamming shut reverberated throughout the house. Startled, the Contessa looked around at the red velvet wallpaper and the gilded rococo statuary that surrounded her on all sides, bafflement on her face. This wasn't Vienna. And she was reasonably sure it wasn't Budapest. But if she was in neither of these places, where was she then? And, more importantly, *when* was she?

Her confused gaze fell to her lap, and she caught sight of the grotesque contraptions that served as her legs. Ah, yes. The New World. The city that sprawled along the shores of the great inland freshwater sea. She stared at a heavily brocaded mahogany love seat and saw a long-dead Chief Justice being fellated by a twelve-year-old boy. She shook her head, dislodging the ghost-memory. It was so easy to forget where and when she was these nights.

If it wasn't for Magda... no, her name was Gretchen. Wait, that wasn't right, either. Phaedra? Yes. That was it. If it weren't for her faithful companion, Phaedra, she would become lost within the world inside herself, wandering the shadow-haunted palaces and ballrooms of centuries past.

"Contessa!"

Phaedra burst into the parlor, her mascara smeared and hair in disarray. That, more than the look of fear on her companion's face, shocked the Contessa back into her senses.

"What is it, child? You look a fright."

Phaedra grabbed the handles of the old woman's wheelchair and began pushing it toward the converted dumbwaiter. "We have to leave! We have to leave *right now!*"

"Phaedra, what's going on?" The Contessa twisted around in her seat so she could face her companion. "Answer me, young lady!"

Phaedra fumbled with the door to the elevator, her eyes blinded by tears. "I'm so sorry, mistress. I'm so, *so* sorry."

"Sorry? For *what?*"

Phaedra's shoulders shook as she began to sob. "I've *failed* you, mistress. Please forgive me."

"Speak plainly, Phaedra! You're starting to annoy me!"

"The Blue Monster is here."

The Contessa gasped as phantom pain shot through the stumps of her legs. She put a trembling hand to her mouth, her eyes wide with fear.

"Are you certain it's her?"

"As sure as sunlight burns," Phaedra replied. "Please, Contessa, we've got to leave right now! Take the elevator to the ground floor and wait for me by the boathouse. I'll go upstairs and get the strongbox and passports, then I'll bring the car around. I'll have to put you in the trunk—just in case sunrise catches us before I can reach a safe haven."

"But I don't want to ride in the trunk," the Contessa said petulantly.

"Please, mistress, not now! Just do as I ask!" Phaedra pushed the wheelchair into the tiny elevator and pulled the doors shut behind it. "I'll be down to get you in a couple of minutes. I promise."

The Contessa sat in the darkened car, staring at the control panel for a long moment, before punching the button.

Phaedra grabbed the top drawer of the bedroom dresser and yanked it out, sending crotchless panties and Wonder Bras flying in every direction. She flipped the drawer over, revealing the manila envelope taped to its bottom. Inside the envelope were numerous identity papers, passports, and documents made out in the various names the Contessa had used over the years. Exactly which pseudonym they would be using to flee the country would be decided later.

Phaedra stuffed the envelope inside a leather satchel, then hurried over to the red leather ottoman and removed its padded lid. Inside the hollowed-out footrest was a metal strongbox containing two hundred thousand dollars in bundled currency, a number of credit cards, seven gold Rolex watches, and various pieces of male jewelry they had yet to convert into cash. Still, it was enough to take them somewhere far away. The French Riviera, perhaps, or maybe the Golden Triangle. Anywhere but here.

As she lifted the strong box from its hiding place, she was surprised to hear the sound of the Contessa's private elevator coming to a stop. She turned and saw the Contessa wheeling herself out of the converted dumbwaiter.

Cursing under her breath, Phaedra put aside what she was doing and strode forward, trying her best to keep the panic from showing in her face. "Why aren't you downstairs?"

"I *can't* leave," the Contessa replied, shaking her head.

Phaedra knelt so she could look her mistress in the face, placing a soft, young hand on the Contessa's withered shoulder. "Why not?"

"Because it's time for my bath," the Contessa said, matter-of-factly, her gnarled hand closing on Phaedra's throat, its grip as tight and inescapable as death's.

There was no mistaking Red Velvet Manor for anything else, even from a distance. The red curtains, lit from behind, caused the windows to glow like the eyes of an animal.

Sonja cut the headlights as she came up the long, winding drive of the house. She could see the Boxter parked alongside the house, the driver's side door still hanging open. She pulled up behind the sports car, blocking its path. She twitched her right arm, cupping her hand so it caught the switchblade as it dropped from its hidden sheath within the sleeve.

The front door was standing slightly ajar, the light from the foyer spilling across the front veranda. Sonja frowned and glanced up at the second floor windows. Her prey was still here. She could feel it. The question was why.

It had taken Sonja twenty minutes to find this place. The renfield had that advantage, on top of a good five-minute lead. She cautiously pushed open the front door, but it swung inward without incident. She stepped inside the grand foyer, eyeing the decor for hidden tripwires or skulking bodyguards. There were none.

She tilted her head, allowing her mirrored sunglasses to slide to the end of her nose, and dropped her vision into the occult spectrum. What had been empty air a moment before was now filled with dark energies that seethed like heat shadows cast against a summer sidewalk.

Out of the corner of her eye she glimpsed men dressed in old-fashioned evening clothes, brandy snifters in their hands, watching a large dog mount a naked woman. But it couldn't be a dog, because it had hands that gripped the woman's waist. As Sonja turned to get a better look, the shades flickered and disappeared.

Sonja shook her head. She had to keep her guard up and not allow herself to be distracted by shadows. The Contessa might be crippled, but she didn't get to be four centuries old on just luck and blood.

Sonja started up the grand staircase, scanning the doors that lined the second floor. They all seemed to be locked save for the one at the end, which stood slightly ajar. She nudged it open with the toe of her boot. The interior of the room was dark, save for a sliver of light from the bathroom that fell across the floor, illuminating the blood-red carpet.

"Do not be so hesitant, my dear," said the Contessa from somewhere inside the darkened room. "You have nothing to fear from me."

"Forgive me if I do not believe you," Sonja replied as she crossed the threshold.

The Contessa sat propped up against the padded headboard of a large oval-shaped bed, dressed in a red velvet robe trimmed with monkey fur. Her hair spilled over her shoulders and across the red satin pillows like ink from an overturned bottle. Her skin was milky white and as smooth as alabaster, unmarred by age or imperfection. Her delicate, long-fingered hands were folded in her lap, cradling what looked like the remote control for a TV set.

Sonja glanced about, probing the shadows for signs of an ambush, but all she saw was a set of prosthetic legs draped over a nearby chair like an empty pair of pants.

"Where is she, witch?"

"She?" The Contessa asked, arching an eyebrow.

"The renfield."

The Contessa pointed in the direction of the bathroom door, which stood slightly ajar. Sonja gave it a wary push. It swung all the way open on its hinges, revealing Phaedra—born into the world as Faye Alice Baker—hanging by her heels over the marble tub, her throat slit from ear to ear like a summer hog. The sight didn't surprise Sonja; she had caught the scent of blood the moment she entered the house.

"I *hated* having to do that," The Contessa said, turning the remote control she held over and over again in her hands. "Really I did. But I had no choice. There was no point in running away again. I knew it, and so did Phaedra, although she could not bring herself to admit it. It wouldn't be fair to her, leaving her on her own... What would she do without me? I did her a kindness, really."

"So you put her down rather than leave her to face life without you. How altruistic. I notice you didn't let her blood go to waste."

"I will meet eternity in no skin but this one."

"Once a vain, psychotic bitch, always a vain, psychotic bitch, eh? Put down the remote, old woman. I'll be as quick about this as I can."

The Contessa shook her head in defiance. "No! I refuse to die at the hands of a monster such as you! My family once strode the world as kings! What right does a lowborn freak of nature have to destroy me? I was Made by my own hand, and by my own hand shall I be Unmade!"

The Contessa pointed the remote at the heavy velvet drapes and pushed the button a final time. The curtains parted like those of a stage and the first rays of the rising sun spilled across the room. Both women instinctively lifted their arms to shield their faces from the sunlight, but only one burst into flame.

The Contessa screamed as her skin and hair caught fire, the flames quickly spreading to her gown and bedclothes. Sonja backed away, both repulsed and fascinated as the ancient vampire's flesh bubbled and melted, dripping from her bones like wax from a candle. Within seconds the Contessa had been reduced to a thrashing skeleton, and yet she continued to scream.

The fire, having consumed the bed, quickly spread to the red velvet wallpaper. The walls ignited like dry kindling, and suddenly the entire room was ablaze. Sonja leapt through the curtain of fire and smoke that had swallowed the door, rolling on the hallway floor to extinguish the flames clinging to her jacket. The hair on the right side of her head was burned to the scalp and heat blisters were rising across her back, but she barely noticed the pain.

The interior of the mansion was already filling with heavy, acrid smoke. As she hurried down the stairs toward the front door, Sonja felt a chill on her spine. Someone, or something, was watching her. She turned and saw what looked like a tall man the color of shadow standing on the landing above her, watching her with eyes made of fire.

Sonja ran out the front door and all the way to her car, throwing it into gear the second the engine turned over. She was halfway down the drive before she bothered to close the driver-side door.

She didn't know why the old blood-witch's patron had chosen to lay low and didn't care. Vampire slaying was one thing, but demon hunting was a whole other ball game.

Inside the funeral pyre the Contessa had built for herself, a shadow shaped like a man stood in the grand foyer and laughed as the grandfather clock with the zodiac face struck thirteen. Upon the final strike, a pillar of fire punched through the roof, and the final visitor to the gilded halls of Red Velvet Manor shut its burning front door behind him.

the
nonesuch
horror

The evil came with the night, adding its shadow to those already cast by the half-moon that hung in the New Mexico sky.

Its arrival was not presaged by the howling of dogs or the shooting of stars, but by a hot, dry wind gusting in from the Continental Divide that made babies whimper in their cradles and the bones of old women creak like ship timbers.

One such old woman, sleeping nose to tail, awoke from a dream of rabbits and lost love and stared with amber eyes at the stars stretched above her head. She sniffed the night air and caught a scent she did not like. The old woman twitched her ears and clicked her teeth, as she was wont to do when uneasy.

There was trouble headed her way. Trouble that walked like a man. It had been a very long time since she had last smelled such a thing, but not so long that she had forgotten the thing that carried such a scent.

The old woman got to her feet and trotted back in the direction of the shelter she called home. There would be no more dreams of better days and chasing rabbits that night.

It wouldn't be fair to call Nonesuch a flyspeck on the map, but it wouldn't exactly be lying, either.

Even back in its glory days, back before the copper mine played out, Nonesuch wasn't much of a town. It was more a collection of houses clustered around a company store than a real community. When the Depression hit for real, Nonesuch took the blow like a hedgehog. By the time World War Two rolled around, it was a legitimate ghost town.

For the better part of seventy years Nonesuch was forgotten, save for the occasional hermit and footloose hippie. Then, about ten years ago, a group of strangers stumbled across the old ghost town, and Nonesuch was reborn.

The strangers who came to Nonesuch were strange indeed, but certainly no less peculiar than many of those who had made their way to New Mexico in the past. In the due course of time they drew up a town charter, elected a town council and appointed someone to keep the peace. That someone was Skinner Cade.

Since Sheriff Cade more or less comprised the entire Nonesuch Police Department, he did not wear a proper uniform, like the lawmen down in Los Alamos or Santa Fe. He wore a pair of dungarees and a denim work shirt with a star cut from sheet metal pinned to his chest, and his squad car was a late model Jeep Wrangler outfitted with an old CB radio that worked when it damn well felt like it. Still, Cade took his responsibility to the citizens under his protection very seriously. After all, everyone had the right to be safe from enemies and live free of fear, no matter what kind of skin they wore.

The day began as it always did for Cade. He woke before the sunrise, careful not to disturb Rosie as he padded into the bathroom for a quick shower. By the time he was finished, Rosie was awake. She sat naked on the corner of the bed, braiding the long, dark hair that hung to her waist.

"Sleep well?" she asked as he dried himself off.

"I had strange dreams," he said, yawning wide enough to display his back teeth. "It felt like I was being watched."

"You look tired," she said, caressing his thigh. "Are you sure you wouldn't rather come back to bed?"

"Believe me, honey, there's nothing that appeals to me more," Cade sighed, dropping down next to her. "But today's perimeter check."

Rosie leaned forward, resting her chin on his shoulder. "Couldn't you put it off?"

"It takes me all day to check on the farthest points. Besides, what if Wiley Simms has fallen down the shithouse again? It'd be another week before anyone would find him."

"You're always using Wiley falling down the outhouse as an example for why you have to go to work."

"Well, it was a pretty traumatic situation."

"For you or him?"

"Hey, I'm the one with the acute sense of smell!"

By the time he finished dressing, Rosie was already frying up a pan of bacon and a skillet full of eggs on the wood stove. The twins sat at the kitchen table, forks ready.

"Morning, Daddy," they chimed in unison.

"Morning, Kachina. Morning, Wyler," Cade said, kissing his daughter on the top of the head while tousling his son's hair. A heaping platter of bacon and scrambled eggs arrived on the table as Cade sat down.

"Now, kids, let your daddy have some food," Rosie chided. "He's got work to do today."

"What do you have to do today, Daddy?" asked Wyler.

"Perimeter check."

"You think Wiley fell down the shithouse again?" Kachina giggled.

"Kachina Cade! Language, *please!*" Rosie admonished, fixing her daughter with a disapproving glare.

"Sorry, Mama. I meant do you think Wiley fell down the *crap* house again?"

"That's better," Rosie said. "But not by much."

"So, what are you kids supposed to be learning today?"

"Miz Nascha is teaching us about the big bomb they built in Los Alamos."

"Is that a fact?"

"Some of the littler kids at school got scared when Miz Nascha started talking about wars and the bomb."

"What about you two? Are y'all scared?"

The twins exchanged glances, but it was Kachina who answered. She had always been the dominant of the pair. "Little bit. Yeah. I guess. But World War Two was a long time ago, right? They don't have bombs anymore, do they?"

Cade pulled up in front of the Nonesuch General Store, which also doubled as the post office and town hall. The store's proprietor was seated on the wide wooden porch in a rocking chair, perusing the newspaper.

"Morning, Uncle Billy," Cade called out as he climbed onto the porch.

"Morning, Skin," Uncle Billy replied, peering over the top of the paper. "What's new in the world?"

"You tell me," Cade chuckled. "You're the one with the newspaper."

"So I am," the older man said with a smile.

Uncle Billy wasn't Skinner Cade's biological uncle, at least not as far as either was aware. The title was more out of respect than kinship. Although the shopkeeper looked to be no more than fifty years old, and was in top physical condition, Skinner knew Uncle Billy was by far the oldest male in the Nonesuch community, and his wisdom and practical knowledge were highly valued.

Although he was a shopkeeper now, Uncle Billy had done damn near everything, at one time or another, from merchant marine to cowboy to ramrod on a railroad gang. He had made and lost several fortunes in his lifetime, and knew how to deliver babies, set broken limbs and nurse sick calves. And, to hear him tell it, he'd been killed more than once.

Uncle Billy was one of Nonesuch's first new citizens. He had not been among the twenty or so original settlers out of Arizona, but had sought them out shortly after they reached the former ghost town. It was Billy who refurbished and stocked the old general store, using his own personal fortune to provide Nonesuch with its necessities and the occasional luxury.

"What's the date on that paper?" Cade asked.

"Relatively fresh. It's just two days old. Cissy brung it in when she fetched the mail." Billy pursed his lips in disgust. "Seems Santa Fe got itself a boney-fide serial killer."

"That a fact? What they calling this one?"

"The Santa Fe Slasher." Uncle Billy clucked his tongue and shook his head. "Sounds like a ball team, don't it? It's a shame what folks get up to, ain't it, Skin?"

"It sure is," Cade agreed. "Cissy already back?"

"Yep. She an' Cully left just as the sun was comin' up. She's inside sortin' mail."

The interior of the store was dark, cool, and smelled of animal feed and aged wood. It was divided into two sections, one side of which was a long wooden counter fronted by a wrought-iron teller's cage.

Behind the cage stood a young woman, little more than a girl, really, her blonde hair hanging to the middle of her back in a tidy braid, dressed in a pair of faded jeans and a poet's blouse. She stood with her back to the door, popping various letters into the appropriate cubbyholes.

"Morning, Cissy."

Nonesuch's postmistress turned and smiled at Nonesuch's sheriff. "Morning, Skin. How are Rosie and the twins?"

"Fine as ever." Cade glanced around. "Where's Cully?"

"He's out back splitting wood."

Cissy and her younger brother Cully were another of Nonesuch's recruits. Six years ago they wandered into town dressed only in rags and dirt, Cissy all of eleven, Cully nearing four. Orphaned and long used to relying on one another to survive, they were as close to feral children as any Skinner could remember seeing. It was Uncle Billy who more or less adopted them, stating that he, too, had once been an orphan. In the intervening years, Cissy had grown into a stunningly beautiful, and impressively strong-willed young woman, while Cully...

Well, Cully had grown.

Twice a week Cissy, with Cully riding in back, drove Uncle Billy's pick-up down to Los Alamos, where she would pick up supplies for the store and drop off and pick up the mail for the entire town at the Mail Boxes Etc.

Cissy was the only resident of Nonesuch who traveled outside the perimeter on a regular basis. The only regular visitor from the outside was Tommy Bronco, the owner of Jicirilla Fuel & Oil, who drove up from the reservation once a month to refill the aboveground tank that served as the community gas station and swap out the propane tanks in various homes.

Others in the community occasionally ventured forth into the wide world, mostly for economic reasons. As head of the Coyotero Tribal Arts Collective, Rosie made quarterly trips to a trendy gallery in Santa Fe, where she sold the traditional blankets, dance shawls and pottery she and the others made by hand. The owner resold them to even trendier tourists and wealthy collectors in New York and Los Angeles. The six-figure income the handicrafts generated were placed in the community treasure chest, which went to pay for those necessities—such as feed and fuel—that Nonesuch's citizens could not generate themselves.

Most of the homes had gardens, where they grew their own corn, squash, and beans, and most also kept chicken coops. The only building with electric lights was the general store, which ran off a generator. The rest of the community warmed itself with stoves fed by propane or wood, while solar panels heated water that was pulled from hand-dug wells by windmills.

The casual outside observer might assume from the proliferation of solar panels and high-tech windmills that Nonesuch was a commune full of back-to-nature, tree-hugging vegetarian hippies. That is the danger of allowing yourself to be deceived by outward appearances. For a casual observer would have no way of seeing that every household contained more than one born hunter, and that there was meat on the table at every meal.

Most of those who lived beyond the knot of homes clustered about the general store and the schoolhouse were ranchers. Some raised sheep for wool, others cattle for meat and all of them bred horses for transportation. However, there were one or two members of the Nonesuch community who were quite different from the rest. These were referred to as the Old Timers, the quasi-hermits who had first settled in the area while it was still a ghost town.

Most of the Old Timers were prospectors, living in primitive shacks that, in many cases, were little more than lean-tos. It was Cade's duty, while on perimeter check, to stop by and briefly visit with each individual rancher and prospector, to make sure that they were doing well and find out if any of them had had any unusual trouble since his last visit.

Wiley Simms' shack had once been the foreman's office for the Nonesuch Mining Company. It stood four feet off the ground on sturdy pillarlike legs and had a front porch, stairs and actual windows, although old burlap bags now covered most of the empty panes.

Wiley's burro, Sookie, sat in the shade under the shack, watching the sheriff warily as she munched on her oats. A hundred yards behind the Old Timer's shack stood the gaping mouth of the old copper mine.

"Wiley? You home?" Cade called out as he climbed the stairs. He pushed on the door of the shack. The door swung open, revealing a table, a chair, a potbellied stove, and a bed made of rags. There was no sign of Wiley.

Cade climbed back down the stairs, scratching the back of his head. He glanced around the tangle of disused mining equipment and ore carts that littered the compound. Wherever the prospector was, it couldn't be far away, since he had not taken Sookie with him. Cade took a deep breath and took a step in the direction of the outhouse.

"Wiley! You in there?"

"Sheriff—! Over here!"

Cade heaved a sigh of relief and trotted over to mine entrance in time to see Wiley emerge from the darkness, a miner's helmet clamped on his head. Wiley Simms was tall and rangy, with shoulder-length gray hair and a grizzled beard. His face was as brown and seamed as a seasoned catcher's mitt thanks to long years spent under the Southwestern sun.

His teeth were yellow and stubby as corn kernels, but nowhere near as tightly spaced as those on a fresh ear. In his canvas jeans, denim work shirt, and square-toed brogans he looked like a cross between Gabby Hayes and Tommy Chong.

Cade didn't really know how old Wiley was, but he assumed the Old Timer was somewhere between fifty and sixty-five. When questioned, Wiley was, himself, somewhat vague on the subject, but from all accounts he had been squatting at the old mining facility since the Vietnam War. Wiley made his living, such as it was, sifting through the old mines that dotted the territory for various semiprecious metals and stones, such as copper and turquoise. Where once he had to carry his finds to the nearest field office, now he sold the pieces of jasper and nephrite and chunks of copper ore he pulled out of the rugged terrain directly to the *coyotero*, who used the stones to make necklaces and utilized the copper in the glazes on their pottery.

The *coyotero* did not pay him in cash, but with vouchers he could redeem at Uncle Billy's store. That way Wiley was able to provide himself with all the foodstuffs and fuel he needed, as well as feed for his beloved Sookie. It wasn't the life of Riley, but it wasn't bad for a man who talked to his burro and had a fear of being around more than four people at a time. As Uncle Billy was fond of saying, no one came to Nonesuch to strike it rich; they came to escape the lives they left behind.

"Sorry I dint hear you callin' th' first time, Sheriff. I wuz down checkin' on th' timbers, seein' they wuz shored up proper," the old prospector explained, switching off the small battery-powered lantern affixed to the brim of his helmet. "You got's t'watch these ole mines, as they're as likely as not to cave in on you."

"So I've heard. You doing okay out here, Wiley?"

"I ain't falled back down th' shit-chute, if that's what you're gettin' at," he replied. "I put in a new floor since then—replaced the one that was et up by the dry rot. 'Tain't right when a man can't take a decent squat without tumbling into th' bowels of the earth. By the by, I ain't never thanked you proper for savin' me, Sheriff. I don't know what would have become of me if you hadn't come along when you did."

"Don't mention it, Wiley. Please. Don't."

Having satisfied himself that Wiley was safe and sound, Cade bid the prospector farewell, climbed back into his Jeep, and sped off in the direction of the next stop on the perimeter check, which just happened to be his mother's place.

"Why won't you let us move you into town?"

"Because towns are not the way of my people," Changing Woman replied simply. She stood in the shade of her one-room adobe, carefully watering her herb garden with a hollowed-out gourd. She was dressed in a skirt and blouse made on her own loom. Her dark hair, liberally shot with gray, hung in twin braids down her back. Although she was the oldest female in the community, she was in good health and possessed a mind as sharp as a knife. "Besides, I can take care of myself."

"I know you're perfectly capable of looking after yourself," Cade said. "I'm just thinking about the kids. Wouldn't it be easier to train them if you lived closer?"

"The training they must undergo is not about ease or comfort," Changing Woman said sternly. "You lived too long among the white men, Skinwalker. You have learned their soft ways."

"You're the one who sent me out among them, Mother."

Changing Woman paused, weighing her son's words, then nodded. "You are correct, my son. I cannot fault you there. I am only your mother by flesh. Another mothered your soul."

He frowned and quickly looked away. Even after more than a decade, it was difficult to think of Edna Cade, the woman who raised him from infancy and loved and protected him as fiercely as any child born of her womb, without a tear coming to his eye.

"Besides," Changing Woman said with a shrug. "It is in the nature of a shaman to live apart. It is how we receive our visions." She turned to study her son. "How did you sleep last night, Skinwalker?"

Cade blinked. "Beg pardon?"

"Your sleep last night. Was it troubled?"

"As a matter of fact it was."

"It is the shaman in you," Changing Woman said, nodding approvingly. "The wolf in your soul recognizes the presence of an enemy."

"Enemy? What kind of enemy?"

"The oldest," she said, her eyes narrowing. "The one your father's blood has battled for millennia. I caught its scent last night. I have been working rituals ever since, trying to determine the exact nature of the beast. It is old, that much I am sure of—and hungry."

"Mother, I still don't understand.... What are you talking about?"

"There is an *enkidu* nosing about the perimeter."

Cade's heart went cold as the word slipped from his mother's lips. "Are you certain?"

"As sure as death," she replied. "Call a council meeting for this afternoon."

"That settles it! You're coming back into town with me!"

"Don't be silly, boy!" Changing Woman said with a dismissive wave of her hand. "I have things to do before the meeting. Give your sister my love."

"You can tell Rosie that yourself. She'll be at the meeting, too."

"Ah! Perhaps I am getting long in the tooth, after all, eh?" Changing Woman said with a sly smile, then dropped onto all fours and loped off in the direction of the sweat lodge.

The Nonesuch council held its meetings in the back of the general store. Each of the various species that lived within the community elected two from their number to represent the whole. Changing Woman and Rosie represented the *coyotero*, Skinner Cade and Uncle Billy represented the *vargr*, and Cissy and Nascha Martinez, the town's schoolteacher, represented the humans.

Cully, the council's unofficial sergeant-at-arms and sole ogre, sat on a chair near the door, alternately scratching himself and staring at his feet. At ten years of age, he stood six-foot-six and weighed three hundred pounds, with a wide forehead that sloped backward, like that of a bull gorilla. A pair of tusk-buds were just starting to jut from his lower jaw. Dressed in nothing but a pair of denim overalls, Cully did nothing to hide the long, curved talons, like those of a wolverine, that grew in place of toenails on his bare feet.

Uncle Billy opened the meeting by speaking aloud what the others were thinking. "Why was this council called, Sheriff?"

Skinner glanced at his mother "I think it's best you address that question to Changing Woman."

All eyes followed the shaman, dressed in a cape stitched together from rabbit pelts, a fetish necklace of turquoise and jasper hung about her neck, as she got to her feet. "Last night I caught scent of a thing I hoped would never cross my path again. There is *enkidu* nearby."

Uncle Billy shifted uneasily and the younger members of the council exchanged blank stares.

"I'm sorry if I am being dense, Changing Woman—but what is this 'inkaidoo'?" Nascha asked.

"It is what you humans call a vampire."

Nascha's eyes widened in alarm and the others began talking rapidly among themselves. Uncle Billy got to his feet, waving his hands for silence.

"Quiet! Quiet, now! We can't let emotion get the better of us!" He turned to face the shaman. "Are you *sure* about that, Changing Woman?"

"There is no mistaking their scent."

"I'll grant you that," Uncle Billy said with a nod. "They might be able to fool the eye, but the nose is another matter."

"What's it doing out here?" Rosie asked.

"Maybe it's come to seek sanctuary," Cissy suggested. "Maybe it wants to join us."

"Wants to destroy us is more likely!" Changing Woman spat in disgust.

"You don't know that!" Cissy retorted.

Changing Woman's eyes narrowed. When she spoke it was with a growl in her voice. "Do not tell *me* what I do or do not know, little one! But I will tell *you* this: Vampires are not like weres or ogres. While we may not be human, we are at least *alive*. We exist within the mortal cycle of birth and age and death. Our span of years is long, but it is not without end.

"The *enkidu*, however, are born of death. They are demons riding around in the flesh of dead men. Theirs is an approximation of life, not life itself. And their appetite is not merely for the blood of the living, but the negative energy that arises from human misery and suffering. Of all the Pretending Races, they are the most devious of all. For countless centuries they have been the blood enemy of the *vargr*."

"But you are *coyotero*, not *vargr*," Cissy pointed out. "What quarrel have you with them?"

"While I may find many things wrong with the *vargr*, I cannot find fault with their mistrust of vampires. And, unlike most of you, I have *seen* an *enkidu*! I know what they are capable of.

"It was a long time ago, back when I was a girl in Arizona. Except it wasn't called Arizona back then. There was a trading post my people frequented that had a small village around it, composed mostly of Pimas. The Pima knew what the *coyotero* were, but did not speak of it to the Anglos or the Spanish, who thought we were some form of Apache. When we would come in to trade, the Pima would simply go inside their shelters and stay there until we left.

"The man who ran the trading post was named Alvarez. His wife helped him with his business and they had a baby girl. Mrs. Alvarez did not seem afraid of the 'natives' as we were called, and Mr. Alvarez did not cheat us much, as white men go, and actually seemed to take pleasure in the company of my father, Crooked Leg.

"Then one day we went to the trading post, only to find everyone there dead. The Pima, the Alvarezes... every last one of them was dead, many of them still in their beds. At first my father thought it was one of the white diseases, like diphtheria or small pox. Then we found several of the Pima hung by their heels like slaughtered deer, their throats slit so that they bled out into pottery jars.

"My father started sniffing around, trying to catch the scent of the man who had slain his friends. With all the dead bodies lying around, the smell of death was everywhere. But soon Crooked Leg caught another scent: something *like* death, but not as natural.

"We found the *enkidu* curled up inside a cedar hope chest in the Alvarez's cabin. It wore the body of a white man, dressed in a fine suit and hard leather shoes, and it had long dark hair and pale skin. The drained corpse of the Alvarez baby was clutched to his breast like a doll. When Crooked Leg pulled the *enkidu* from its hiding place, its eyes flew open and I could see they were red and full of blood.

"The vampire struggled, but his movements were sluggish, like those of a drunken man wakened from a stupor. When we dragged him outside, the *enkidu* began to scream and, to our surprise, his skin turned black and blistered and, after several seconds of agony, he caught fire.

"Crooked Leg consulted with the shaman, who poked through the charred remains of the *enkidu* and told my father to place all the bodies in the trading post and burn them, as we would diseased horse blankets. In the end, the Mexicans used it as an excuse to launch another strike against the Apache in the region.

"Decades passed before I learned that the thing responsible for the massacre was a vampire. I have counted myself lucky I have not made the acquaintance of another of their kind. There is too much sun and open space for their liking in this part of the world. But that is changing now, with the growth of cities like Phoenix and Albuquerque. Wherever there are human cities, you will always find three things: rats, pigeons and vampires."

"Now, Changing Woman. I wouldn't say *all* the *enkidu* are like the one you mentioned." Uncle Billy held a hand up to stem her protest. "True, they *do* have a reputation for evil unique even among the shadow races. But they ain't *all* bad. One of the best friends I ever had was a vampire! We rode together for a while, back in the old days. He met his final death tryin' to save my life. Granted, our friendship was an unusual one—but it *was* genuine. For all we know this *enkidu* is like the one I was partners with. He was looking to start things anew in this country, just as we are. We shouldn't be quick to assume the worst. After all, there is not one of us here—Miz Cissy and Miz Nascha excepted—who ain't tasted human flesh."

"What about me, Uncle Billy?" Cully asked, raising his hand as if he were in class. "I ain't et nobody, neither!"

"I'm sorry, Cully," Uncle Billy said, smiling indulgently at the young ogre. "I didn't mean to leave you out."

Cully smiled broadly, pleased with being acknowledged by one of the elders.

"You can put your hand down, now, Cully," Nascha said gently.

"Yes, ma'am," Cully replied, lowering his arm.

"Uncle Billy is right," Cissy said. "Not *all* vampires are bad. Before Cully and I found our way here, the only person who *ever* showed us *any* kindness at all was a vampire. At least I *think* that's what she was. She had fangs, and my stepmother called her by that same word you used. She saved me from Fiona, my father's wife, and she was going to kill Cully, but I begged her not to, and she spared his life. Would a vampire do something like that?"

"Both Uncle Billy and Cissy have a point, mother," Rosie said evenly. "Maybe you're jumping the gun. We don't *know* what this vampire wants. Maybe it's just passing through. Maybe it's looking for a place to start over, just like everyone else here. It's not fair for us to judge him before hand."

"This is utter foolishness!" Changing Woman snapped, getting to her feet, her eyes flashing with anger. "The *enkidu* are diametrically opposed to *everything* we're trying to do here! They have no interest in humans and Pretenders living together in open accord! The *vargr's* attempts at infiltrating human political and religious organizations are child's play compared to what *they* have done over the millennia! They *thrive* on secrecy and manipulation! We have to bring the humans in from the perimeters and keep them under lock and key for the next few days, until we can hunt down and eradicate this danger!"

"You want to do *what?*" Nascha said in stunned disbelief. "You talk about us as if we were sheep!"

"And that's exactly how this *enkidu* sees your kind. You're no more than livestock in his eyes."

"It sounds like he's not the only one who sees us that way!" the schoolteacher retorted.

"Nascha's right," Cade agreed. "The humans aren't going to take kindly to being rounded up, even if it is for their own good."

"Why us?" asked Cissy. "Why not everyone within the perimeter, if this thing is so dangerous?"

"This is madness!" Changing Woman snarled. "We sit here chewing the fat when we should be out securing the town and trying to hunt down this monster!"

Rosie turned to address the elder *coyotero*. "Mother, you, more than anyone else, know that Nonesuch was created as a safe haven for nonhumans weary of the predator lifestyle. Is it so hard for you to imagine a vampire who has decided to exist in harmony with the living?"

"For all your experience, you are naive in the ways of the Real World, child," Changing Woman told her daughter. "The *enkidu* exist to feed on the living and perpetuate their kind. Everything they do is designed to either put them in the proximity of their next meal or insure their continuance. Any other emotion or desire they might display is merely a pretense, designed to help them pass for human." The shaman got to her feet, glaring at the others seated about the table. "If you are not willing to bring the humans into town for protection, then at least warn them as to what is out there."

"Do you think that's wise?" Uncle Billy asked. "It could make people jumpier than they already are. The last thing we need is panicked farmers blowing the heads off everything that moves."

"This is a question that can only be answered by the humans on the council," Rosie said "Cissy? Nascha? What do you think should be done?"

The women exchanged uneasy glances.

"The idea of a vampire being on the loose is... disturbing," Nascha admitted. "But Uncle Billy is right—we have to be careful with this information. I mean, we don't *really* know if there really *is* a vampire out there, do we? I mean, no one has seen or heard it. And even if there *is* one out there, we don't know what its intentions are toward us."

"Yes," Cissy said, nodding her head in agreement. "Until we know more about what he wants from us, we should keep quiet for the time being."

Changing Woman shook her head, unable to believe what she was hearing. "It is impossible for *enkidu* not to bring death and devastation with them! Wherever they go, there is pain and suffering in their wake. Once this thing establishes a foothold, you will *see* how interested it is in maintaining Nonesuch's ideals of inclusion and openness! The most ancient of battles—that of the weres and the *enkidu* for control of the human race—is about to be fought once again, here in Nonesuch. I will not lend my blessings to such madness." Changing Woman stalked to the door of the general store, turning to fix the council with one final, withering stare. "Fools! You are endangering not only yourselves, but your children as well! That is the problem with the young ones today: too much thinking, not enough instinct."

Wiley Simms' definition of a good day and a bad day were extremely basic. A good day was when he found something that could be converted into supplies and feed for Sookie. A bad day was where he hurt himself, like when he fell through the rotten floor of the outhouse. Using that yardstick, today had been a very good day, indeed.

He had been tempted to say something to Sheriff Cade when he came by earlier but managed to hold his tongue. He didn't want to jinx his good luck by talking about it too early. Besides, he could very well be wrong. It wouldn't be the first time that had happened.

Wiley couldn't really remember the time before he lived in Nonesuch. Some of that had to do with the relentless New Mexico sun parboiling his brain for a decade or two, but a good deal of it was because the life he had known before Nonesuch had been a hollow one. Oh, it had been full of material possessions, deadline pressures and expectations from everyone from his parents to his school to society, but at its core it had proven an empty, unfulfilling existence, which, in the end, made it easy to throw away without looking back.

Living rough in the high country wasn't easy, but it was a hell of a lot better than being a corporate wage-slave. In the brave, new world Wiley had chosen for himself, success wasn't measured in promotions or salaries, but in keeping his belly full and his bedroll dry. When all was said and done, it really didn't bother him that he was surrounded by werewolves.

Although Wiley didn't have much use for people, he did like the newcomers who had moved into the old ghost town. Maybe that was because most of them weren't really people. The newcomers pretty much minded their own business and allowed him to do whatever he pleased. Every so often he would catch sight of one of them in their fur skins, running down rabbits or antelope, but he wasn't any more scared of them than any man should be of his neighbors. After all, they had an understanding: He wouldn't go shooting at them, and they wouldn't prey on Sookie.

One of the biggest benefits of the newcomers' arrival was that Wiley no longer had to worry about mountain lions any more, despite all the sheep and cattle in the area. The big cats cleared off the minute they caught wind of what had taken up residence in Nonesuch. Now he could leave Sookie stabled in the mine at night with a bale of hay and not have to worry about her.

The rising and the setting of the sun proscribed his activities, as it did for most people who lived without electricity. As the light began to fade, Wiley prepared a humble meal of black beans, flour tortillas and jerked beef, washed down with cold coffee. After checking on Sookie one final time to make sure she had plenty of feed and water for the evening, he retired to the cabin to enjoy a shot of whiskey and a pipe of tobacco before turning in for the night.

As he was finishing his pipe, a horrible shriek shattered the quiet. He instantly recognized the cry as coming from Sookie, although he had never heard the burro in such distress before. He grabbed the Coleman lantern from the table and his double-barreled shotgun from its resting place behind the front door and hurried toward the mine.

"I'm comin', girl!" he shouted, holding the lantern aloft.

The burro was lying on her side just outside the mine. She had run as far as her tether allowed. She wasn't breathing and there was foam smeared about her muzzle.

"Sookie!"

Wiley's knees gave out at the sight of his beloved burro stretched, cold and unmoving, on the hard ground. He dropped beside the felled beast, heart-stricken. "What happened, girl?" he moaned as he stroked her stiff mane, as if she could somehow answer him. He and Sookie went back a long way; he found her as a foal, wandering the hills after being orphaned by a mountain cat.

As he touched the burro's throat, he felt something warm and wet. He pulled his hand away and stared at the blood smearing his fingers and palm. He lifted the lantern and saw twin punctures in Sookie's neck.

There was a sound from inside the mine, like a footstep on loose rock. Wiley raised his shotgun in the direction of the noise.

"Who's there? I *know* somebody's there!" he shouted. "You either answer me or I'll open fire!"

There was movement from deep within the shadows, and a pale figure emerged from the darkness. He was tall and thin, dressed in expensive dark clothes smeared with blood and dirt. Wiley noticed that the stranger's hands had very long, narrow fingers that ended in hooked nails, and while the stranger's face was as pale as milk, his mouth was red as crushed berries.

"Who are you, mister? Speak up, before I blow you full of holes!"

The stranger smiled as if something the prospector had said was amusing.

"Where you headed, Skin?" Uncle Billy asked as he gassed up Cade's Wrangler.

"I'm going on perimeter check again. Until we know what that vampire's intentions are, I'll rest easier knowing I've kept tabs on everybody."

"Not a bad idea," the older man said, nodding his head.

Cade retrieved an Army Surplus issue walkie-talkie from the back of the Jeep and tossed it at Uncle Billy. "I want you to keep this on you for the time being. I gave one to Cissy, too. In case something goes down out there, I want to be able to bring in back-up as soon as possible."

"I read you loud and clear, my boy," Billy said with a crooked smile. "Just give a shout and I'll come a'runnin' like a dawg to the hunt."

Cade scratched his head as he looked around the abandoned mining camp. Wiley wasn't in his cabin and Sookie was nowhere to be seen. Perhaps they had gone off into the hills to look for turquoise. Or, more likely, the prospector had taken the burro with him into the mine.

Cade walked over to the entrance, sniffing cautiously. He could smell the distinct reek of burro dung and piss, but there was another odor underneath it. While he could not identify the scent, there was no mistaking it as a being that of a predator. Cade's hackles came up instinctively.

"Skin! Skinner, do you read me? Over!"

Cade blinked, distracted by the squawk of the walkie-talkie, the mine temporarily forgotten. "This is Skinner. I read you loud and clear, Uncle Billy. What's wrong? Over."

"Nate Ferguson's boy just rode into town, fit to bust. Says his pappy needs you out at the farm. Says there's something hidin' out in his barn. Over."

"I'm on my way! Billy, I need you to get hold of Cully and bring him to the Ferguson place. Do you copy? Over."

"Roger, I copy."

"Good. I'll meet you at Nate's. Over and out." Cade returned the walkie-talkie to its canvas sling. He eyed the yawning mouth of the mine for long moment, then turned and headed back to the Jeep.

Nate Ferguson emerged from his wooden geodesic dome as Cade's jeep pulled up in the dooryard. He held a rifle close to his chest, like a soldier on parade.

"Thank God you're here, Skinner!"

"What's this about there being an intruder on your property, Nate?"

"My boy Jimmy went out to milk the cow, as usual," Ferguson said, pointing at the barn that stood a hundred yards from the house. "He comes runnin' back, fit to be tied, sayin' he heard someone movin' round in the hayloft. So I went to check it out, and I'll be damned if the first thing I see when I climb up into the loft is a pair of boots sticking out from behind a bale of hay! That's when I sent Jimmy into town to fetch you, Sheriff."

"I see," Cade said. He removed his gun from its holster, flipping the chamber open for a quick spot-check. "You been back out to the barn since then?"

"No, sir!"

"Good," Cade said, reholstering his gun. "I'm gonna go have a look-see. I want you to wait here for Uncle Billy and the others."

"Will do, Sheriff!" Ferguson called after him.

The interior of Nate Ferguson's barn was dark and smelled of fresh hay, old straw and cow shit. Yet there was another, stranger scent mixed in with the manure and cattle feed, one that was unfamiliar to him. But whatever it was, it definitely smelled dangerous.

He paused when his head cleared the edge of the loft. There were several bales of hay stacked to his right, from behind which poked a pair of scuffed black boots, toes pointed toward the ceiling. Cade quietly stood up and maneuvered himself so he could get a clearer view of what inhabited the boots.

Stretched out on a bed of clean hay was a young woman dressed in a battered black leather motorcycle jacket, filthy black jeans, a torn T-shirt, and a pair of mirrored sunglasses. Her hair was blacker than a King James Bible, and shorn in such a fashion that it suggested she had cut it herself without the benefit of a mirror. Her skin was as pale as a shut-in's and her hands were folded over her breast like that of the dead in repose. She did not seem to be breathing.

Cade pushed the brim of his cowboy hat so that it rested on the back of his head. So *this* was the vampire his mother was so worried about. Although she did not look particularly dangerous, her scent told a different story. The odor that radiated from the unconscious woman rose from her in waves, like heat from a summer sidewalk. She reeked of blood, darkness, and violence, mixed with a tinge of madness. He felt an instinctual ill ease in her presence and fought to keep a growl from boiling in his gut.

If what he had been told about vampire habits was accurate, the *enkidu* in Nate's barn would remain immobile until sunset. This meant he had a few hours to get her out of the hayloft and into the lockup. Then he could question the creature at his leisure—and destroy it, if need be. He just had to get it out of the barn and into town without raising any suspicion from Nate. Transients wandering through the area were nothing new, so it would be relatively easy to pass the intruder off as a road tramp seeking a safe place to sleep. All he had to do was find a tarpaulin to wrap her in to keep the killing rays of the sun off her skin before hauling her off to the pokey.

Cade grasped the vampire's legs by the ankles and began to drag her across the loft, leaving himself unprepared for the kick to his gut that sent him flying across the loft and slammed him into the wall hard enough to make the entire barn shudder.

Cade grimaced in pain and clutched his midriff. His spleen was ruptured, damn it. To hell with inclusion and living in harmony and all that other politically correct crap! The kid gloves were off!

He closed his eyes and allowed the change to wash over him. There was a wet popping sound, like that of someone pulling apart a stewed chicken, as his bones realigned and his musculature warped and twisted itself. His body hair thickened and grew coarse, spreading to cover his entire body. His ears became longer and moved higher up on his skull while his fingernails thickened and curved in on themselves, becoming talons.

He growled and grabbed the encumbering remains of his shredded shirt and tore it from his body as he got to his feet, balancing on his crooked hind legs, his yellow eyes blazing with anger. He didn't like shapeshifting while in uniform, but sometimes it couldn't be helped. In total, it had taken thirty-three seconds to effect the change from sheriff to werewolf.

As he turned his snarling head toward the vampire, Cade saw that she was now on her feet, her stance that of a martial artist cautiously awaiting an opponent's first move. Cade bared his teeth in ritual challenge and the vampire hissed in response, exposing a pair of ivory-white, razor-sharp fangs.

He came in low, clipping the vampire square in chest with his left shoulder. The force of his lunge carried them through the unsecured hay doors, and sent the two plummeting to the hard-packed earth of the barnyard.

Although the stranger absorbed most of the impact, their rough landing barely seemed to have fazed her. As she pushed herself upright, Cade quickly moved out of striking distance. He nervously pawed the ground with his hind legs as he watched her casually knock the dirt off her jacket. Despite having fallen fifteen feet onto a hard surface, her mirrored sunglasses were still in place.

What the stranger did next truly amazed him. Instead of burning, baking, melting, crisping or otherwise spontaneously combusting, she pulled a switchblade and opened it with a flick of her wrist. The knife blade was silver. Cade's eyes widened in alarm.

The stranger began circling him, knife at the ready, her movements as smooth and sure as water poured over a rock. Cade was pretty sure vampires didn't move around in open daylight, and he knew for damn sure that they didn't handle silver weapons. But whether this woman was a vampire or not was beside the point. Whoever or whatever she was, she definitely seemed to know a thing or two about killing werewolves.

Although he was graced with inhuman speed, strength and stamina, as well as a body that could shrug off otherwise fatal wounds, the damage done to him was still very real, as was the pain that accompanied it. In a head-to-head battle with another *vargr* or an equally powerful nonhuman, he could find himself seriously crippled. And, in the case of the woman he was fighting right now, he could very easily die of toxic shock if the silver knife so much as pierced his skin. And, judging from what he had seen of her speed and strength so far, that scenario was a distinct possibility.

"Now wait a minute, ma'am," Cade said, holding up his forepaws, hairy palms outward. "I think there's been a misunderstanding." He tried his best to smile, but his snout made it look like a snarl. "This is all a *big* mistake."

"Yeah, and you made it, dog-boy," she replied with a sneer.

The stranger made a straight-ahead thrust at Cade, the switchblade clutched in her right hand. Cade pivoted quickly on his left hind foot, swinging his left arm inward and his right foot backward, deflecting the knife thrust. Cade pivoted sharply, coming in close to his attacker, and delivered a hard right punch to her kidney.

The stranger groaned loudly but remained on her feet and did not drop her weapon. She staggered backward, spat a streamer of blood onto the barnyard dirt, and wiped the corner of her mouth with the sleeve of her leather jacket. But before she could make a second lunge, a shotgun blast ripped through the stifling afternoon heat like a thunderclap from on high. Both combatants turned to stare at Uncle Billy, who had a pump-action shotgun pointed at the stranger's head. Cully stood behind his adoptive father, looming over him like a statue carved from granite.

"Freeze, lady!" Uncle Billy barked. "This thing's loaded with silver buckshot!"

The stranger grinned broadly, exposing her fangs. "Go ahead and shoot—silver is no threat to me!"

"Perhaps so. But I suspect gettin' your head blown into itty-bitty pieces ain't something you can shrug off." He motioned with the barrel of the shotgun toward the knife. "Now drop the weapon. That's right. Now kick it over to me. No funny stuff, or I'll part your hair startin' at your chin."

The stranger grimaced as if she'd bitten into a sour persimmon, but did as she was told, kicking the switchblade to Uncle Billy with a sharp scuff of her right boot.

"Nate! Grab the knife!"

Nate Ferguson emerged from his hiding place behind Cully and scooped up the surrendered weapon.

The stranger shook her head in amazement, a crooked smile on her face. "*Vargr*, ogres and humans—what is this place, a Pretender dude ranch?"

"What this *is*, ma'am," Cade said, trying his best to keep the snarl out of his voice, "is a law-abiding community of decent, peaceable folk. And *you* are under arrest."

The stranger turned to look at Cade, who was still in his wolf-skin "What for?"

"Trespassing, for one. Not to mention assaulting a peace officer."

"*Peace officer—?*" She paused for a long moment to stare at Cade, then began to chuckle. "Don't tell me *you're* the law around here?"

"Yes, ma'am, I'm afraid that's so. Now are you gonna come along peaceable, or do we have to get rough?"

"What the hell!" she said, throwing her hands up in mock surrender. "Whatever gets me out of this damned heat the fastest!"

Nonesuch's jail was one of the few buildings left over from the boomtown days that had been made of stone, not wood, and still had the original iron bars on its solitary jail cell. The moment Cade locked the door the stranger laid down on the cell bunk and returned to the deathlike state he had originally found her in.

He mulled over what little he knew about his prisoner as he shifted out of his wolf-skin and back into his human persona. On one hand she looked like a vampire: She had the pale skin, fangs, strength, indifference to pain, and instantaneous healing traditionally associated with the *enkidu*. But, on the other, she was capable of withstanding contact with direct sunlight and seemed completely immune to the silver that was lethal to both werewolf and vampire alike.

As he pinned his homemade sheriff's badge onto the new shirt requisitioned from Uncle Billy's dry goods department, the door opened and Changing Woman entered the cramped confines of the front office. She was dressed in her shaman robes, an intact coyote pelt, its hollowed-out skull resting atop her head, the forepaws wrapped about her throat.

"You caught the dead thing." It was not a question. Cade did not ask her how she knew. His mother had her ways of finding things out.

"I've got her locked up."

Changing Woman sniffed the air, a puzzled look on her face. "Her smell is strange. It is *like* that of the *enkidu*, but it is not the scent of the creature I sensed the night before."

"That's what I was afraid you were going to say," Cade sighed as he sat down behind his desk. "However, I think you'll want to see what our visitor back there had on her." He reached inside the top drawer and pulled out a large manila envelope, dumping its contents onto the desktop. A Zip-Loc plastic baggie containing the stranger's knife, the blade extended, fell onto the blotter with a weighty thud.

Changing Woman gave an audible gasp and stepped back from the desk. Her eyes widened at the sight of the silver blade shaped like a frozen flame.

"Mother—what is it?" Cade asked, alarmed by the fear he saw on the shaman's face.

"That is not *just* a knife, Skinwalker! It is a thing of power, like the Wolfcane," she explained, referring to the totem-staff of the *vargr*, used for millennia by the alphas to denote their supremacy over the pack. "The magic that abides within this blade is far older and angrier than any I have ever seen before!" She quickly turned her head, as if fearful of looking too long upon it. "Please, put it away."

Cade did as she asked, gingerly picking up the baggie by one corner and dropping it back into the drawer.

He had hoped Changing Woman would have helped solve the puzzle the stranger posed. But now it looked like he would have to wait for sundown to find out exactly what it was he had locked up in his jail.

The thing that used to be Wiley woke up with meat on the brain.

The urge to taste warm, living flesh between his teeth was as urgent as a full bladder. There was no language, no emotion, no memory—nothing but the need to feed. All other thoughts and concerns were wiped away, enslaved to a hunger that was as boundless as it was nameless.

He got to his feet, wobbling like a freshly foaled colt, and then took an unsteady step forward. He sniffed the stale, damp air of the mineshaft. There was no live meat here. He staggered up the tilted floor toward the entrance, which seemed to shine like a magic gate. He instinctively knew that where the darkness was as bright as noonday was where the live meat could be found.

He stood at the mouth of the mine, his head tossed back like a hound catching scent, then set off in the direction of the nearest meat, the drool pooling in his mouth and spilling from his lips in a steady stream.

The stranger opened her eyes as the sun set behind the mountains and the cool of the evening began to replace the heat of the day. She unfolded her hands and sat up right.

"It *is* you."

The stranger turned to stare at the young woman who stood on the other side of the jailhouse bars.

"I never thought I would ever see you again. But when Uncle Billy told me about the strange woman in Nate's barn, and the knife you were carrying, I knew it had to be you. Who *else* could it be?" Cissy laughed with a nervous toss of her head. "You helped me a long time ago. You said your name was Sonja and you saved my family from a monster. Do you remember?"

Sonja Blue smiled, revealing a brief glimpse of fang. "Of course I remember you, Tiffany." She walked over to her visitor, resting her hands on the crossbars of the cell.

"Nobody calls me that anymore. Everybody here knows me as Cissy. That's what Cully calls me."

"You've grown up. Has it been that long?"

"Ten years."

"I take it that wall of muscle I saw earlier was your brother."

Cissy smiled at the mention of her half-brother, her eyes lighting up with pride. "Yeah, that's Cully. He's one of Sheriff Cade's deputies. Sort of."

"And your father—?"

Cissy's smile faltered and her gaze dropped to the floor. "Daddy— Daddy's dead. He killed himself a long time ago."

"I'm sorry to hear that, kid," Sonja said, although there was something in her voice that hinted that she was not surprised.

"He took the money you gave him and got us as far away from New York as possible, which turned out to be Taos. But he was never the same after

Fiona. Six months after we came to New Mexico, he hanged himself in the closet of the motel room we were living out of. Then it was just me and Cully."

"So how did you end up here—wherever 'here' is?" Sonja asked, gesturing to their surroundings.

"I knew if Social Services got hold of me and Cully, they would split us up. And I knew no one else could understand Cully the way I do. So I kept us on the move. We wandered around on our own for a long time. Then I started hearing these stories from other runaways... stories about a place up in the mountains, where the people who lived there weren't people at all. So we went in search of the town, hoping maybe we could find someone who would see Cully for what he really was, someplace where we would not have to leave after Cully forgot his manners and ate another cat. We've been here six years."

"I'm glad y'all are catching up on old times, but I'm afraid I'm gonna have to ask you to leave," Cade said from the doorway that lead to the cells. "I've got a few questions I need to ask your friend—Sonja, is it?"

Cissy glanced at Sonja, nodded her head and quickly left, leaving the vampire alone with Cade. Sonja turned her mirrored gaze on the sheriff and smiled crookedly. "You know my name—but I don't know yours."

"True enough," he replied with a nod. "The name's Cade. Skinner Cade. I'm the sheriff around here. But you knew that already. You also know I am what's commonly called a werewolf. Well, that's not one hundred percent correct. I'm half were-coyote, but that's beside the point. Now, if you don't mind me asking, ma'am—what exactly are *you*, and what is your business in Nonesuch?"

"Is that what this place is called?"

"Yes, ma'am."

"How apropos," she chuckled. "To answer your question, or at least part of it, I am an oddling, if you will. By all rights, I should be just another undead chippie. I was taken to hospital after being attacked by a vampire, where I died on the operating table. The doctors pumped me full of new blood and got my heart going again, trapping the vampire's seed within a living host. As such I'm both human and vampire. I must feed on human blood in order to live, and I have all their strengths and none of their weaknesses—at least, not yet."

"So what is it that you do, Miz, uh—?"

"Blue. I hunt and kill vampires."

"Isn't that a rather *unusual* occupation, given your condition?"

"Who better to kill monsters than another monster?" she replied with a shrug.

"You got a point," he conceded. "So what're you doing in our neck of the woods?"

"I was tracking down a vampire who goes by the name of Vasek. He fled Santa Fe after I killed his minion—a ghoul."

"Ghoul?" Cade grimaced at the thought. "I've heard about such things, but I've never seen one."

"You haven't missed much. This Lord Vasek character creates them to cover his tracks. The ghoul abducts victims and brings them back to his lair. Once they have been drained, Vasek allows the ghoul to eat its fill and dispose of the leftovers elsewhere. The abductions and deaths are usually blamed on random serial killers."

"The Santa Fe Slasher!" Cade gasped, his eyes widening as he made the connection.

"Give the man a Kewpie doll!" Sonja drawled, doing her W.C. Fields imitation. "Vasek fled the city when he realized I was on to him. He ended up here by accident, I suppose—although it's not impossible that he somehow learned of this place and thought he could trick you into providing shelter to a fellow Pretender."

"It's your opinion, then, that he did not come here out of a genuine desire to give up his existence as a predator?"

"Are you kidding? Vasek knows he's being hunted. The first thing he is going to do is make another ghoul to replace the one I killed, then he's going to set about building a brood as fast as he can. In Santa Fe he was allowing his ghoul to devour the bodies of his victims before they could resurrect. After all, he didn't need the competition. But the situation's different now. He needs others of his own kind to help protect him from his enemy. Vasek will immediately start remaking every human he can get his hands on in his own image. And with each conversion, his contagion spreads exponentially. In less than a week he could have every human in the vicinity transformed into a vampire."

Cade stared at the leather-clad stranger for a long moment, and then unlocked the cell, swinging the door open. "If what you say is true, then I need your help, and I suspect you just might need mine as well."

Sonja followed Cade from the cell into the front office. He reached inside his desk and removed the evidence folder, upending it so that the knife slid out onto the desktop. She snatched it up so quickly he did not see her move. One moment her hand was empty, the next it held a knife.

"That's a real, um, interesting weapon you got there, ma'am. Care to tell me how you came into possession of it?"

"It was a present from a friend," she said as she slid the switchblade up the right sleeve of her leather jacket. "I have no idea where he originally got it from. All I remember him telling me was that it was very, very old and that it was supposed to be foolproof defense against monsters."

"Do tell. You and I need to talk in greater detail—we can do that far more comfortably at my house. Besides, my wife should have dinner waiting, and I'm hungry enough to eat the tail off a hobby horse."

Skinner Cade's home was a two-story adobe located near the Coyotero Tribal Center. A bedraggled chicken with feathers the color of dirty laundry strutted about the front yard, clucking to itself. The otherwise rustic appearance of the building was offset by the solar panels affixed to its flat roof.

"Kachina!" Cade called out. "Penny's loose again!"

The front door banged open and Kachina shot past her father and his guest, her ears back against her head.

"Sorry, Daddy! I'll get her!"

The chicken took off in a dead run, but was quickly snatched up by its owner.

"Henny-Penny is my daughter's pet," Cade explained. "But she hates being cooped up, so to speak. She's always escaping and getting into the garden." He motioned to the neatly arranged rows of squash, corn, and other vegetables that occupied the back yard. "If my kids weren't so attached to the damned thing—and if she wasn't such a good layer—Penny would have ended up in the stew pot awhile back."

"How many children do you have?"

"A boy and a girl. Twins, actually." He looked around, sniffing the air. "Speaking of which—Kachina, where's your brother?"

"He's playing over at Tommy Spotted Pony's."

"You go on over to Tommy's house and fetch him. I want both you young'uns close to home tonight."

"Yes, Daddy!" Kachina dashed off on her errand, clearing the low adobe fence in a single bound.

"Lord, that child loves to run," Cade chuckled, shaking his head in paternal admiration. "You'd think she was part greyhound!" He held the front door open and removed his hat with his free hand, ushering Sonja ahead of him. "Come on in. I'll introduce you to my better half."

The interior of the Cade home was cool and shady, organized around a wide hallway that ran in a straight line down the middle of the house, from front door to back. The fifteen-inch thick adobe walls were coated in softly hand-troweled stucco the color of buttercups. Thick wooden vigas dominated the twenty-foot high ceiling of the central great room, which served as the Cade family's combination living and dining area. A fire was already crackling in the kiva fireplace in the corner, providing protection against the cold of the coming high desert night.

"Skin? That you? We're having chili con carne tonight." An attractive young woman with butternut skin and ebony hair stepped out of the kitchen, followed by the warm, welcoming smell of simmering spices and corn bread.

"Yep. And I've brought company."

Rosie froze, staring at the stranger at her house like a coyote bitch blocking the entrance of her den. "Is that her? The one you found in the barn?"

"Yes and no. She's the one I found in the barn—but she's not the vampire Changing Woman caught scent of."

Sonja stepped forward, smiling without showing her teeth. "My name is Sonja Blue. I'm pleased to meet you, Mrs. Cade. Lovely home you have here."

Rosie's gaze traveled up and down Sonja's person, from her mirrored sunglasses to her scuffed boots and back again before she spoke. "Yes, well, it's Skin's design. It's all part of his master plan for Nonesuch. Please excuse me," she said, with a smile that was more a show of teeth. "I have to get back to my cooking..."

"Don't worry about setting a place for me, Mrs. Cade. I don't eat chili." Sonja turned to Cade and stage-whispered to him. "I'm afraid your wife isn't quite sure whether or not she likes the idea of having me in her den."

"Please don't mind Rosie, Ms. Blue," Cade said as he unbuckled his gun belt, placing the holster inside the roll-top desk near the fireplace. "I don't think you were quite what she was expecting."

"Believe me, it cuts both ways!" Sonja chuckled. "You're not exactly what I was expecting, either. A werewolf lawman with a wife and kids? I can honestly say I have never run across anything even vaguely resembling you and your family, Sheriff Cade. What, exactly, did your wife mean when she said this house was all part of your master plan?"

Cade laughed. "Nonesuch is designed to stay below radar. That means remaining independent of the public utility companies. Doing without electricity, public sewers and natural gas is easy enough for us weres. However, the same can't be said for our human friends. And, to be frank, many of us in the were community have become accustomed to the niceties of modern technology as well. There is no electricity outside of the general store, and what few appliances we have are gas-powered, including the refrigerators. As you may have noticed on our walk over here, most of the homes in Nonesuch are equipped with solar panels, which are used to heat our water.

"Every home is also outfitted with a rainwater harvesting system, which is used for bathing, cooking, and irrigation of private gardens. Most of the homesteads, such as ours, also have freshwater wells. Because of the critical importance of well water in such an arid climate, there are no septic tanks in Nonesuch. The majority of the homes within the town itself have been retrofitted with graywater systems, which recycle the wastewater generated by each household. By utilizing aerobic micro-organisms to biologically convert solid waste into fertilizer, each family is able to provide much of its own compost for their garden over the course of a year."

"You sound more like an architect than a lawman," Sonja said, shaking her head in admiration.

"Well, I *was* thinking about majoring in city-planning back in college," Cade admitted bashfully. "But I never dreamed I would be attempting to build a community from the ground up—especially not one like this!"

The front door banged open and Kachina and her twin brother, Wyler, thundered into the house. Both children were grinning ear to ear, their eyes glowing like freshly minted gold coins.

"Mama! Daddy!" the twins chimed. "Fella's back!"

A shaggy, four-legged shape the size of a young adult bear stood framed in the doorway behind them. The beast lifted its massive head and thumped its tail in greeting, a red tongue lolling from the corner of its mouth like a velvet sash.

Cade knelt before the creature sandwiched between his children. "You old bastard!" he grinned, taking Fella's head between his hands and scratching it behind the ears. "Where you been, boy? Were you out huntin' for antelope and bighorn in the high country again?"

As Sonja stepped forward to join Cade, the great beast's hackle came up and a low, throaty growl rumbled in its chest.

"She's okay, Fella!" Cade said, taking a double handful of the animal's nape so that they were locked eye-to-eye. "She's a *friend*," he said slowly and distinctly, stressing the last word. He motioned for Sonja to draw closer. "Ms. Blue, I'd like you to meet Fella. He's one of my closest and most trusted friends. Fella, say hello to the nice lady."

Fella looked at Cade, then back at Sonja, before offering his right front paw. Her eyebrows lifted upon catching sight of the opposable thumb.

"You didn't mention there was a half-wolf among your number. Your friend is *very* rare, indeed."

"Yes, I'm aware of the *vargr* eugenics council's stand on half-wolves," Cade said with a weary sigh. "They don't want them polluting their precious pedigrees. For some reason, they consider werewolves mating with true wolves bestiality."

"And *vargr* raping humans is normal?" she shot back.

"I don't *agree* with their policies, I only know of them. I'd appreciate it if you could remember that."

"You're right, Sheriff. Please forgive me."

Rosie stuck her head out of the kitchen. "Kachina! Wyler! Go wash your hands. You too, Fella! Dinner's ready!"

Nate Ferguson was awakened from his bed by the sound of horses screaming. He looked to where Little Bird normally would have been beside him before remembering she had taken their son to stay with her relatives on the reservation earlier that day. The incident with the stranger in the barn had spooked his wife in a way nothing else in this strange land ever had before.

Nine years ago, while on a rare trip down to Albuquerque, Skinner Cade had spotted a band of young toughs in a culvert, kicking around what looked like a scarecrow. The scarecrow just happened to be Nate. Skinner scared off the punks and offered to drop Nate off at a hospital. Nate had begged him not to do so—there was bench warrant out on him for drunk and disorderly.

So instead of leaving him to die in the ditch, Skinner took Nate back to Nonesuch, where he was nursed back to health by a collection of Native Americans, social rejects, and werewolves. Nate hadn't set foot outside Nonesuch since that day, save for a brief foray into the Navajo Nation to find a wife.

In the years since Skinner had dragged him out of the culvert, Nate had achieved more than he had ever dreamed possible. He had a home, a wife, a son, friends, neighbors, along with enough livestock and food to provide for his family and their simple needs. He wasn't living the life of a Rajah, but it was pretty damn good for a Sterno-swilling bum who used to live under an overpass. And he would be damned if some woman was going to scare him off his land.

He threw back the blankets, snatching up the pair of pants draped over the foot of the bed. He grabbed the loaded thirty-aught he kept behind the front door and hurried out across the yard. The noise coming from the barn was horrific. The last time he heard animals make such a sound was when he'd worked as day labor at a dog-food factory. It had taken a gallon of Mad Dog to wash the echoes of the mustangs' screams from his head.

As he drew closer, Nate could see that the barn doors were standing wide open. Cloverleaf, his prize mare, bolted clear, her eyes rolling in equine terror. Nate leapt out of the way, narrowly avoiding being trampled by the frightened horse as it fled into the night. He stepped into the barn, gun ready.

"Who's there? Show yourself! I got a gun!" He shouted over the frantic lowing of the agitated cattle and the sound of horses and mules kicking at their stable doors. Nate retrieved the battery-powered flashlight he kept just inside the door and played the beam around the interior of the barn. Panicked livestock stared back at him, their eyes showing white.

Nate focused the flashlight beam on Cloverleaf's stall. The mare had reduced the slats to splinters in her desperate attempt to escape. He then pointed the light at the stall next to Cloverleaf's, which housed one of the plow mules. At first he thought it was empty as well, then he saw a dark bulk sprawled in the hay. He moved closer to get a better look, and saw that the poor beast's mouth hung open, its tongue dangling to one side, bloody froth covering its muzzle, its eyes glazing over. Wiley Simms raised his head from the dying mule's flank, his face smeared with blood and straw, and hissed at Nate like an angry possum.

Nate cried out, dropping the flashlight as he stepped back from the animal pen. Never in all his life, not even during his days hanging out drinking hooch under the overpass, had he seen such bestial hunger in a person's eyes. It was as if every last vestige of humanity had been stripped away, leaving only stark, staring madness.

"Stay where you are, Wiley!" Nate said, leveling the gun at the gore-covered figure crouched before him. "I don't want to shoot you, but I will if I have to!"

Wiley grinned up at Nate, bloody drool dripping from his quivering lips. The flesh of the mule was good, but nowhere near as tender as the flesh of man. The ghoul no more knew why this was true than a bird knows why it's warmer down south. But as the thought of eating the man crossed the dark, cold clay of its mind, the ghoul felt something twitch in its hindbrain. Something that told him that the man was not to feed his hunger, but destined for another's need.

Following dinner, Rosie and Cade cleared the dishes from the table. After checking their homework, Rosie shooed the twins off to bed. After dispensing goodnight kisses, Cade returned to the great room to find his guest seated in a chair, staring into the fire in the kiva, her fingers steepled. The half-wolf, Fella, was sprawled at her feet like a bearskin rug.

"I'm impressed," Cade said. "Fella doesn't normally relax in front of strangers."

"We understand each other," Sonja said simply. "He knows I pose no threat to the pack. In fact, he cut short his hunting trip because he caught wind of the *enkidu* I seek."

"How did you figure that out?" Cade asked half-jokingly. "Read his mind?"

"Yes. To a certain degree," Sonja replied, surprising him with her seriousness. "Please, sit down. There is much we have to discuss if we are to work together. I'm interested in learning more about you and this town of yours."

"Why don't you just read my mind? That would save some time, wouldn't it?"

"Yes it would, but I doubt you would find the experience very pleasant. Besides, I would rather hear it from you. Tell me about yourself, Skinner Cade."

Cade shrugged his shoulders and sat down in a chair opposite his guest. "Very well. If you insist. But, remember, you asked for it. Like I told you earlier, my name is Skinner Cade. But that was not the name I was born with. My real name, my birthing name, is Skinwalker. My father was a *vargr* lord called Feral. My mother is a were-coyote named Changing Woman. And I am the product of rape.

"My mother and her mate had been lured to a meeting with the *vargr* under the pretense of signing a peace treaty. My mother's mate was slain and his killer mounted her in victory. The *vargr* probably would have slain her as well, but she managed to escape and return to her people. When I was born I was one of a set of demi-twins. My wife, Rosie, was my littermate. We share the same mother but have different fathers.

"My mother would have killed me at birth if not for the human midwife who helped deliver my sister and myself. The midwife took me to a foundling home where I was adopted by the people I would grow up believing to be my parents, William and Edna Cade.

"The Cades cherished me as only those who know the true value of a child can. I never once doubted the depth and sincerity of their love for me, no matter what. They knew I was different from other children, but it never changed how they felt toward me. Like most *vargr* reared among humans, I had a hard time being accepted by my peers, and was often the butt of cruel jokes and vicious pranks. I could have become embittered and twisted, like so many other secret monsters, but the love of my parents kept me strong. I never knew how incredibly lucky I was to have been adopted by the Cades until I went out into the world and met others like myself who had known nothing but abuse at the hands of the humans who raised them. My mother, rest her soul, loved me even after she discovered the truth about me. I was only ten years old at the time..."

Cade fell silent and his gaze became distant, as if he was looking at something far away. After a few seconds he swallowed hard and resumed speaking, but there was now a slight hitch in his voice.

"My father had taken me deer hunting for my very first time. When I bagged my first buck, he said it was a rite of passage, marking my transition from boyhood into manhood. He blooded my cheeks— smearing my face with the fresh blood of the deer I had brought down. And, without meaning to, I changed for the first time.

"My mother found me crouched over his dead body, gnawing on his carcass like a rabid beast. Instead of killing me for the monster I was, she took me home, cleaned me up, and protected me, not only from others, but from myself as well. She succeeded so well I had no memory of what I had done that horrible day until I shapeshifted for the first time as an adult.

"When I discovered the truth about myself, I thought, at first, I should find others of my kind. I thought I might fit in better with other werewolves than I did with humans. But I discovered that I could never truly fit in among them. The purebred *vargr* proved to be ravenous, blood-drunk maniacs who used humans to sate their appetites. Faced with the possibility of centuries of life as a cannibal and serial rapist, I was on the verge of suicide.

"It was not until I met my mother's people, the *coyotero*, that I realized there was indeed hope for myself. The *coyotero* know how to live in balance with their world and those who share it with them. That is why the *vargr* hate them so. The *vargr* came to this country with the white man, and like the white man, they were an arrogant and greedy breed. They came very close to wiping the *coyotero* off the face of the earth.

"The *coyotero* taught me that just because I have wild blood in my veins, that does not mean I have to live like a beast. The *coyotero* have coexisted in relative harmony with the native peoples of the Southwest for millennia. While they have been known to eat the occasional human now and again, their relationship with the desert tribes has been benevolent—hence the importance of the trickster-god Coyote in the Native American mythologies.

"With the *coyotero* I saw how it was possible for human and Pretender to live together, work together, and fight together against a common enemy. I know from personal experience that the role of monster is a cruel one. To live the life of a predator means you can never truly be at peace, either with the world or yourself. You are constantly on the prowl, fearful of exposure or challenges from more powerful, far deadlier predators. All Pretenders play at being humans, but not all of us do so simply in order to prey upon the flock. Some of us pretend because we dream of having a family and a home and a place in a society where we can live without fear.

"Nonesuch was born of that dream. We have worked hard to make this a place where human lives beside werewolf, where werewolf hunts alongside were-coyote. Any Pretender who has wearied of the endless cycle of hiding and killing and living in fear is welcome to join us and start a new life, one free of predation and exploitation. We hope as word of what we're doing spreads through the underground that more and more Pretenders will find their way to us. There are those on the town council who still believe we owe this Vasek a hearing."

"Believe me when I tell you, Sheriff Cade: Never trust an *enkidu*."

"Does that include you as well?" Cade asked, lifting an eyebrow.

"Yes," she answered. "I could not hunt and destroy these creatures as well as I do if I did not have their darkness inside me. I can be a very dangerous woman, even when I don't wish to be."

"Perhaps that is true," Cade said with a shrug. "But I have learned to trust my instincts when it comes to people, whether they're human or not."

"And what do your instincts say about me?"

"That you're conflicted. And I have no doubt in my mind that you can be lethal when crossed. But, basically, I believe you are a decent sort. Whatever that sort may be."

Before he could continue, a muffled ringing sound came from the roll-top desk.

"What's that?" Sonja asked.

"It's the hotline," Cade explained, levering himself out of his chair. "We don't have telephone service, per se, but there are a few army-issue field telephones scattered among the older human citizens. My phone rings automatically the minute whoever is on the other end of the line picks up their receiver." He rolled the top of the desk back and pulled an old-fashioned telephone receiver from its olive-drab canvas carrying case.

"Sheriff Cade speaking." He frowned, as if having trouble identifying the voice on the other end. "Mrs. Cowpers—? Is that you? What? I'll be right out! Maisie, I need you to lock your doors and stay away from the windows! Do you hear me? Don't let *anyone* in until I get there! Now stay put—help's on the way." He glanced up at Sonja as he returned the field telephone receiver to its case. "Maisie Cowpers says there's something in her chicken coop, and whatever it is, it's laughing."

The Cowpers place was a small parcel located a mile or so up the road from Nate Ferguson's spread. A couple of weeks ago, Maisie's husband of forty-seven years, Kerwin, upped and died of gut cancer, leaving her to raise chickens and candle eggs on her own. As Cade pulled up in front of the Cowpers' house, Fella leapt out of the back of the Jeep before it came to a full stop. The half-wolf loped over to the chicken coop then went on point, like a bird dog in the presence of hidden quail, his teeth bared and his hackle raised from nape to tail.

Taking his gun from its holster, Cade motioned for Sonja to flank him as he kicked open the door. He glanced inside, grimaced, and then returned his weapon to its holster.

"Whatever was after Maisie's chickens has flown the coop. No pun intended."

"Could it have been an animal?" Sonja asked.

"You tell me," he said, motioning for her to look inside.

The walls of the coop were coated with blood, matted feathers, and the dripping yolks of shattered eggs. Chicken carcasses, fifty in all, lay scattered about like gory feather dusters. Each and every bird was missing its head. The nesting boxes were overturned and what few eggs that had not been hurled against the walls had been trodden underfoot. Sonja turned back around to speak to Cade, but he was already running toward the farmhouse.

"Mrs. Cowpers! It's me! Sheriff Cade!"

He was answered by silence. As he stepped onto the front porch, he could see the front door was hanging open on busted hinges. Whatever it was that had raided the chicken coop had also kicked open the door, despite the heavy crossbar. All the furniture in the front room was smashed into kindling. Skinner dashed into the kitchen and then into the bedroom, only to find each room dark and empty.

He returned to the front room to find Sonja standing in the middle of the demolished furnishings, studying a shattered piece of Blue Willow china she had picked up off the floor.

"She's gone," he said, trying to keep the fear from his voice.

"Vasek's minion has claimed her for his master," Sonja said, dropping the fragment of ruined china back onto the floor as she turned to face him. "If your friend is lucky, she'll die of a heart attack before the bastard has a chance to feed."

"Damn it! This ain't how it's supposed to be!" Cade spat, kicking the gutted remains of the Cowpers' sofa hard enough to reduce it to splinters. "I *promised* them a safe place for humans and Pretenders alike, and they *trusted* me!"

"Don't be too hard on yourself, Sheriff," Sonja said. "There's no undoing what has been done. Once he converts a few humans, though, you can kiss your little attempt at utopia goodbye. We've got to find Vasek's lair and take him out before he can surround himself with others of his making. But where to begin? This territory is full of abandoned mines and old graveyards..."

"Mine?" Cade took his hat off and hurled it to the floor. "*Damn* it! The old copper mine! I was there earlier today, just before I got the call about Nate's barn! I *knew* something was wrong out there, but I just couldn't put my finger on it! *Damn it!*" He kicked the remains of a broken chair across the room in his anger. "I should have followed my instincts and gone into that fucking mine! If I had, this never would have happened!"

"Don't be so rough on yourself," Sonja said gently. "Chances are you would have simply gotten yourself killed. Being a werewolf isn't much help in a vampire's lair—especially if he's got a minion with him. And judging from the mess in the coop, our friend didn't waste any time replacing his ghoul."

"Do you think there's a chance Maisie's still alive?"

"The only humans vampires keep alive are renfields," she said, shaking her head sadly. "They are psychics who serve as watchdogs for their masters during the day. Unless your Mrs. Cowpers is a telepath or clairvoyant, her only use to Vasek is as an addition to his brood."

Cade sighed and picked his hat up off the floor, knocking the dust off it. "You're the vampire hunter—what do we do now?"

"We wait for the sun. There's no point in trying to find him before then. As long as he remains underground, Vasek is capable of moving about during daylight hours. However, *enkidu* don't like interrupting their beauty sleep. He'll be somewhat sluggish, as will whatever by-blows he's got down there with him."

"In that case, political correctness be damned! I'm rounding up the rest of the human homesteaders tonight and bringing them inside the perimeter for the duration. I'm not going to let that son of a bitch claim another life on my watch! Filthy bloodsucker! Uh, no offense, ma'am."

"None taken, Sheriff."

As dawn arrived, two vehicles pulled up to the old abandoned copper mine. The first was the Jeep, with Cade at the wheel, Sonja riding shotgun, Fella wedged in between them. The second vehicle was a pick-up truck, containing Uncle Billy and Cissy, with Cully riding in the bed.

Cade hopped out of the Jeep and cupped his hands to his mouth. *"Wiley! Where are you?"*

"I doubt he will answer," Sonja said. "From what you've told me, your friend was probably one of Vasek's earliest victims."

"I still have to try and find him," Cade replied as he mounted the stairs to Wiley's cabin. "His safety is my responsibility."

"Any sign?" Uncle Billy called up from the truck.

Cade shook his head. "His bed doesn't look like it's been slept in." He hurried back down to join the others. As he reached the bottom of the stairs something brownish-gold and low to the ground flickered at the corner of his eye. As he turned toward the thing at the edge of his vision, Changing Woman rose up onto her hind legs, her three rows of teats barely discernable through the thick fur covering her belly.

"Good morning, mother," Cade said evenly. "I see you've chosen to join us."

"Of course. You are my son, matters of conception aside. I would not allow you to go into battle alone. And, to speak straight, I have my doubts about your new friend." She gestured with one talon to where Sonja stood, talking to Uncle Billy.

"What about her?"

"I do not trust her. There is a shadow on her soul, one that waxes and wanes like the phases of the moon. Sometimes her face shines, other times it is in eclipse."

"Could you say that a little louder? I don't think she can hear you from where she's standing!" Cade snapped at Changing Woman. "Look, if Sonja was going to kill me, she could have done it several times by now. Jesus, mother—one of these days you're going to *have* to learn to trust other species!"

"I remember how this land was before the white man," Changing Woman replied curtly. "Speak to me of trusting strangers in another century or two."

Exasperated, Cade turned on his heel and went to where the others were gathered, trying to ignore the burning in his ears.

"You're mother's right," Sonja said. There was no trace of anger or insult in her voice. "There is no reason for her to trust me. For all you know I'm one of Vasek's minions leading you into a cleverly orchestrated death trap."

"Are you?" Cade asked, arching an eyebrow.

"No," she replied. "But I *could* be. You never can tell—whether it's with people or things that pretend to be people. Now let's get this show on the road."

As they neared the mouth of the mine, Uncle Billy grimaced. "Christ A'mighty! You smell that?"

"Yeah," Cade replied through clenched teeth.

"Smell what?" Cissy asked, looking confused. "All I smell is dirt and machine oil."

"Sorry, girl," Uncle Billy said. "I forgot your nose ain't as keen as ours. Even Cully's picked up on it." He nodded toward the young ogre, whose nostrils were flared like those of a nervous pony.

"Bad. Bad in dark," Cully rumbled anxiously.

"It's the odor of nesting undead," Sonja explained. "That means there's more than one down there."

"Sonja and I are going in. Uncle Billy, Changing Woman—I want you to wait here with Cissy and Cully. If anything comes out, I want y'all to blast it, understand?"

"Gotcha," Uncle Billy said as he opened his shotgun and slid a couple of cartridges into the breach.

"Whatever you do, make sure you shoot it in the head," Sonja explained. "It doesn't matter whether you're using regular buckshot or the silver loads. If you blow out its brains, it ain't goin' nowhere. If you can't manage a headshot, try for the spine. Cutting them in two won't kill them, but it'll slow them down."

"Yes, ma'am," Uncle Billy snapped his shotgun back together. "Here, you better take this with you, Skin," he said, handing Cade a nine-volt flashlight. "I realize neither of y'all have much trouble in the dark, but there's a limit to even *vargr* night vision."

"Thanks, Billy," Cade said, hefting the flashlight in a salute. As they moved toward the yawning mouth of the old incline shaft that lead down into the mine, Fella dropped into step behind them. Cade turned and shook his head, pointing toward the others. "Fella! *No!* You can't come with me this time, big guy! You've gotta stay here with Uncle Billy and the others."

Fella made a snuffling noise and shook his head, his ears flapping like stubby wings.

"You heard me! I said *no!*" Cade's tone was stern and loud, as if he was talking to a Labrador retriever who was insisting on following him to school. "You can't go with me!"

Fella's ears drooped, his shoulders slumped, and his tail dropped. After a long moment, the half-wolf turned and plodded back in the direction of the others, and Cade and Sonja continued into the mine. While they followed the narrow-gauge tracks that once ran the ore cars, Cade glanced over his shoulder and saw the half-wolf framed against the daylight, watching after them with an anxious expression on his face.

"Damn hard-headed beast," he sighed.

"He's extremely loyal," Sonja commented, not without some admiration. "You are lucky to have him as a friend."

"He's more than a friend. He's family," Cade explained. "And I don't mean it in the usual way people do when they talk about their pets. He's a first cousin on my dad's side. Good Lord—what's that stink?" he swung the flashlight beam in the direction of the reek. The dim light reflected off the peeled skull of a burro.

"That's Sookie, Wiley's pack animal, or at least what's left of her." He grimaced and looked away. "Did—did that Vasek asshole do this?"

"Judging from the puncture wounds on the animal's throat, I'd say he was responsible for part of it. But I'm betting most of that damage was done by a ghoul. They're equal opportunity carnivores. Horses, chickens, humans, whatever. They prefer living meat, but they'll eat the dead if there's nothing better on hand." She glanced around at the various side tunnels that branched off the main shaft. "I wouldn't be surprised if the ghoul wasn't using these passageways to excavate bodies from the local graveyard."

"He wouldn't have to go that far," Cade replied. "This mine is one huge tomb. There was a cave-in in one of the lower galleries back in the 1920s that trapped at least fifty miners. The company decided it was more cost-effective to leave them there rather than excavate them. Not long after that they closed down the mine for good."

"How quaint," Sonja grunted in reply. "No wonder Vasek chose this place to nest in. The very walls are impregnated with the horror and suffering of those miners left to die. *Enkidu* are drawn to scenes of human misery like flies to shit."

As they moved farther into the mine, the incline grew steeper and the atmosphere increasingly close.

"God, the air's stale down here," Cade grumbled, coughing into his fist.

"That doesn't mean much to a creature like Vasek. Vampires don't need to breathe like living things do."

Cade paused, tilting his head to one side like a hound. "Do you hear that?"

Sonja stood still, lending her ears as well. "Yes," she whispered in reply. "It's coming from over there." She pointed to one of the side tunnels off the main passageway.

Cade turned the flashlight in the direction she had pointed, casting its beam onto an image born of nightmare. A pallid figure, nominally human, squatted on its haunches in the darkness, naked save for the bushy mane and beard framing its face and the blood and chicken feathers smeared across its chest. It was busily gnawing on a human thighbone that had been snapped in half.

Cade stepped forward. *"Wiley—!"*

The ghoul jerked its head in Cade's direction, baring its teeth at the intruders, spittle and blood dripping from its curled lips.

Sonja grabbed Cade's arm to stop him from getting too close, but it was too late. The ghoul leapt forward, swinging the thighbone like a crazed caveman, knocking the flashlight from Cade's hand. The passageway was plunged into darkness deeper than any grave. The ghoul's powerful hands closed upon Cade's throat, bearing him to the ground with a strength born of something beyond madness.

There was fierce growling and the smell of fur. The ghoul's face suddenly contorted in pain and its blood-wet mouth opened wide in an agonized shriek as it was dragged off the prone body of the sheriff. Fella pulled the ghoul down the tunnel, his powerful jaws locked onto its hind leg. The half-wolf whipped its massive head back and forth, savaging the captive ghoul like a terrier with a rat. The ghoul yowled and plunged the jagged end of the thighbone into Fella's shoulder, causing him to yelp in pain and let go of his prey. The ghoul quickly got to its feet and disappeared into the darkness, dragging its right leg behind him like a broken kite. Sonja dashed after the wounded thing, her silver knife drawn.

Cade turned his attention to Fella. The half-wolf lay on his side, panting rapidly, the thighbone jutting from his shoulder, not far from a major artery. Cade gripped the makeshift spear and pulled it free with a single tug. Fella turned his head to lick his wound, whimpering like a pup on the tit.

"Damn it, boy! I told you to stay put!" Cade said as he saw to his friend's shoulder, wrapping a strip of cloth torn from his shirt over the puncture. Fella licked his face as he bandaged his wound. "Don't try making up to me right now!" Cade said sternly, pushing Fella's muzzle away. "You disobeyed a direct order! Now go back up top and stay there!"

"Take this with you."

Cade looked up, startled by Sonja's sudden reappearance. One second she wasn't there, the next she was standing at his elbow, Wiley's head held in one hand like a perverse lantern. She tossed the gruesome souvenir onto the ground between the half-wolf's paws. Fella eagerly snatched it up, careful not to tear the skin with his fangs, and trotted off like a dog with a new chew toy.

"It was a quick enough death, as such things go," she said as Cade got back onto his feet. "Your friend felt very little, assuming anything of him remained inside that creature. You okay?"

"I'll live," he wheezed, massaging his bruised throat.

"I didn't dare interfere when it jumped you," she explained. "If I nicked you while trying to stab the ghoul..."

"I understand."

"We're close to the nest. I can feel it," she said. "I can take over from here. You go back up top with Fella."

"No. This is my town. I am the law here. It is my responsibility to see that justice is done."

"Nobody would think the less of you for letting me take care of this, Cade. After all, you have a wife and kids depending on you."

"That's exactly why I can't turn tail at a time like this."

Sonja took a deep breath, as if preparing to argue the matter, then let it out again like a weary horse. "Suit yourself. It's your jurisdiction."

"Which way do we go, then?"

"This way," Sonja said, gesturing in the direction the ghoul had fled. "Wounded minions invariably flee in the direction of their masters. For some deluded reason they think they'll protect them."

"Do they?"

"Nah. Usually they just kill them."

"Do you think he knows we're down here?"

"Oh, he knows, all right. They always know when you kill one of their posse. Don't ask me how, they just do. So be on your toes."

The narrow passageway eventually opened onto a large gallery, the solid rock ceiling of which had been carved into the rough semblance of a cathedral. The air was foul and heavy with moisture from the seeping walls.

"How far—how far down do you think we are?" Cade gasped as he bent over to catch his breath.

"I'd say at least four, maybe five thousand feet," she replied. "And I don't care if you swore a blood oath on a stack of Bibles ten feet tall, I'm not taking you any farther. You need air, Vasek doesn't."

"What about you?"

"I can take it or leave it," she replied, shrugging her shoulders.

There was a sound of loose pebbles sliding underfoot. Cade froze. "Did you hear that?"

"Yeah," she replied. "They're close."

"Sheriff..." The voice was frail and querulous, sounding frightened and lost in the darkness. *"Sheriff Cade... help me..."*

"That's Maisie Cowpers," Cade said, his voice tinged with hope.

Sonja shook her head. "It just *sounds* like her."

"You don't know for sure," he shot back. "Besides, I thought it took three days and nights for a human to resurrect as a vampire."

"God damn it, who told you that? Peter Cushing?" Sonja spat in disgust. "We're not talking hard rules like in Monopoly! Sometimes it only takes a few hours for the host body to be taken over."

The scrambling sound came again, this time from a different direction than before. An elderly woman dressed in a tattered and filthy housecoat lurched out of one of the connecting tunnels. Her silver hair was in disarray as she groped her way through the darkness, her arms extended in front of her like a child playing blind man's bluff.

"Sheriff Cade... where are you? It's so dark... I can't see anything... where am I? I'm so afraid! Please... I want to go home!"

"It's okay, Maisie," Cade said, smiling comfortingly, even though he knew she could not see his face. "You're safe now." He took the old woman's elbow in his hand.

Mrs. Cowpers' head whipped around, the look of fear and confusion on her face replaced by a demonic grin, her eyes gleaming in the dark like those of a sewer rat.

Her dentures flew out of her mouth, displaced by the fangs that sprang from her barren gums like spring-loaded darts.

"God damn it, Cade!" Sonja snarled as she pulled the werewolf free of the vampire's clutches. "What the fuck is the point of bringing me down here if you're going to ignore *everything* I tell you? Now get out of the way and let me do my job!"

Sonja rammed her switchblade into the vampire's chest, going up under the ribs to skewer the heart like a black olive. The thing that used to be Mrs. Cowpers screeched like a cat with its tail caught in a door and dropped to the ground, where it twitched and flopped about at their feet. Cade grimaced as the old woman's skin blackened and peeled away from her skull, revealing a naked mass of muscle and bone.

"Sorry you had to see that. Silver poisoning in vampires isn't a pretty sight," Sonja said.

"Thanks," Cade said, swallowing the bile crowding the back of his throat. "Next time I promise I'll listen."

"Fuck this sneaking around in the dark!" Sonja snarled, kicking the liquefying mass that used to be Maisie Cowpers. "*We* know he's down here, *he* knows we're down here, and *he* knows that *we* know he's down here!" She threw back her head, arms opened wide as if inviting attack, and shouted at the cathedral-like ceiling of the cavern. "*Vasek!*" The vampire's name echoed throughout the tunnels honeycombing the mountainside. "*Show yourself, you bastard!*"

A voice spoke in the darkness, although it was impossible for Cade to pinpoint exactly where it was coming from. "I see you brought the local law with you. I'm quaking in my boots."

"You *better* be, asshole!" Cade growled. "If I don't walk out of here alive and in one piece, my friends up top are under orders to bring this overglorified prairie dog town down around your ears! Now show yourself like the lady asked!"

"As you wish, Sheriff," Vasek sighed.

A tall, gaunt figure dressed in the tattered remains of a fashionable Italian suit, now grimed with mud and gore, stepped out from behind a nearby outcropping. Vasek's face was as pale as a winter moon, save for his lips, which were full and wetly red, as if he had just feasted on fresh raspberries. His cheekbones were as sharp as the blade of a knife, and a white pigtail hung between his shoulders like an albino snake. The vampire stood and stared at them with eyes that shone like glasses of claret held before a fire while he nervously dry-washed his hands, the fingers of which were as long as knitting needles.

"Your little escape plan didn't turn out like you figured, dead boy," Sonja said, taking a step toward her prey. "You've got more than me to contend with now."

"I'm *so* frightened!" Vasek sneered.

"You arrogant stiff—!" Sonja laughed humorlessly, shaking her head in disbelief. "Take a good look at my buddy here, worm bait. Now tell me what you see."

Vasek frowned, but did as Sonja said, focusing his attention on Cade. The vampire's eyes widened in alarm and he took an involuntary step backward. "*Vargr!*" he hissed.

"Bingo!" Sonja grinned. "And not merely a loner or a mated pair, either. You brought your little road show slap-dab in the middle of a pack, dead boy! You queered your own game before it had a chance to get started! There's only room in this county for *one* species of super-predator, Vasek—and these guys called dibs!"

Vasek took yet another step backward, his arms held close to his body as if in fear of accidental contact, a look of angry disbelief on his sallow features. "Kill them!" he shouted at no one in particular. *"Destroy them!"*

The cavern floor underneath Cade's feet exploded in a shower of dirt as a hand—the fingers as white as grubs—burst through the soil and grabbed his shin. Cade looked down and saw the loose dirt slough away, revealing Nate Ferguson's face, pale as death, grinning up at him. The rancher's eyes were red as traffic lights and his canines as long and curved as a wild cat's fangs.

"Let go of him, dead boy!" Sonja snarled, punting Nate Ferguson's head like a place-kicker going for a goal, her boot smashing the vampire's skull like a rotten watermelon.

As Sonja tried to shake Nate Ferguson's clotted brains off her foot, a second figure lurched from one of the tunnels, its fangs bared. A couple of days ago the vampire had been an extreme sports enthusiast looking for a rugged mountain trail to explore, and he was still dressed in his elbow pads, and a half-shell crash helmet. Sonja easily sidestepped the erstwhile mountain biker, severing his spinal cord with a single flick of her knife. The vampire made a pathetic bleating sound, like that of a frightened goat, and collapsed into a pile of twitching, flailing limbs.

Sonja spun to face Vasek, her hands dripping with the cold, black blood of the undead. She pointed a finger at the vampire lord and grinned; "You're next, dead man!"

As Sonja advanced upon him, Vasek's impassive mask cracked and the vampire shrieked and disappeared into one of the mine's many passageways. Sonja bounded after him like a hound after the fox. She chased Vasek through the perpetual midnight of the tunnels, his milk-white pigtail waving in the darkness before her like a truce flag, until the passageway opened onto yet another gallery nowhere as grand as the one chosen for his nesting ground.

She looked around, but there was no sign of her prey. However, she did spot a pickaxe and a large canvas bag propped against one of the walls. The canvas bag had 'Property Of Wiley Simms' stenciled on it in big block letters. Frowning, she moved closer to investigate. As she bent down to retrieve the bag, Vasek grabbed her from behind, raking at her eyes with one hand while he dug his knitting-needle fingers into the inner elbow of her knife arm, his nails piercing the leather jacket like it was made of tissue paper. Sonja cried out as her right arm went numb from shoulder to fingertips, the switchblade falling from her spastic fingers. Cackling gleefully, Vasek kicked the switchblade out of reach with a powerful swing of his Italian half-boot.

"That's all I'm ever going to take from you, bitch!" he snarled, hurling Sonja to the ground with a single shove. "Who do you think you are, chasing me—Lord Vasek!—from pillar to post as if I were mere vermin to be exterminated! You kill my minions! You destroy my gets! You even bring a damned *vargr* into my lair! What matter of monster *are* you, woman?"

"I'm the one that's going to kill you, you bloodsucking son of a bitch!" she growled.

"You nasty little impertinent upstart! Just for that, I'm going to tear off your head and shove it up your cunt!"

Sonja didn't doubt for a moment that Vasek was perfectly willing and able to make good on his threat. Her right arm still hung numb and useless at her side.

"But first I think I will pluck out your eyes out and use them for marbles!" The vampire lord said with a grin, his long fingers twitching like the legs of an Alaskan king crab as he leaned over her.

"Fuck you, freak!" Sonja spat, using her good arm to throw a fistful of loose dirt into the vampire's face.

Vasek chuckled as he wiped the soil from his face. "Come now, my dear. Is that the best you can do?"

A deep, racking cough abruptly replaced Vasek's chuckle. The vampire put a hand to his mouth and it came away sticky. He stared in open bafflement at the black, stinking blood coating his palm, then touched his face to discover that the ichor was pouring from his nose like stout from a freshly tapped keg. Vasek's neck began to swell rapidly, as if his throat was being filled with air from a bicycle pump. The swelling continued until his face and head resembled an overinflated water balloon, his eyes and nostrils reduced to narrow slits through which blood and other less identifiable fluids oozed in a steady stream.

The flesh covering his skull tore like sodden tissue paper, dropping away in great, wet sheets, exposing the wetly gleaming bone and tendons underneath. The vampire lord clawed at his diseased head, tearing away huge chunks of flesh as it blackened, withered, and peeled away like the skin of an overripe banana. With a final, ultrasonic shriek of agony, Vasek collapsed onto the floor of the mine, the shock of the impact sending spinal fluid squirting out his ears.

Sonja got to her feet, staring in rapt fascination at the dying vampire sprawled before her. Using her good arm, she picked up Wiley's canvas prospector's bag and managed to flip the pouch open. She stared at the ore samples inside, and then back at Vasek, who was already starting to trickle out of his suit.

"Sonja! Ms. Blue—where are you?" Cade's voice echoed through the mine. The young werewolf sounded very concerned.

"I'm over here, Sheriff!" she shouted back in answer.

"Are you okay?"

"My right arm is hurt, but otherwise I'm fine!"

"What about Vasek?"

"He's dead!"

"Stay put! I'm on my way!"

"No! Don't come any further than you already have! It's dangerous for you down here! "

"Why? What's wrong?"

"What kind of mine did you say this was?"

"Copper!"

"Not anymore! It's a *silver* mine, now!"

"Are you sure you won't stay a little longer, Sonja?" Cade asked one final time as they stood outside the general store. The sun had yet to rise and the mountain air was crisp enough that his words were accompanied by little puffs of steam.

Sonja stood beside Uncle Billy's truck, one hand resting on the door handle. Cissy sat behind the wheel, Cully huddled in the bed like a concrete Buddha, as their passenger said her final good-byes.

"You needn't worry. My arm's completely recovered. Besides, it's time I went back to work. "

"You don't have to leave at all, you know."

"I appreciate the offer, Sheriff," Sonja said. "But I'm afraid I'm not ready to settle down to the country life. At least, not yet. As it is, Nonesuch is going to have its hands full trying to figure out what to do with a brand spanking new silver mine."

"That's God's own truth if ever it was spoke. I reckon Wiley must have struck that vein by sheer accident. He spent his life lookin' to strike it rich, and what does he get for his trouble?" Uncle Billy sighed, shaking his head. "Poor old bastard. But Skinner's right, ma'am—you're always welcome here."

"You sure about that? You haven't seen me on one of my bad days. There is something like Vasek inside me, only it's a lot meaner."

"You're not telling any of us something we don't already know," Cade said. "There is something dark in each and everyone of us here, Human and Pretender alike. But we have all made the decision to not allow it to rule our lives. Sometimes we succeed, and sometimes we fail. But at least we try. You and I are not so different, Sonja. We both fight to maintain our humanity in the face of monstrosity. And, in the end, that is all any of us has got."

Sonja flashed a sad, sweet smile as she clasped Cade's hand in her own. "You're a good man, Skinner Cade, werewolf or not. I wish you good luck with your town and your family."

"Come back and see us some time."

As she climbed into the passenger seat beside Cissy, she glanced over her shoulder at him one last time. "Perhaps I'll do that—in another thirty years or so, say? It would be nice to find out how far along Nonesuch will have come."

"It's a date," Cade said, touching the brim of his hat. "See you in thirty."

"Yeah. See you then."

She got into the truck and slammed the door shut. Cissy threw the transmission into gear and the pick-up jounced its way down the dirt road that passed for Nonesuch's main street, headed in the direction of Santa Fe.

Cade watched until the truck disappeared from sight, then turned his gaze up at the sky above, which was still filled with stars without number. Nonesuch had faced the first true threat to its existence, and it had survived the encounter. He was not so naive as to believe it would be the last. Maybe the next danger would wear a human face. Maybe it would have no face at all. In any case, it would have to deal with him if it wanted to start trouble in his town.

He tossed his head back, sniffed the brisk morning air and caught the scent of sausage links frying in the pan coming from his house. He grinned and dropped down onto all fours and loped back to his home and his wife and children, tongue lolling in anticipation of breakfast.

person(s) unknown

A patrol car was waved down at the intersection of South L Street and South 57th Street at 10:30 p.m. on Saturday by a member of the Help the Homeless Outreach charity, who alerted the patrolmen to an altercation transpiring in a nearby alley. When the police arrived to investigate, they saw what appeared to be a violent physical confrontation between a man and a woman. When ordered to stop by the authorities, the woman fatally stabbed the man and fled the scene. The officers gave chase but were unable to capture her. She is described as being a Caucasian woman in her early twenties, tall, and dressed in a black leather motorcycle jacket and mirrored sunglasses.

The following is a transcript of the interview of Humphrey "Hump" Johnson:

(Tape recorder being turned on)

DETECTIVE CLEMENCE: This is Detective John Clemence of the Tacoma Police Department, Homicide Division. I am about to conduct an interview with one Humphrey Johnson, regarding the homicide that occurred on Saturday, February 16th, 2002, in the alley near the intersection of South L Street and South 57th. The interview begins Sunday, February 17th, at 3:20 a.m. Please state your name, age and place of residence for the record, sir...

JOHNSON: My name is Humphrey Johnson, but I go by "Hump." I'm fifty-two years old, and I ain't got no address, 'less you count that fridgerator carton you boys hauled me outta.

CLEMENCE: Mr. Johnson, could you describe, as best you can, what exactly transpired earlier tonight?

JOHNSON: Well, I started out hustling change, trying to scare up enough scratch for a forty. Then I went to see what Dimebox was up to.

CLEMENCE: "Dimebox"? That would be Mr. Polk?

JOHNSON: Yeah, I guess. I only knows him as Dimebox. Anyways, Dimebox and me split his bottle of Mad Dog. Then we got a tin of sardines and some crackers from the corner store and had us a real fine supper. While we was eating, Dimebox he got to talking bout this friend of his, Greasy Jim. Him and Greasy was in the shit together, back in the day.

CLEMENCE: You mean they had served together in the Army...?

JOHNSON: Yeah. In Nam. Anyways, Greasy Jim had the croup something awful, according to Dimebox. He was afraid he weren't getting proper attention, what with him being camped out in a packing crate in the alley off 57th. So I tell him that if he's so worried bout his homey, we ought to go pay him a call. So we goes round to the alley where Greasy Jim got his crate, and I be damned if he ain't lying there in his own whiz, making a noise like a clogged crapper when he breathes. Dimebox, he gets all upset and tries to get Greasy to come out of the crate so's we can take him to the Mission, but he's out of his head with fever and putting up a fight. Then Dimebox remembers them do-gooders that come round the hood ever so often...

CLEMENCE: That would be the members of Help the Homeless Outreach?

JOHNSON: Yeah, that's them. Anyways, they hand out free sandwiches and hot soup out of this van, and sometimes they got this doc that hands out rubbers and penicillin. Anyways, I tell Dimebox we got to see if they can't get Greasy Jim a bed in Tacoma General, y'know? Better a bed there than a drawer in the morgue, I always say. Anywho, Dimebox axes me to stay with Greasy and keep an eye on him like until he comes back. So's I'm watching him, okay? But he ain't doing nothing but lying there, right? So I make a quick stop at the liquor store, to get me more hooch. After all, it's cold out there. I needed something to keep my blood warm. Anyways, I ain't gone five minutes—ten, tops. When I get back to the alley I seen this dude pulling Greasy out of the packing crate by his legs. At first I think it's the doc, right? Then I get a good look at what he's wearing, and it ain't nothing no doctor would have on his back.

CLEMENCE: Can you describe the clothes the man was wearing?

JOHNSON: It was some kind of suit. Not a new one either, but more like one of the hand-me-downs you can get down at the Mission. It was dark, like deep blue or black, but you could see there was dirt, mud, or some kinda crud smeared on the sleeves and legs, like he been sleeping in a dumpster. This asshole is dragging Greasy Jim out of the box, and I can see Greasy don't want none of it. He's shaking his head back and forth, but he's too weak to call out. So's I run up and yell at him to leave Greasy be. The dude, he turns on me and hisses like a cat or something, and I can see his eyes are all red...

CLEMENCE: You mean they were bloodshot?

JOHNSON: Shit no, they weren't bloodshot! They was red. Like when you drive up on a dog or something at night. It threw such a scare in me I dropped my damn bottle. The dude, he turned back to whatever the hell it was he was doing to Greasy Jim. Whatever was going down, I knew I didn't wanna be there to see it. That's when I turned around and run smack into the bitch.

CLEMENCE: Did you get a good look at the woman?

JOHNSON: Hell, yeah, I seen her. She was fine, too. Tall, real pale, like them junkie gals can get, you know? She was wearing a leather jacket, jeans, and had dark hair.

CLEMENCE: What color were her eyes?

JOHNSON: Damned if I know. She was wearing sunglasses.

CLEMENCE: She was wearing sunglasses? In an alley? After ten o'clock at night?

JOHNSON: What did I just tell you, fool? If I seen her eyes, I'd tell you what damn color they was.

CLEMENCE: Okay. Then what happened?

JOHNSON: The girl, she tells me to get lost and pushes me aside, then next thing I know she jumps onto the dude messing with Greasy.

CLEMENCE: When you say she jumped onto the man, do you think she was possibly helping him?

JOHNSON: Hell, no! She was on the fucker like white on rice. The dude, he stops what he's doing and they start going at it like pit bulls in the ring. That's when I lit out. I knew better than to get in the middle of that shit! I get up the street, I seen Dimebox with the doc. I tell them what I seen, and I guess after that's when the cops got waved down. I didn't stick around long enough to find out any more. I seen enough for the night. I found me another forty, went back to my place, and stayed there until your boys rousted me and brought me in for questioning.

CLEMENCE: Mr. Johnson, have you ever seen the man who attacked Greasy Jim—I mean, Mr. DeGrese—before?

JOHNSON: No sir, I have not.

CLEMENCE: What about the woman?

JOHNSON: Nope, I ain't never seen her before, either. I would have remembered her if I did. Say, is Greasy okay?

CLEMENCE: He's in a coma. They have him in the ICU over at County. Your friend, Mr. Polk, suffered a broken arm and several fractured ribs attempting to come to Mr. DeGrese's aid. It's uncertain whether the man or the woman caused his injuries. The man you say was attempting to harm Mr. DeGrese is dead.

Do you have any idea what this man may have been trying to do?

JOHNSON: Shit, I reckon he was trying to eat Greasy Jim.

CLEMENCE: Eat him?

JOHNSON: Yeah. We got a real problem with vampires in the hood. Ask anyone.

**From the Incident Report
filed by Detective John Clemence,
Homicide Division of the
Tacoma Police Department:**

    Following interviews of the eye witnesses Mr. Humphrey Johnson, a/k/a "Hump," and Mr. Edward Polk, a/k/a "Dimebox," it has been determined that the John Doe found at the scene was attempting to rob or otherwise cause bodily harm to Mr. James DeGrese, a/k/a "Greasy Jim." There is also reason to believe that the John Doe may be the same perpetrator responsible for the disappearance of several members of Tacoma's homeless community over the last few weeks. The Jane Doe who stabbed the John Doe in full view of Patrol Officers Stanley and Shaw appears to have been attempting to come to the aid of Mr. DeGrese, but there is also evidence to suggest that she may have been an accomplice of some kind. All attempts to identify the Jane Doe have drawn a blank with the local community. Either they do not recognize the woman or are unwilling to admit to knowing her. Despite Mr. Johnson and Mr. Polk's fanciful insistence that Mr. DeGrese's attacker was a vampire, until such time as a positive identification can be made, the murder of the John Doe will be listed as having been committed by a person(s) unknown.

HELL COME SUNDOWN

Award-winning author Nancy A. Collins returns in the upcoming horror/western collection **Dead Man's Hand: Five Tails of the Weird West**. This volume includes her celebrated novellas "Lynch" and "Walking Wolf," the hard-to-find short stories "The Tortuga Hill Gang's Last Ride" and "Calaverada," and the all-new novella "Hell Come Sundown." This last tells the story of Sam Hell, an undead cowboy who rode long before Sonja Blue. Following is a preview of that tale.

DEAD MAN'S HAND: FIVE TALES OF THE WEIRD WEST

by Nancy A. Collins

ISBN 1-58846-875-4
WW12995

Coming in Autumn of 2004

Hiram McKinney glanced up from his Bible as the cherry-wood mantle clock chimed eight o'clock. The timepiece, with its hinged convex glass lens and elegantly embossed Arabic numerals, was one of the few luxuries that had managed to survive the family's trip from Tennessee into the wilds of Texas.

"It's time you got off to bed, young man," Hiram told his son, who was toiling over his McGuffey's Reader workbook.

"Please Pa, can't I stay up a lit'l while longer?"

"You heard your daddy, Jacob," Miriam McKinney countered, without looking up from the sock she was darning.

"Yes ma'am," Jake replied glumly, setting aside his schoolwork as he scooted his chair away from the table.

The seven-year-old walked over to where his parents sat before the fieldstone fireplace to bid them good night. His mother put aside her sewing and leaned forward, pecking her son the cheek.

"Night, Jake."

"Night, Ma. Night, Pa," the boy said, turning to his father.

Mr. McKinney glanced up from his reading and gave his son a fond smile and a nod. While their son would never be too old for his mama to kiss, Hiram had recently decided that the boy was beyond any such mollycoddling from his father.

As Jake headed for his room, Mrs. McKinney called out after him one last time: "Pleasant dreams, sweetheart."

Neither saw the boy flinch.

The McKinneys came to Texas fifteen years ago, setting down stakes on some prime ranching land along the Nueces River, near Laredo. For the first five years they lived out of a one-room cabin. Then, as time moved on and they gradually became more prosperous, Hiram added a second room, so that he and Miriam no longer had to sleep where they ate. Then, three years later, Jake was born.

Jacob was not the McKinney's first child, but he was the only one to survive the cradle. An older brother and sister had both succumbed to disease before they got their first teeth. For the first three years of his life, Jake slept in the family bed. Then he was moved to a pallet in the corner for two years.

When Jake reached the age of five, it was decided that he was old enough to be moved to the lofted area above the communal room. For the next two years Jake drifted off to sleep to the sound of his parents discussing their day's activities or planning out what needed to be done to keep the homestead running smooth.

As the McKinney family's fortunes continued to rise, Hiram decided they could afford constructing a room for their son, placing it opposite their own, so that the layout of the house resembled a capital letter T.

Most boys Jake's age would have been thrilled to have their very own room. And at first, Jake was very excited by the prospect. But all that soon changed. His very first night alone, his screams woke up the house. His father charged into the room in his long johns, shotgun in hand, convinced that Comanches were dragging his son out the window. Once Hiram realized that was not the case, he cussed to beat the band.

When Jake told his parents about the thing that came out from under his bed, they listened for a moment and then exchanged looks. Pa was more than a little put out by the whole thing, but when he saw how frightened Jake was, he made a show of getting down on his hands and knees to prove there wasn't a boogeyman hiding under the bed.

Ma McKinney said it was only natural for a young boy to be frightened the first time he had to sleep on his own. All his life Jake had slept within earshot of his family. Sleeping by himself in a separate part of the house would take some getting used to. His father had grudgingly agreed to that point—after all, he himself hadn't slept in a separate room until after he was married, and even then he'd never truly slept alone.

However, as Jake's night terrors recurred night after night, his father's tolerance rapidly eroded. Pa was of the opinion that Ma was mollycoddling the boy, where Ma felt that Pa was in too big a hurry to make a man out of a child.

This was not a new argument between the McKinneys, but it was becoming an increasingly larger bone of contention with each passing birthday. Since Jake loved his parents with all his heart, knowing that he was the reason for them not getting along tore him up something fierce.

Jake wanted to be a man and make his daddy proud, really he did. But there was something going on that neither of his parents truly understood. The reason for his night terrors wasn't bad dreams or fear of being alone. No, it was something far worse. The simple fact of the matter was that his bedroom was haunted.

Jake wasn't real certain how that could be, as no one had ever lived in it before. He'd always been of the impression that it took someone dying in a place to make it haunted, but apparently that wasn't a hard and fast rule. He had learned, however, that whatever it was that lived under his bed did follow a pattern of behavior.

Whatever it was didn't come out every night—just those that coincided with the dark of the moon. He also knew that the thing was scared away by screaming and light, even if it was the weakest candle flame. Just a hint of lamplight appearing under the crack of the door as his mother came to check on him was enough to cause the apparition to fold in upon itself like a lady's lace fan.

At first he thought that the thing that haunted the room could only harm him if he looked at it, so he slept curled up in a tight little ball, the covers pulled up over his head. This seemed to stymie the thing from under the bed, but only for a while, and it eventually figured out that it could force him to throw back the blankets by sitting atop his huddled form until its weight threatened to suffocate him. As terrible as the creature was to look at, the very knowledge that the thing was sprawled across his bed was even more horrifying.

After the first couple of weeks, his father forbade his mother from checking on him whenever he cried out during the night. When it became clear his mother would no longer be coming to his aid, Jake realized that it was up to him, and him alone, to solve his problem.

He first tried to battle the monster by keeping the lamp burning beside his bed all night long. That only worked until Pa complained about the amount of oil being wasted. The general store was in Cochina Lake, over ten miles away, and the McKinneys only went there once every six weeks. Because of the increase in consumption, they were close to being out of fuel with two weeks to go before the next trip.

Jake's nights were seldom restful, and his dreams rarely pleasant. Even on those nights he was not haunted by the thing from under the bed, he slept fitfully, waking every time a timber groaned or a branch scraped the side of the house. Still, as bad as things were, he could not bring himself to tell his parents the truth of his situation. For one, he knew they wouldn't believe him, and for another, he didn't want his father to see him as a frightened little boy. If being born and raised in Texas had taught him anything, it was self-reliance. This was his problem by damn, and it was up to him to solve it, come what may.

The light cast by Jake's lamp chased the shadows back into their respective corners as he entered the darkened room. The curtains his mother had fashioned from old flour sacks were pulled tightly shut against the moonless night. Outside of the bed the only other furnishings in the room were a nightstand, a footstool, and a double chifforobe, since the room had no closets. The walls were made from planks his Pa had cut at the local sawmill, and the chinks between the boards were caulked with river clay to keep the wind out. That the solitary window in the room boasted panes of glass instead of waxed cloth was a testament to the McKinney family's newfound prosperity in this most unlikely of promised lands.

Jake carefully placed the lamp on the nightstand and began to undress, neatly folding his clothes over the foot of the bed as he did so. Once he was in the altogether, he removed his nightshirt from its place under his pillow and pulled it on over his head. Jake gave the room one last apprehensive look before blowing out the light and jumping under the covers. The interlaced ropes that supported the mattress groaned slightly as he tried to get comfortable under the pile of quilts that covered the bed.

Instead of burrowing down to the heart of the bed like a prairie dog as usual, Jake lay on his back and stared up at the ceiling, as rigid as the rafters above his head. His arms were stiffly extended along his sides atop the covers, his hands balled into tight fists, as if prepared for a fight.

A finger like the tine on a pitchfork emerged from the shadowy region under the bed. It was followed by its brothers, each as long and narrow as the first. The spidery, overlong digits were joined to a wide, flat palm, which was attached to a narrow, bony wrist. The fingers hooked themselves into claws, digging into the floorboards as the thing dragged itself clear of the bed. Once it was free it stood up, unfolding itself like a pocketknife. Its knobby back made a clicking sound as it shrugged its shoulders, locking its spine into place.

It was pale as a frog's belly, with skin like that found on a pitcher of milk that's been left to sit too long. Its body was hairless, save for the tangle of lank, greasy curls that hung from its lopsided head like a nest of dead snakes. Its legs were as long and thin as tent poles, and bent backward at the knee, so that it seemed to be both walking away from and towards its prey at the same time.

Its face, if you could call it that, was toad-like, with wide, rubbery lips, a pair of slits in place of a nose, and two huge, blood-red eyes that glowed like an angry cat's. When the thing smacked its lips, Jake could see the inside of its mouth was ringed with jagged teeth.

When the fiend stared down at Jake, the boy saw a brief glimmer of surprise in its hideous eyes. Clearly it had not expected its victim to be so exposed. Still, it knew better than to question its good fortune. The thing moved so that it loomed over the boy, bending low so that its hideous face was mere inches from his own, its spidery talons poised to spear the terrified child's eyeballs.

Although the thing before him filled him with terror, Jake bit his tongue to keep from crying out. The time had come for him to face that which frightened him and become its master.

The horror that hovered before him blinked an inner eyelid, and its nasal slits dilated sharply, catching scent of the subtle change in the chemistry of fear. Emitting a low growl, the thing abruptly turned its head on its shoulders like an owl, so that it was staring over its shoulders at the chifforobe.

The moment the monster took its murderous gaze off him, Jake kicked back the bedclothes, causing the creature to swivel its head back in his direction. *"Now!"* the boy screamed at the top of his lungs. *"Do it now!"*

The doors to the chifforobe flew open with a bang and out of its depths stepped a man dressed all in black, from his scuffed cowboy boots and floor-length duster, to the hat on his head. He brandished a pistol in hands so pale they looked as if they'd been dipped in whitewash. His face was equally pallid, save for his eyes, which burned like red-hot coals dropped in a snow bank. About the pale man's neck was cinched a bolo made from a polished stone the color of blood.

"Step back from the boy, critter," the pale man said in a voice that sounded as if it was coming from the bottom of a well.

The thing from under the bed flipped its head back around on its shoulders and snarled at the intruder, displaying a ring of razor-sharp teeth. A sane man would have fainted dead away or fled the scene, but the pale man opened fire instead. The thing clutched its midsection, a look of confusion and pain crossing its hideous face before it collapsed onto the floor.

"You did it!" Jake shouted gleefully, jumping up and down on the bed. "You killed him!"

"Don't get too excited there, son—you can't really kill these critters," the pale man replied, holstering his pistols.

There was a loud slam as the door to Jake's room flew open and Hiram McKinney entered the room, galluses dangling from his pants, shotgun at the ready.

"Who in Hell are you, mister, and what are you doing in my boy's room?" he thundered.

The pale man raised his hands slow and easy, so as not to tense the rancher's trigger finger. "The name's Hell. Sam Hell. And I'm here at your son's request."

"That's right, Pa!" Jake said excitedly, jumping up and down on the bed. "This here's the Dark Ranger! He come here to get rid of the monster! See?!? It's real! It's really real! And it came out from under my bed, just like I tol' ya!"

Hiram looked to where his son was pointing. "Sweet baby Jesus!" he gasped, his eyes started from their sockets. "What in Heaven's name is that?"

"Heaven has nothing to do with it, Mr. McKinney. May I put my hands down now?"

"Hiram, honey? What is going on in here—?" Mrs. McKinney poked her head around the doorjamb, a homespun shawl about her shoulders and her hair gathered into her nightcap. She gave out with a squeal of horror upon seeing the thing sprawled across the floor.

"Tell you the truth, Miriam—I have no earthly idea what's going on."

"I sent for him, Pa! I saw his advertisement in the back of this magazine, and I wrote him, telling him what was wrong, and he wrote back and said he could help and tol' me what to do what to when he got here!"

"Excuse me, folks—but as I've been trying to explain to your boy here, this dance ain't over yet."

The man called Hell stepped over the body of the fiend on the floor, pushed back the sackcloth curtains and opened the window, which swung inward on a hinge. A second later a woman dressed in the fringed riding chaps and beaded pectoral of an Indian warrior clambered over the sill.

"Comanche!" McKinney shouted in alarm, lifting his weapon.

Hell turned and grabbed the barrel of the shotgun in one milk-white hand, forcing its muzzle to the floor. Hiram tried to yank the shotgun free from the pale stranger's grasp, but there was no budging it.

"Yes, Pretty Woman is a Comanche," Hell said matter-of-factly. "And I would kindly appreciate it if you did not point your gun at a lady—and one who happens to be my business partner, at that."

The Comanche woman acted as if she did not see or hear what was going on about her as she kneeled beside the creature on the floor. Muttering a chant under her breath, she removed a grass rope lariat tied about her waist and hogtied the unconscious creature like a steer ready for branding. Just as she finished trussing it up, the thing made a wailing sound, like that of a wounded elk, and began to struggle.

Mrs. McKinney screamed and snatched her son off the bed, clutching him to her in an attempt to shield him from attack. Hiram McKinney attempted to pull his shotgun free of the stranger's grip in order to fire on the thing, but it was still held fast.

"There's no need to panic, folks," Hell said calmly. "Pretty's got it under control."

The Comanche medicine woman learned in close to the fiend's wildly gnashing mouth. She raised a clenched fist to her lips and blew a quick burst of air into it. A cloud of grayish-white powder enveloped the creature's face, and it abruptly ceased its howling, becoming as limp as wet laundry.

"Is it dead?" Mrs. McKinney asked, her curiosity having overcome her dread.

"Like I told the boy—there's no killing such critters," Hell said flatly, letting go of Hiram's shotgun. "You might as well try and murder a stone or stab the sea. Best you can do is making sure it can't do you more harm."

Pretty Woman removed a leather bag from her belt and emptied its contents, mostly dried herbs and other less identifiable artifacts, onto the floor. She glanced up her partner with eyes as dark and bright as a raven's, and he nodded in return.

"Come along, folks," Hell said, motioning for the others to leave the room. "We better leave Pretty to finish the breaking in peace. Something tells me y'all could do with a cup of coffee right about now."

Hiram McKinney sat in his favorite chair, his shotgun resting across his knees, while his wife busied herself with making coffee. He stared at the pale-skinned stranger who called himself Hell, who was now sitting opposite him in his wife's rocking chair. At first Hiram had thought the stranger was an albino, but now that he was able to get a closer look, he could see that Hell's complexion was more like that of the consumptives who had come out west for the Cure.

Uncertain of how to proceed in such an unusual situation, he finally decided there was no wrong way to go about it, so he opted to grab the bull by the horns. "Jake said something about him writing you—?"

"Yes, sir. That he did."

"Here, Pa—this is what I was talking about." Jake handed his father a copy of *Pickman's Illustrated Serials*, which was tightly rolled in order to fit in a boy's back pocket.

Hiram took the periodical and flattened it out as best he could across his knee. He frowned at the lurid illustration that adorned the front cover, which showed a band of outlaws shooting up a town, all of whom had swooning damsels and bags of loot clutched in the hands that did not hold smoking six-shooters. Floating over the desperadoes' heads was the title of the lead story, in ornately engraved script: *The Tortuga Hill Gang Rides Again*.

"You been wasting money on penny dreadfuls?" Hiram said sternly, glowering at his son in disapproval.

"Far be it from me to step in between a father and his son," Hell said. "But don't you reckon you're being a tad harsh on the boy, considering the situation?"

Hiram opened his mouth, as if to argue to point, then realized the foolishness of it. "I reckon you're right on that point, mister."

"Here, Pa—here's where I saw his advertisement." Jake pointed to a quarter-page ad, located just below an advertisement for Dr. Mirablis' Amazing Electric Truss. Unlike the other advertisements, it did not boast steel-engraved pictures or florid script, even though what it claimed to be selling was far more esoteric that the patent medicines and seed catalogs that surrounded it.

Troubled by Specters, Ghosts and Phantoms? Fear No More! There Is Help! Call For The Dark Ranger: Ghost Breaking A Specialty! No Spook Too Small, No Fiend Too Fierce! Write Care of: Box 1, Golgotha, Texas. Our Motto: 'One Wraith, One Ranger.'

"Dark Ranger?" Hiram rubbed his forehead, baffled by what he was reading. He glanced over at the man seated across from him with something akin to awe. "You a Texas Ranger, mister?"

A look of profound sorrow flickered across Hell's face and was quickly gone, like a cloud scudding across the moon. "I was. Back before the troubles."

Hiram raised an eyebrow. "Cortina?"

Hell took a deep breath and nodded, as if the very memory caused him pain. "Yep. I was at Rio Grande City. Now that the Rangers have been replaced with those carpetbaggin' State Police, I break ghosts and scare off things that go bump in the night."

"Any man who rode with Cap'n Ford and Robert E. Lee is more than welcome in my home," Hiram said, putting aside his shotgun. He stood and offered Hell his hand. "And I am eternally grateful for you helpin' out my boy here."

"You've got a very brave and resourceful son, Mr. McKinney," Hell said, accepting the rancher's handshake. The Ranger's grip was hard as horn and as cool and dry as a snakeskin. "Not many boys his age would have had the gumption to do as he did."

"No, I reckon not," Hiram agreed, a hint of pride in his voice. "I'll be damned if I can figure out how you got into the house in the first place, though."

"I let him in, Pa!" Jake explained. "Miss Pretty Woman rode up this morning, while you was out tendin' the herd and Ma was out in the coop seein' to the chickens. She gave me this note that said Mr. Hell needed me to leave my bedroom window open so he could sneak in and hide before I went to bed. That way he could catch the haint unawares."

"Well, I'll be jiggered," Hiram said. "But, son—why didn't you tell your Ma and me what was goin' on?"

"I didn't think you'd believe me. Besides, I was afraid it might hurt y'all. I didn't want anything bad to happen to you and Ma on account of me."

Hiram looked into his son's face with a mixture of amazement, respect, and love. "So you just kept goin' to bed, even though that thing was waitin' for you every night?"

"It weren't there every night. But yes, sir, I did."

"Here you go, dear," Mrs. McKinney said, handing her husband a tin cup full of hot coffee. "How about you, Mr. Hell? Would could care for something to drink?"

"No, thank you, ma'am," he replied, smiling without showing his teeth. "I don't drink—coffee."

Pretty Woman stepped out of Jake's room and coughed into her closed fist. Hell stood up, visibly relieved that he no longer had to make small talk.

"Ah! Pretty's finished with your unwanted guest. It's safe to go back in now."

"Are you sure?" Mrs. McKinney asked uneasily.

"Ma'am, there's not a lot of things in this world I'd bet good money on—but Pretty Woman's medicine is one of 'em."

As they re-entered, the creature scuttled into the far corner of the bedroom, its head ducked low like that of a dog that's been kicked once too often. The speed of its movements made Mrs. McKinney cry out in alarm and clutch her husband's arm.

"No need to be fearful, ma'am," Hell said calmly. "The fight's been took out of it." He strode over to the creature and grabbed the grass-rope noose about its neck. "Come along, you," he snapped.

"What—what, exactly, is that thing?" Hiram asked, trying to keep the unease from his voice.

"I'm not rightly sure. I'll have to ask Pretty." Hell turned to the medicine woman and said something in Comanche.

Pretty Woman wrinkled her nose as she replied in her native tongue, pointing to the walls as she spoke. Hell nodded his understanding.

"According to Pretty, this here's a nature-spirit of some sort. These critters attach themselves to things like rocks, trees, creeks and the like—I reckon you could say they live in them. Some are friendly towards folks, others ain't. Seems this one attached itself to the tree that the planks used to build this room were milled from. By using various incantations and spells, in combination with a specially prepared rope, Pretty has succeeded in rendering this particular spirit harmless—as long as y'all keep the noose about its neck, and feed it nothing but salt."

"Beg pardon?"

"Salt weakens unnatural things," Hell explained. "That is why the signs of power used in calling down the things from between worlds are drawn in salt; it saps their strength and binds them to the will of the conjurer." Hell stepped forward and handed the loose end of the rope to Jake. "I reckon he's yours, if he belongs to anyone. You'll find having your own private fiend has it advantages. For one thing, they chase off bad luck, as well as snakes. You feed this bogey a tablespoon of salt a day and he'll be yours until the oceans run dry and the mountains crumble. Provided you never take off the noose.' "

"What happens if it's removed?" Hiram asked, eyeing the creature cautiously.

"Just see that you don't," Hell replied gravely. "I don't do refunds."

After a few minutes of haggling, it was decided that five dollars cash money and a spool of ribbon was just pay for a night of ghost-breaking and fiend-binding. Although the McKinneys offered to let Sam Hell and Pretty Woman spend the rest of the night in the barn, the pair politely declined.

"It is most kindly of y'all to extend such a invitation," the Ranger said, touching the brim of his hat. "But the nature of our business demands that we be on our way long before sun-up."

As they rode off into the night, Hell turned to look one last time at the McKinney clan as they stood in the dooryard of their homestead. Hiram leaned on his shotgun as he waved goodbye. Miriam McKinney stood close to her husband, occasionally casting worried looks in the direction of her son, who was busy poking the captive fiend in the rump with a sharp stick.

After they rounded a bend in the road and were no longer within line of sight of the McKinney ranch, Sam reached inside his duster and retrieved a long, thin cigar shaped like a twig.

"See? I told you advertising in the back of penny dreadfuls would pay off," he said, biting off the tip of the cigar with a set of very white, inhumanly sharp teeth.

"I'll grant you that," Pretty Woman replied in perfect English. "But I do not see how it will help you find the one you seek."

"Texas is a big place. I could wander forever and a day and never find him. But if something spooky is happening, odds are he might be near at hand. Kind of like high winds and hailstones mean a twister's nearby."

"There is something to your way of thinking," the medicine woman conceded. "But I still think it was a waste of perfectly good money."

"I wouldn't say that. After all—you got yourself a nice spool of ribbon out of the deal, didn't you?"

"That thing could have torn me apart like fresh bread! That's hardly worth a spool of ribbon."

"Yes, but it didn't, did it? And that ribbon should look real nice wrapped around your braids."

"Point taken," she replied with a smile. "Still, do you think it was wise telling them so much about yourself?"

"I didn't let on too much. There was plenty of Rangers that fought at Rio Grande City and Brownsville. Besides, they don't know my real name. And there's no Rangers headquarters left to contact anymore, even if they did decide to try and check up on me. As far as the State of Texas is concerned, Ranger Sam Yoakum is long dead."

ABOUT THE AUTHOR

Nancy A. Collins is the author of several novels and numerous short stories, as well as having served a two-year stint as a writer for DC Comics' *Swamp Thing*. A recipient of the Horror Writers Association's Bram Stoker Award, the British Fantasy Society's Icarus Award, and the Deathrealm Award, as well as a nominee for the Eisner, International Horror Guild, and World Fantasy Awards, her works include *Knuckles and Tales: A Southern Neo-Gothic Collection*, **Sunglasses After Dark**, and **Darkest Heart. Dead Roses for a Blue Lady** features her cult character, Sonja Blue, which has been optioned for film and television development. Ms. Collins currently makes her home in Atlanta with her husband, underground artist/provocateur Joe Christ, and their two dogs, Scrapple and Trixie.

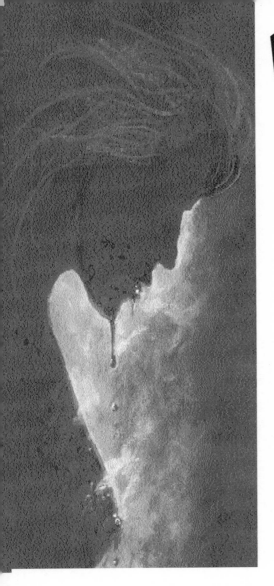